How to Stir a Baker's Heart

Candice Sue Patterson

How to Stir a Baker's Heart
COPYRIGHT 2019 by Candice Sue Patterson

Contact Information: customer@pelicanbookgroup.com

Scripture quotations, unless otherwise indicated are taken from the King James translation, public domain.

Cover Art by *Nicola Martinez*

White Rose Publishing, a division of Pelican Ventures, LLC
www.pelicanbookgroup.com PO Box 1738 *Aztec, NM * 87410

White Rose Publishing Circle and Rosebud logo is a trademark of Pelican Ventures, LLC

Publishing History
First White Rose Edition, 2019
Paperback Edition ISBN 978-1-5223-0216-2
Electronic Edition ISBN 978-1-5223-0214-8
Published in the United States of America

Dedication

To my grandparents, Eddie and Delores Self, who both struggled with dementia. I thought of you while writing nearly every page of this book, cherishing my childhood memories with you, wishing I could know you as an adult. How I wish you could meet my children, for I know they would love you as much as I do.

Thank you, Grandpa, for the postcard you sent me from Florida when I was three. I still have it. And believe it or not, that postcard is what prompted me to begin my writing journey. I look forward to seeing you both again someday. Until then, I will take imaginary journeys with you on your fictional boat on the lighthouse tour mentioned in this story.

Acknowledgments:

A huge thanks to the sisters of my heart--The Quid Pro Quills--Robin Patchen, Pegg Thomas, Kara Hunt, Jericha Kingston, and Marge Wiebe. Your support, prayers, wisdom, and honesty push me to be a better writer. I couldn't survive my fictional world without you.

Nicola Martinez, your editing skills and your amazing talent in cover design make writing books a pleasure. Thanks for all you do.

Adam, not only do you provide inspiration for my stories, but you calm me down when I'm freaking out over deadlines, you're patient when the house is a mess and the laundry is overlooked due to said deadlines, and you help me brainstorm plots when I need an idea from an entirely different angle. Thanks for being my real-life hero.

To my little men--Levi, Silas, and Hudson--who aren't so little anymore. You are wonderful boys, and I'm beyond blessed to hold the title "Mom." Even if I sometimes question whether or not I'm going to survive these teenage years. ;)

Above all, I thank my Lord and Savior Jesus Christ. I may not always understand the path He puts me on, but I'm glad He's in control. I'm grateful He has let this writing dream of mine come to fruition. All honor and glory is His.

And thank you, dear reader, for taking time out of your busy life to spend it with my characters.

1

For Olivia Hudson, starting over was like trying to bake an award-winning pie out of olives and sauerkraut. No matter what ingredients she added to balance the flavors or how she arranged them, it wouldn't work. Life was not a beach or a box of chocolates. Though chocolate did help.

The delectable, fudgy scent of her triple layer chocolate cake stirred Olivia's senses as she stretched across the bakery counter and placed a fresh slice in front of her favorite customer. In the four months Olivia had lived in Stone Harbor, Maine, she'd formed an attachment to Arianne Anderson. The sugar-craving bridal boutique owner had an honest, down-to-earth personality Olivia found refreshing.

"Thanks." Arianne lifted her fork as though it weighed a hundred pounds.

"Vanilla latte?" Olivia picked up a disposable cup and started the process, already knowing Arianne's answer.

"With a shot of espresso."

"Wow, someone's had a rough day."

Arianne stared at the thick brown frosting in a daze, sighed, and swallowed her first bite. Her eyelids fluttered closed, and her shoulders relaxed.

Olivia chuckled. All would be well in Arianne's world now—at least until the plate was empty.

"It's hot." Olivia placed the latte in front of her friend then leaned her elbows on the counter and clasped her hands, her lower back grateful for the reprieve. "What's got you down?"

Arianne's dark blue eyes pooled with tears. She swallowed and tucked a strand of curly blonde hair behind her ear. "I...." Arianne glanced down at the cake. "I'm cheating on my husband."

Olivia straightened.

A tear dropped onto the granite countertop. Arianne swiped away the dampness on her cheeks and sighed. "Two evenings a week for the past three months, I've had things to catch up on at work,"—she made air quotes over the last word—"when really I've been driving twenty miles to escape my husband and indulge in the sinful ecstasy of your baking."

The tight band around Olivia's throat eased. "There isn't another man?"

Arianne shook her head. "No. But the way I lust after this cake when I'm with Huck is adultery."

Relief almost swept Olivia's legs out from under her. She threw a wadded napkin at her friend, satisfied when it made contact with Arianne's nose. "You scared me."

More tears. Now that Arianne's faucet was running, there was no turning it off.

Olivia checked the time on the tea-stained clock with a cupcake from an old Victorian postcard decoupaged to the face. Close enough. She locked the front door and flipped the sign to Closed. "What's got you running?"

Olivia joined Arianne on the customer side of the counter and took the next wooden stool beside her. She pressed her fingertips to her lower back.

Through the wall of paned windows, an orange sunset lowered against the icy harbor, giving an ethereal look to the lobster boats and dories coated with frost. Perfect for wall art.

Arianne fidgeted with the napkin, now damp and covered in mascara stains. "I can't get pregnant. We've been trying for almost two years and every time we're...*together* I feel like a complete failure. Sometimes it's so bad I avoid Huck entirely. Like tonight."

This sweet woman wanted a baby more than anything. Meanwhile, other women conceived unwanted children all the time. The world wasn't right.

"I'm sorry." Arianne sniffed. "The hormone therapy to help the fertility wagon along makes me a little emotional. Combined with the stress of expanding the boutique and building a wedding chapel, I'm a mess."

A little emotional? The woman was a basket-case. "How does your husband feel about you *working* late?"

Arianne forked a bite. "He doesn't suspect a thing."

"He will if you don't get rid of that smear of chocolate icing on your upper lip."

Arianne snatched up the napkin, made a face at the black stains, and smiled at Olivia's offer of a fresh one.

Both women giggled.

"I've no right to complain. God has already blessed me with a beautiful daughter from my first marriage. But she keeps asking for a sibling, and I know Huck wants a baby as much as I do, no matter how hard he tries to hide the disappointment in his eyes month after month."

Olivia stood and started cleaning the tables with a bleach-soaked rag. "Infertility doesn't mean failure. Your husband may be disappointed, but I'm sure he's not disappointed with you."

The pungent smell filled the room as strongly as the words hit her heart. It was true in Arianne's case. It didn't apply to Olivia's situation. That's why work was such a great distraction. Her legs and feet ached, and her back complained by closing time every day, but the twelve-hour schedule did her good. She couldn't dwell on regrets when she was too exhausted to think. Sleep, of late, had been blessedly quick and deep.

"In my head, I know you're right. But my heart says something different."

Don't believe the lies. How many times back home had Olivia said that to patients in her office? Easy for her to say, but harder to believe now that she'd experienced the dark side of the rainbow.

"Hmm...this is divine," Arianne said around a mouthful of cake. "What's your secret anyway? I've never had frosting this perfect."

Olivia shook off the black cloud. Her stomach grumbled, reminding her she'd skipped lunch. She paused her cleaning to smooth a knot from her shoulder. "Can you keep a secret?"

Arianne nodded, curls bouncing around her shoulders.

"Cola."

"The carbonated drink?" Arianne stared at the remaining nugget of cake on her plate in wonder. "You're a genius."

Olivia swallowed the bark of laughter that almost escaped. "People have been using it for years."

A cobweb dangled from one of the nautical lanterns suspended from a hand-hewn beam above Olivia's head. She stood on a chair, reached up, and brushed it away. Though both the building and the menu needed updates, the boat oars, fishing nets, and anchors adorning the whitewashed walls and the glass jars displaying colorful sea glass and shells gave the pastry shop a seaside, magazine-quality feel. Especially after she'd added thin crown molding to the display cases and then distressed them with white chalk paint.

Silence reigned until a ping on the glass caught their attention. The predicted wintry mix had arrived.

Arianne slapped five dollars on the counter and pushed it toward Olivia. "Tip." She winked. "I'll be back for another session on Thursday."

"Session?" The bill crinkled as Olivia slipped it in her apron pocket. How had Arianne found out her secret?

"Your desserts. They work better than any therapy available. I always feel better when I leave here."

Words Olivia had always loved to hear, though she'd never expected to hear them in a bakery. However, rumor had it the shop carried a confection to cure every problem. Like the gingersnaps that had helped ease Mrs. Watson's queasy stomach, or the iced, red velvet brownies that erased local author Maggie Mahonen's writer's block. Of course, the claims were ridiculous. Something for small-town folk to talk about. But the rumors had boosted business all the same. Olivia unlocked the door for her friend. "See you Thursday."

Arianne pointed her finger. "Next time, we talk about you."

"Oh, I don't—"

"You." Arianne gently squeezed Olivia's elbow. "Don't think I can't see the heartache lurking behind your eyes. I've been there myself. There's a reason you came to Stone Harbor that involves more than caring for your grandma." After a quick hug, Arianne put up her hood and dashed for her car.

So much for anonymity. There was truth to that women's intuition thing.

Olivia sucked in a deep breath. The cold air shocked her lungs. Indiana winters had been cold, but Maine felt like the tundra. She needed some heavier gear.

After sweeping the small section of floor she'd missed earlier, she turned out the lights and pushed through the swinging doors to the kitchen. Gleaming stainless steel and the lingering smell of lemon cleaner made her smile. She was grateful for such a hard-working crew. And grateful they'd all left for the day. A quiet kitchen fed her creativity, revived her soul.

She cocked her head. The building was too quiet. Had Grandma fallen asleep while organizing her new desk? Olivia rushed to the office, where she'd left her grandma reading earlier. Other than typical office stuff and a small loveseat, the room was empty. A young adult mystery novel lay bookmarked upside down on a cushion.

Dousing the light, Olivia closed the office door and checked the bathroom. On her way to the other side of the kitchen, her foot hit an object that scraped across the tile floor. Grandma's glasses. Olivia knelt to pick them up, and her gaze traced an invisible trail to the cracked-open back door. Dread coiled inside Olivia's stomach and squeezed. "Grandma?"

The rear parking lot was void of cars and people

but was quickly filling with sleet and snow.

"Grandma?" she yelled louder.

Where on earth had she gone?

Panic set in. Olivia grabbed her purse and locked the doors behind her, the display case of treats the last thing she spied through the glass before icy drops pelted her head.

If only her desserts could heal all the messes in her life. A cookie to regenerate her life's purpose. A muffin to rebuild the declining bakery. An olive and sauerkraut pie to find a missing woman with Alzheimer's.

2

Sleet smacked the windshield, pulling Blake Hartford's focus from the Co-Op meeting and back to the road. The weatherman had predicted a warming trend in April with a high chance of heavy frost in early May. Every farmer in New England would spend the next month on their knees. If Blake lost another crop to frozen blossoms or disease it would do him in.

He turned up the defrost and slowed the vehicle. The wipers slapped time with the radio, giving him a glimpse of the pavement before the icy glaze stole his view again. Warm air blasted at full speed. With a swipe, the glass cleared, presenting a ribbon of road in the path of his headlights—and a person walking along the center lane.

Blake swerved and then pumped the break until the truck came to a safe stop along the shoulder. Gut in his throat, he inhaled a deep breath and flipped on the hazard lights. The figure remained an obscure dark blob in his rearview mirror. He scrubbed a hand down his face to rid the images of what had almost happened. Obviously, whoever that was needed help.

Blake left his truck, and his breath caught as icy rain pummeled his face and shoulders. Swaying pines on the opposite side of the road made menacing shadows, while the ocean beyond the guardrail churned waves against the cliff.

The pedestrian walked closer, seemingly unaware of the icy moisture.

"Is everything all right? Can I give you a ride?"

When the figure moved within five feet of his truck, the red glow of the taillights revealed a thin, frozen frame. A woman. With no coat. "Miss, are you hurt?"

The scared gaze that latched onto his didn't belong to a miss at all but to a woman he'd guess to be in her seventies. She opened her mouth to speak but a tremble stole through her body, and she closed her lips.

Sleet coated Blake's hair and eyelashes. He cleared them with a swipe of his fingers. "Ma'am, are you hurt?"

No bleeding or bruises from what little he could see, only a small icicle clinging to the end of her nose. He hadn't passed any stranded vehicles on this stretch of road. Had she wrecked? Been attacked?

"Ma'am?"

Frail, wrinkled hands reached for his arm as another shiver overtook her. He'd been in the elements less than a minute, and he was chilled clear through. No wonder she couldn't speak. The sweatshirt she wore offered no protection. If she'd been walking any length of time at all—and by looks of her stiff clothes she had—hypothermia was probably setting in.

With a firm gentle tug on her hands, Blake led the way back to his truck. "Is there anyone I can call for you?"

The poor woman shook so badly he feared her legs would give out. He needed to get her warmed up, and now. He opened the passenger side door and lifted all of what felt like ninety-eight pounds of her onto the seat, praying she understood he was trying to help and not harm her.

"My name is Blake," he said, his foot slipping on the pavement as he backed away. "I'm going to get you warm and safe." He closed her door and went around the back of the truck, slipping once on the road.

The cab brought instant relief from the cold. He switched the vents to defrost and floor panels and then cranked the temperature as hot as it would go. "Where can I drive you? Do you have family close by?"

The woman stared at the dashboard. Shock? Blake ran his fingers through his hair. Or tried to. The ends had crusted over. What should he do? Hospital or police station? "Can you tell me your name?"

Nothing.

Watching to be sure there were no other cars on the deserted highway, he jerked the wheel in a U-turn and headed back toward town. No matter where he ultimately decided to take her, both places lay that direction.

His wet palms kept slipping on the steering wheel, and he swiped them along his damp jeans. "How'd you come to be out in this mess?"

The woman only shivered.

"Again, my name is Blake. I'm here to help you."

He hoped making polite conversation would put her fears at ease, if she had any. Her face was as placid as a summer lake. Blake talked about everything that popped into his head—what he'd worked on that day, who he predicted would win the World Series, his favorite foods. By the time they reached Stone Harbor, the woman began rallying around.

She studied a rip in her slacks. "I-I don't know you."

Streetlights bathed the truck enough for him to witness the confusion in her pale eyes. "No, ma'am." Blake repeated his name and how she'd come to be in his truck.

"I don't know you." She gripped the door panel, raising the thick veins in her hands. Her gaze darted around the cab. Her chest rose and fell in panic. "I don't know you!"

Blake hesitated to move or speak, unsure how to handle the situation. The police station was closest. He'd take her there. They could determine whether or not she required medical care. He eased the truck to a stop at the town's only stoplight, the police station a long two blocks away.

The woman groped for the door handle. "I don't know you," she yelled, over and over.

Blake grabbed her arm, not only to reassure her but to keep her from jumping out. Despite not weighing more than a wet blanket, she managed to best him and opened her door. She jumped off the bench seat and onto the ground with the stealth of someone half her age. Apparently, fear and adrenaline were a powerful combination.

Blake slapped the wheel, threw the truck into park, and followed her. "I won't hurt you. I'm trying to get you home."

She spun and pointed a finger at him, stuttering words he couldn't make out, eyes wild.

Oncoming headlights highlighted them, and a sports car fishtailed to a halt at the curb. The driver's door opened. "Grandma?" A young woman in a hooded coat scrambled out and ran at them. "Oh, thank God, you're safe." She gripped her grandma's arms and pulled her into a hug, pushing the hood off her hair.

The older woman's face twisted in annoyance but the savage look in her eyes dimmed.

Cold rain spattered around them.

Blake exhaled, glad the woman had family and grateful to exit this scenario. "I found her walking down Highway One just past Rim Road."

The woman released her grandma and turned as if she only just realized he'd been standing there. The bluest eyes he'd ever seen met his. Even with her dark hair mussed, the freezing rain, and the petrified grandmother, his mind declared she was absolutely beautiful.

"That man...that man," the grandma stuttered, jabbing her bony finger at Blake.

Blake took a step back, unsure what he'd done to make the woman angry.

"That man," she repeated.

"Calm down, Grandma, and tell me what happened. Are you hurt?"

"Hurt." The elderly woman put distance between herself and Blake. "That man...hurt...hurt."

The younger woman gazed at her grandma's torn slacks and mud-stained sweatshirt. Those blue eyes bounced from him to her grandma then back again. "Did this man hurt you?"

The grandma jabbed a finger at him again. "Hurt."

Blake threw up his palms. "I didn't—"

"Back off." Those stunning eyes turned to blue fire, and she gripped her grandma's arm, walking them both backwards to the sports car. Blake stepped forward to defend his character, not wanting this woman to think he'd harm anyone.

She thrust out a palm like a traffic cop. "Don't

come any closer or I'll...I'll..." They continued backing away as she glanced around the sidewalk in search of something. She raised her chin. "I'll kick you."

If the circumstances were different, he'd laugh. Unfortunately, nothing about this evening was funny. Why would the grandma lie about something he didn't do? "I found her walking in the storm, unresponsive. I was taking her to the police station."

"That man...hurt...me," the grandma lied again.

Blake kept his response calm. "I didn't."

"Hurt!" The old woman screamed the word over and over.

With every backwards step closer to their car, the granddaughter's gaze darted from him to her grandma. Her forehead crumpled, as if trying to decide whose position was most logical. If her grandma would stop screaming maybe the woman could judge accurately.

Before Blake could regain equilibrium of the situation, he was staring at the sports car's taillights in the distance. Drizzle coated his skin. The town was silent and unmoving, the businesses having closed hours ago. The stoplight reflected green off the slick pavement.

His attempt at Good Samaritan had just exploded.

Blake returned to his truck and waited for the now-red light to turn green. He was soaked, cold, and tired, but what troubled him more than anything was that the granddaughter—and the elderly woman, who'd obviously lost her faculties—thought him a monster. Or a pervert.

With no way to rectify the misunderstanding, Blake went to the police station, reported the incident to the authorities so they'd be aware of what had happened, and then drove home. After a hot shower and a late dinner out of a can, he tried to focus his thoughts on the weatherman. If the man's predictions were correct, Blake needed to review his options. But as he fell into bed and listened to his house settle, he chased the question that had plagued him since his first look into those disarming blue eyes.

Who was that beautiful woman?

3

Olivia fought the dregs of sleep. Two lattes, plus espresso, sat like a boulder in her stomach. Her heart raced, but her eyes struggled to focus on Sheriff Miller and the gingerbread he held in his meaty hand.

He'd offered to meet her at the bakery before they opened to discuss the grandma-napping stranger. When he arrived, he said the stranger had stopped by the station last night and explained the situation while she waited in the ER for clearance to take Grandma home. Three hours of sleep just wasn't enough for a woman to function properly. She covered a yawn with her hand and leaned her arms on her office desk.

The sheriff swallowed his bite and chased it down with coffee. "I assure you, Elizabeth wasn't in danger with Blake. I've known him and his family for years. His record is spotless. Not even a traffic ticket."

Positive the sheriff had just broken some kind of citizen confidentiality protocol, Olivia rubbed her aching forehead. "You're saying there's no possible way this man had intentions to harm my grandmother?"

"Exactly." He packed in another bite.

So, this guy—Blake—was an outstanding citizen. Grandma's lack of bodily harm, minus the scratch where her slacks had torn, probably from a fall, agreed with what the sheriff had said about his integrity.

Meaning Olivia owed him an apology. And her gratitude. If only she'd have slowed down to connect the dots last night, she'd be avoiding this today. "Where can I find Blake Hartford?"

Sheriff Miller held up his finger while he chewed then swallowed. "He comes through town now and then. Mostly keeps to himself, though. He keeps busy farming and restoring his Victorian farmhouse."

The tidbit had her passion for antiquated architecture salivating. The farming thing, however, confused her. Yes, her city-girl upbringing made her ignorant of farming, but she couldn't picture fields of cattle and goats on the coast of Maine.

The sheriff chuckled, and she realized she'd been making a face.

"He owns a blueberry farm," he said.

Ah.

"Tell you what." The sheriff wiped the bread crumbs from his lips. "I'll let Blake know to stop by. You can thank him then."

"Works for me." That would buy her time to rehearse an explanation as to why her grandma had been wandering the roads alone, disoriented, and shouting false accusations. And why Olivia had resorted to threats a toddler would make.

The sheriff rose from the chair and shook her hand. "Welcome to Stone Harbor, Miss Hudson."

And what a welcome the past four months had been. Polar ice cap temperatures. The stroke that sent Grandma further into the abyss of Alzheimer's. A barrage of doctors' appointments. Managerial and shift changes at the bakery. But last night's incident topped them all. She'd come for healing and found chaos. "Thank you, Sheriff."

He made for the exit but paused when his hand met the doorknob. He turned to her. "You know, I heard your gingersnaps have helped Wanda Watson's digestion issues. I didn't believe it, but my ulcer's been killing me for a while now, and your gingerbread has me feeling better than I have in ages."

She smiled instead of groaning and told him to take a loaf on his way out, no charge.

The decadent aroma of strawberry buttercream drifted in from the now open door. In the far corner of the kitchen, Grandma stood at the mixer with the ever curt and sulky Darlene. The woman despised Olivia, though her reasons were unclear.

The hum of industrial mixers and the ovens' warmth tempted Olivia to dreamland. Except she couldn't go. Right now she had time, however short, to delve into the exciting world of order invoices, bills, and property taxes before the bakery opened its doors to customers.

At least these issues were in black-and-white and could be organized in neat stacks according to importance. The issues in her personal life—not so easy.

~*~

Three weeks into April, Blake stood next to his twenty acres of lowbush blueberries, grateful the cold front had stayed a few degrees above freezing. Even better—the weatherman's prophecy had been false. A hurricane pushing along the southern coast was bringing warmer temperatures Blake's way. The sun's warmth spread across his back, and the hundreds of white, star-shaped blossoms beginning to dot the bushes.

Twelve feet away, Huck Anderson knelt beside a stack of wooden beehive boxes, laughing.

Blake frowned. "It wasn't funny."

"I'm laughing 'cause I'm usually the one trying to claw my way out of awkward situations." Huck stood. "Have you seen 'em since?"

"No. The sheriff told me to stop by the bakery because she wanted to apologize, but I haven't."

"Why not?"

"Clearly, both women were scared and confused. An apology isn't necessary."

Huck replaced the bee-box lid, covering the frames where the honeybees were making their comb. Several insects had landed on his arms and shoulders as if he were a bee magnet.

Blake stayed put. He respected the bees and their vital role in pollination and sustaining human life, but he didn't want to mess around with them either. His southern-born friend, however, loved the challenge.

"Is she hot?" When Blake stuttered, Huck's laughter echoed across the field. "That says it all, buddy." Huck sobered and picked up his pry bar and bee smoker from the ground. "How'd the lady end up on the highway?"

Blake shrugged. "Sheriff said she wandered off while the granddaughter was closing up shop. I guess that's why she's here, to take things over."

Blake hadn't seen Mrs. Hudson for years, which was why he hadn't recognized her that night. The owner of the area's once-famous award-winning bakery was shorter and frailer than he remembered. Bad enough that tourism had plummeted, now the merchants themselves were fading too. Blake reconsidered his earlier decision to avoid the bakery. He didn't need an apology, all things considered. But he was curious to know if this Olivia's eyes really were as blue as he remembered. As though he needed fool thoughts like that right now.

Blake inhaled a deep breath of sunshine and salty air, filling his lungs and mind with something sensible. If Madison had taught him one thing, it was that infatuations were just that—infatuations. When Blake fell in love, he fell hard, and he'd been balancing pretty good on his own for a while now. No need for any stiff breezes in the form of pretty granddaughters to knock him down.

He assisted Huck in checking the remaining hives by offering moral support from his farm utility vehicle. Over the next several days, the bees would work together pollinating the blossoms and turning their hard work into a golden profit for Huck and a sustaining farm for Blake.

If only he and the rest of the town merchants board could revive Stone Harbor as easily.

4

Olivia fastened the delicate string of pearls around Grandma's neck and smiled at their reflection in the dressing table's mirror. "You look beautiful."

The antique furniture, reminiscent of the Revolution, was in excellent condition. Its pristine top held a lace doily with two bottles of perfume, a framed picture of Olivia's grandparents at their wedding, and a small oak jewelry chest. Grandma sat atop the matching upholstered chair and studied her reflection. She reached for the black-and-white portrait of herself. A knotted finger traced the lines of her once-flawless, porcelain skin. Grandma sighed.

Without words, that sound represented every woman's feelings toward the enemy of time. Grandma had aged gracefully up until her stroke. The first couple of months had been rough, but she'd regained her physical strength quickly. Her speech was choppy and broken now, and Alzheimer's sometimes had her scrambling for words and repeating things to the point of madness. Today was one of her quieter days.

Olivia adjusted the short collar on Grandma's shirt to rest beneath her puff of salt-and-pepper hair. A spray of department store perfume filled the space after a spritz to Grandma's neck and wrists.

The scent took Olivia back to childhood summers when she'd visited. She'd always been fascinated by the house's old nooks and crannies, the lobster boats bobbing in the harbor, and the bustle of the bakery. She didn't recall much about her grandfather, only that he smelled of vanilla pipe tobacco and captured beauty wherever he could with his vintage cameras. His passionate artistry hung on almost every wall of the house, with a few prints at the bakery, too.

Maine was vastly different from the straight highways and cornfields she was used to. There had been no farmland near her loft apartment in Indianapolis, of course, but every once in a while she liked to drive south for some quiet and fresh air.

None of it was home anymore.

The overwhelming emptiness, the black hole that liked to surround her, threatened the moment. But it was easy to get lost when her moral compass had been stolen by the person who'd given it to her. When the wool over her eyes had been removed, to reveal that her life, in essence, was a lie. *Don't believe the lies the enemy whispers in your ears. You are still you, despite your circumstances.* To think people had paid her good money to hear words she herself failed to practice. Too much deception. Too many unanswered questions.

Grandma wrapped her hand around Olivia's wrist and squeezed. "Don't worry. Be happy."

Olivia swallowed and then smiled, remembering the song she and Grandma used to dance to in the kitchen when Olivia was a teenager. "You're right. Ready to go?"

Grandma rose from the chair, smoothed a wrinkle from her bed's quilt, and turned for the door.

Olivia stepped on the woven rug protruding from beneath Grandma's bed and turned off the Tiffany lamp on the bureau.

Don't worry, be happy. Four of the simplest words in the English language. Yet some of the hardest ones to live by.

~*~

The orange sun setting against the harbor reflected off the windows of Town Hall, nearly blinding Olivia as she and Grandma walked toward the door. Olivia balanced a box of the day's unsold desserts in one hand and steadied Grandma with the other. When they entered, voices filled her ears.

Glenda Harrison, owner of the corner B&B, stood from her metal folding chair and rushed to greet them. "I'm glad you made it. I told Darlene you'd come, despite her certainty you wouldn't." Glenda clasped her hands at the waist of her fleece sweatshirt and rocked back and forth in her black quilted mocs.

Darlene was here?

"Come on now." Glenda ushered them forward, her sea-glass bracelet glinting under the florescent lights. She transferred the box from Olivia's hands to her own, stirring the scent of its sugary contents. "I saved you both a seat right up front."

So much for sitting in the back to observe her first meeting as the official new manager of the Harbor Town Bakery. At least thirty people were in attendance, including the five huddled at a table in the front, presumably the board officers.

"Hazelnut brownies, cherry scones, and chocolate chip cookies. Get 'em before they're gone, folks."

Olivia chuckled at Glenda's attempt to morph her east coast accent into a raspy Tennessee auctioneer's. Half the attendees flocked to the snack table.

The heat from all these bodies crammed into such

a tiny space was like an afternoon in the south. Olivia wouldn't complain, however. It was a nice change from the Siberian tundra she'd endured the last few months. She helped Grandma to a chair, then took the one next to it and removed her sweater.

The Seaside Book's owner, Mr. Greene, limped toward the food wearing green plaid pants and a matching cardigan. He stopped to shake both Olivia's and Grandma's hands. "I'll take two of those brownies," he shouted to Glenda. "And I call this meeting to order." He winked at Grandma and leaned in closer. "I hear hazelnuts are good for arthritis."

A beautiful shade of pink colored Grandma's cheeks.

Olivia grinned. She was following her own prescription by forcing her newly introverted self to be social, even though she wanted nothing more than to bury her head beneath her blankets. A bit of the heaviness weighing her down eased, and she relaxed against her seat.

The board leaders took their places at the head of the room.

Her smile plummeted. Before her sat not only Darlene, the bakery's faithful long-time employee who didn't hide how much she despised Olivia, but also the grandma-rescuing farmer, Blake Hartford.

Their gazes locked. A crooked grin slid up his unshaven face. A baseball cap shadowed dark eyes. Brown hair, the color of vanilla bean, brushed the collar of his brown flannel shirt. Didn't he exude the gorgeous, rugged catalogue model?

How annoying.

~*~

For the life of him, Blake couldn't concentrate on this meeting. Not when his blue-eyed accuser was going out of her way to avoid looking at him. No need. When her gaze had met his, he'd seen that her eyes were as striking as he remembered. Her presence had stunned him.

Blake was new to the board, elected six months ago, and since Elizabeth hadn't attended a meeting for almost a year, Darlene had represented the bakery. She'd practically run the place anyway.

Sheriff Miller had relayed that Elizabeth's granddaughter was now in charge, so Olivia's attendance tonight shouldn't have him as dry-mouthed as a pubescent teenager on a first date.

Glenda wiped brownie icing from her finger with a napkin. "Third order of business: how do we entice tourists to come back? My B&B hasn't seen a full house in four years. If this continues, I'll be forced to close the doors and move on."

The crowd murmured agreement.

Arthur Greene interrupted the buzz from the audience. "The Rock House has been in your family for generations."

"I know, and it would kill me to leave," Glenda said, "but when Craig died, I took out a second mortgage to remodel. I didn't foresee our economy taking a nosedive."

"None of us did." Ralph Bollero rubbed his thick palms together, the grief of losing his service station etched in the lines of his face. People didn't mind driving more than ten miles out of their way to get gas, as long as there was a connecting fast-food chain.

Darlene tapped her pencil against the table. "And

our suppliers have threatened to drop us because our orders aren't meeting their minimum yearly quota."

Olivia's head jerked up.

"Sales are down," Darlene continued, "and funds aren't available to place larger orders. Not to mention that most of the fresh ingredients would go to waste before we could utilize them."

Posture as straight as a flagpole, Olivia swept her thick, dark bangs to the side. "Actually, sales are up twenty-five percent from last quarter. I spoke to said supplier yesterday and assured them we'd meet their quota by year's end."

Darlene put down her pencil and folded her hands together. "How Pollyanna."

Either Olivia always turned green when provoked, or she was going to be sick. Even so, she was wicked cute when riled.

Elizabeth patted Olivia's hand. "Don't worry. Be happy."

Glenda slapped her palm on the table. "That's right, Lizzy. The power of positive thinking."

To her credit, Olivia never broke eye contact with Darlene. "I refuse to have it any other way."

"Ha!" Glenda poked a finger at Olivia. "This girl has spirit. I believe you're exactly what we need around here."

"We've been doing just fine without her," Darlene mumbled loudly enough to reach Blake's ears.

He was surprised at Darlene's viciousness. After years of service, it seemed as if Darlene wanted the bakery to fail. Uncharacteristic. She'd worked at the bakery since her son, John, was in middle school. Blake had been John's classmate. He'd known the family most of his life.

Glenda groped for her reading glasses, snatched her pen, and jotted something in her notebook. "The Maine Tourism Association is already taking ads for next year's travel planner. We have the necessary funds. The price includes the magazine ad as well as an ad on their website. All we have to do in the meantime is make our town more appealing. Any suggestions?"

Arthur proposed having a new welcome sign made for those entering town. Miranda recommended hiring a professional photographer to capture pictures of Stone Harbor, and then investing in a web designer to create a separate website specifically for the town, something they should've done years ago. But that was part of Stone Harbor's charm—they were behind the times.

"All great ideas, people," Glenda said. "How do we get it done?"

Olivia raised a timid hand, her cheeks a couple shades lighter than her silky, red shirt. "A friend of mine is a marketing director. He owes me a favor. I can call him tomorrow."

He?

Blake cleared his throat. "I can make a new sign."

The task shouldn't be too hard. He had the right tools in his woodshop.

Darlene slouched and crossed her arms. "It's false advertising if we don't have anything tourists want when they arrive."

Miranda motioned around the room. "There's *us*."

Glenda nodded, giving Darlene a *what's your deal* look. "Only one of us here can offer an objective opinion, give us an idea of what people see when they look at us from the outside." She turned to the only newcomer. "Olivia, what do we need to do? What are we missing?"

Olivia shifted in her chair. "Oh, I...um."

Darlene chuckled. "Who better to know what's best for this town than the people born and raised here?"

This time, Glenda didn't even try to hide her annoyance. She leveled a glare at Darlene. "We'd still like her opinion."

Agreement flooded the room, and all eyes turned to Olivia.

Yep, Olivia definitely turned seasick–green when put on the spot. She stared at her grandmother, who was engrossed in studying the stitches on her purse. Then Olivia took a deep breath and squared her slim shoulders.

"When I'm traveling, I search for places that pique my interest *and* have the conveniences I desire. A reputable hotel with restaurants and shopping or museums within a few blocks. Stone Harbor has those qualities, but the town needs a facelift."

The entire room leaned in.

Olivia swallowed. The green tinge darkened a bit.

"Grandma and I have discussed offering new services at the bakery. For example, specializing in wedding cakes, since coastal Maine is a popular wedding destination. We're also updating the menu. I'd love to remodel the old storage closet into a casual area where customers can read while they snack or utilize Wi-Fi. Maybe expand the deck that overlooks the harbor, add some tables and chairs...give folks a place to eat, relax, and enjoy the scenery—locals and tourists.

"If everyone will take the effort to add modern improvements to their businesses, I think Stone Harbor will become the bustling summer town I remember as a child."

She'd summered here? Blake hadn't known that.

"Money." Darlene's finger-rubbing interrupted his thoughts. "All that takes money, sweetheart."

Olivia addressed the group. "Far less if we do the work ourselves and help each other."

Darlene snorted. "This isn't Mayberry, city girl."

The shiny lips matching Olivia's shirt flattened into a straight line. Then her entire face glowed in a smile. "Why not? We could reinvent ourselves as the *Mayberry of Maine*."

The room exploded with voices. Nods. Smiles.

Arthur stood and began clapping. "Well done, young lady."

Olivia nodded. "I'll contact my friend right away."

Glenda whistled to quiet the room. "I'll offer fifty percent off available rooms to any local who agrees to leave an honest review on the website."

For the next thirty minutes the group brainstormed ideas. Charlie's Bike Shop would start renting bicycles by the hour so tourists could explore the peninsula. Brush Strokes Art Gallery would start hosting an art festival every August. Season's End Winery would offer wine-making classes. And Eddie and Delores Self would bring their lobster boat out of retirement and give lighthouse tours during peak season to nearby Machias Seal, Libby, and Great Wass Islands.

By meeting's end, every business had a plan and volunteer workers to help them execute the changes.

Except the bakery.

Between farm work and Little League, every minute of Blake's time was already spoken for. But something about Olivia Hudson drew him, and he commended the way she'd put Darlene in her place using positive actions instead of cutting words. So when the idea popped into Blake's mind, he threw it out there. "I'll remodel the corner of the bakery."

Olivia assessed him much the same way she had the night he'd found her grandma. Wary. Intrigued. Defensive. Thankful. However, another something told him she didn't like being beholden to anyone.

"In exchange for purchasing my blueberries during harvest, of course," Blake continued. "I also have some contacts you might want to consider. Buying local could save you money."

"An exchange." The tension of her forehead eased. "I think we can work something out."

"A plan indeed!" Glenda clasped her hands and looked heavenward. "We've got enough to keep us busy for months." She ripped out the paper she'd been scribbling on. "Blake, Olivia. You kids are perfect for organizing this facelift. Whoever's in favor of electing Blake and Olivia to run Project Mayberry, say 'aye.'"

The voices boomed in the tiny space before he or Olivia could protest.

"Meeting adjourned." Glenda slapped the table like a gavel. "See everyone next month." The sneaky board president pushed back her chair and hugged an unsuspecting Olivia, who stood with her arms at her side. Glenda patted Olivia's cheek and then walked toward the exit singing *I Will Survive*.

What had just happened?

While other members cleaned tables and straightened chairs, Blake approached Olivia, who seemed bent on strangling her wrist with her purse strap. "I think we'll work fine together as long as you can follow my rules."

The wrist-choking stopped, and her eyebrows arched over eyes beaming with so much sass they could melt ice. "Your rules?"

Blake smoothed the front of his flannel and leaned closer. "No kicking."

It took a few seconds, but Blake got the reaction he was hoping for.

She giggled—half wry, half amused. "You've come to collect on that apology now."

He grinned. "Apology accepted."

"That was easy."

"Misunderstandings happen."

"Thank you." The tension in her shoulders eased, and they relaxed into a normal line.

"All these great ideas will take some time to sort through." He held up the paper Glenda had given him. "Do you have time later in the week? We could talk over coffee. Or dinner."

Man, his skills were rusty.

"Oh." She frowned at his boots. "I'm really busy with the bakery and Grandma. I'll help how I can, but I don't have any extra time to head a project like this. Maybe you should consider someone else."

Was it his dinner offer that had her running away? "Tell you what. Everyone in town knows how to get ahold of me. If you change your mind, let me know." He stepped from the building and into the cold air, fully expecting never to hear from Olivia Hudson again.

5

Mayberry of Maine? What had she been thinking? This was reality, not a backlot with cameras and actors.

Warm water pooled into Olivia's hands, and she splashed her face to rinse away the creamy suds that scrubbed away her makeup and the day's grime. She patted her skin with a fresh towel. They wanted her—this broken therapist staring back at her in the mirror, the one who masqueraded as a baker—to lead the project as though she were the answer to all their problems. Well, she'd lost her talent for problem-solving the day she'd lost her identity. Now she could no longer tell where lies ended and truth began.

Among all the unknowns in life, one thing was certain: people would hurt you.

That's why she loved baking. A list of ingredients, precisely measured, blended, and cocooned at the right temperature had an expected end. Comfort.

No tears. No hurt. Unless one ate too much.

Cold bathroom tiles against Olivia's feet prompted her to cut short the pity party in exchange for a sweatshirt and double-lined socks, which the salesman had assured her would warm even the wimpiest Mainer. They'd lived up to their guarantee, however, she had to be careful on the smooth, plank floor unless she wanted to go ice skating.

Olivia gripped the sturdy banister on her way

downstairs, where she'd left Grandma watching reruns. The Massachusetts-style home had always captivated her with its twelve-foot ceilings and tall windowpanes. All four fireplaces were still in working order. A crackling fire sounded heavenly right now, except they had no firewood. Something she would rectify before next winter.

Grandma snored from Grandpa's worn recliner, an eighties relic kept for reverence more than functionality. A book spread open across the throw blanket. Careful not to disturb her slumber, Olivia lifted it from Grandma's lap.

She rifled through the pages. It was a scrapbook-journal of some sort, compiled mostly of photographs accompanied by a short story. It appeared to contain adventures Olivia's grandparents had had together, captured in black-and-white moments of time. She inspected the cover. *Volume One, Courting and the Newlywed Years.*

Were there others? Masculine cursive letters on the inside cover drew her attention. Olivia sank onto the sofa and settled under a throw blanket of her own.

"Living is like tearing through a museum. Not until later do you really start absorbing what you saw, thinking about it, looking it up in a book, and remembering—because you can't take it in all at once."
—Audrey Hepburn

Cherish these memories, Elizabeth, lest you forget we've had good times, too. Whatever the future holds, I will love you in health and sickness, joy and sorrow.
Cliff, 1968

Olivia's fingers curled around the book. 1968—

eight years after her dad was born. *"Lest you forget we've had good times too."*

Why would Grandpa fear she'd forget? His eloquent words held the weight of both love and sadness. A pleading of sorts. What had prompted such a gift?

Grandma woke herself snoring and changed positions. In less than three seconds, she was sleeping again. Lamplight bathed her bony frame, enhancing her pale skin and slightly sunken cheeks. So frail. So peaceful at the moment.

Her Grandpa's cryptic message whispered across the years to his wife now riddled with Alzheimer's. Today, Grandma had remembered something to make her want this book. Olivia longed to know the woman more intimately. Twelve hundred miles had kept them from connecting the way grandparents and grandchildren should. And since Olivia's dad had rarely taken the time to visit after Grandpa died, she really didn't know her grandma at all.

The journal began with how her grandparents had met at the Starboard fishing weirs in 1949.

On a warm July day with my pants rolled to my knees, I sat on the wharf, feet in the water, photographing inbound sardine boats and the area's many lagoons. What I captured through my lens instead was the most beautiful woman I'd ever seen, fishing with her father at the prime age of eighteen. The father who scowled at me for invading your privacy.

I approached and offered to deliver the memento once I'd processed the film, delighted to gain your address and an excuse to see you again. That was the day I fell in love with Elizabeth Marion Turner of Winter Harbor.

In the picture, Olivia's great-grandpa had classic

pomade-doused black hair and a thin mustache. She'd never seen a picture of him before, nor had she known his name. Her dad had always been reluctant to discuss family, a trait she'd dismissed but now pondered.

Lest you forget we've had good times too. Had something tragic happened?

Grandma needed tailored care. Olivia needed to understand where she'd come from, who she was. If she started at the roots of this family tree, maybe she'd find her branch again.

~*~

Blake stepped out of the barber shop into the afternoon sunshine. Talk of baseball and the smell of aftershave gave way to crisp, salty air and The Clam House's daily special. He ran a hand over the back of his head. He always felt a little naked after a spring cut.

A flash of pink past the rotating barber pole caught his attention. Olivia strode down the sidewalk, flipping through the letters in her hand. Blake changed direction to go after her.

She paused. Her shoulders slumped. Now may not be the best time to chat, but it was a good three blocks from the post office back to the bakery, and she still hadn't committed to helping him run the *Mayberry of Maine* campaign.

Blake made short work of the distance. "How's our town hero?"

She startled, then pinned him with those amazing eyes and frowned. "I don't know. When I find him, I'll ask."

"Aren't you as warm as a Midwestern summer."

She held up the mail in her hand and sighed. "Sorry. Bad timing."

He'd figured. "Anything I can do to help?"

The breeze stirred short strands of hair that refused to stay in her ponytail. Blake shoved his hands into his pockets to keep from acting like an idiot and pushing those hairs behind her ears. Something about this woman knocked his good sense loose.

Olivia shook her head. "Family stuff." She continued walking. "What are you doing in town today?"

He matched his steps to hers. "Picking up lumber from the hardware store."

"And getting a haircut, I see."

Blake raised a brow. "You noticed."

Her cheeks turned rosy. She seemed to be having trouble deciding between embarrassment and anger.

Blake laughed.

Her lips curled into the barest of smiles. "What are you building? Business or pleasure?"

"Both. I'm restoring my house."

"A Victorian. I heard. They're one of my favorite designs. I love the way they were built both for functionality and entertaining."

"You sound like you've studied architecture."

"Some." Her lips pressed into a straight line.

Trees shaded the sidewalk for the next block. They walked in silence most of the way.

"So." Olivia shifted the letters to her other hand. "You farm blueberries, help run the town council, and restore relic homes. What else do you do, Blake Hartford?"

"You forgot to mention rescuing little old ladies."

That earned him a genuine smile. "Yes, you're a regular knight in shining...flannel."

He chuckled and ran a hand down his shirt. Little spitfire. "I coach Little League and help with our local 4-H. What do you do besides run a bakery and care for your grandma?"

She shrugged. "Between the bakery and Grandma, I don't have time for anything else."

"I guess that means you haven't changed your mind about helping me."

They'd reached the bakery. Vanilla and warm sugar scents filled the space between them.

"I'd like to help but..."

But someone or something had done a number on her. "I don't see why two people of the opposite sex can't save a town while remaining professional. Who knows, we might even become friends."

She ran her tongue over her top teeth. "Is that why you think I'm hesitant?" Her gaze skittered away, and she shifted. "Truth is, I'm not the right person for the job. I honestly don't have anything to contribute."

"You're wrong. What you've already contributed meant everything to these people."

She blinked.

"You gave them hope."

Olivia swallowed then disappeared through the bakery's entrance.

Blake let her go. He'd pushed her far enough.

For today.

6

Hope. The word had been circling Olivia's brain for the past five days. *"You gave them hope."* The sincerity in Blake's voice, in his piercing dark eyes, held on and refused to let go.

The sweet smell of the bakery curled around her on the bakery's outdoor patio. She gazed up at the swirl of orange and purple cresting the tree tops across the harbor. The still water reflected the scene, broken only by the occasional lobster boat or brightly colored buoy.

If hope had an image, this would be it.

Olivia pulled her grandma's journal from her hoodie pocket and scanned the entry she'd read last night. Her grandparents had enjoyed a similar sunrise on Cadillac Mountain in the fall of 1949. They'd been courting a few months and had to be chaperoned by Grandma's big brother, Bobby.

Those last couple of years had been a dark time for me, trying to return to civilian life after the war, after the things I'd seen. Then I met you. And you kept agreeing to let me see you. Once again, my life was filled with light. That light was hope.

That morning on the mountain with you on one side and, unfortunately, Bobby on the other, I knew I wanted to spend the rest of my life with you. You gave me hope. Now I'm giving it back.

Rejoice in hope, Elizabeth. Be patient in tribulation. Continue in prayer. Romans 12:12.

Her grandpa's advice had collided with Blake's words in such a way that Olivia could no longer remain idle. One of the first things she counseled her patients to do was to find a place to serve. A soup kitchen, daycare, church—anywhere they could serve others. That simple gesture took the focus off self for a while and proved that no matter where a person was in life, there was always someone else worse off.

She hadn't followed her own prescription, though. After her father had initiated the divorce, and her fiancé, Justin, had buried himself in his work, her mental health had spiraled at a rate too fast for her to keep up. Before she knew it, she was the patient in the facility where she volunteered twice a month.

Olivia couldn't guarantee that helping Blake on this town project would reap positive results, but there was something about Stone Harbor she couldn't ignore. As if every wave that rolled ashore brought her a small piece of hope.

The weight of the phone in her back pocket prodded her to take the leap. She removed it and pressed send on the text she'd spent too long typing before bed last night. Brittany, one of her hardest working employees, had offered Blake's number when Olivia asked if anyone knew how to contact him. Apparently, Brittany had dated him a few times, which chafed Olivia for reasons she'd rather not examine, and warned her that even a simple friendship with this man was dangerous.

Blake was too good to be true with his earthy lifestyle, rugged attractiveness, and pristine reputation. Territory best left uncharted.

Olivia had more baggage than O'Hare International and not six months ago had been engaged. That was enough to remind her even the closest people couldn't be trusted, promises were broken every day, and she was better off alone.

The chilly temperature weaved its way beneath her layers. Olivia retreated to the warm kitchen, where a smooth tenor crooned from the radio. The smell of yeast and sugar solidified her resolve to nix any thoughts of a relationship and concentrate on building the bakery's reputation. She'd work with Blake to help this town, but she had to keep her priorities in focus. Not to make friends with the local farmers.

Brittany whizzed past carrying a large tray of packaged sourdough bread. "Red velvet's in the oven."

Olivia inhaled. "Smells amazing. Employee meeting in five. Spread the word."

The leggy, twenty-something brunette disappeared through the swinging doors to transfer the bread to the display case.

Grandma wiped the remnants of flour from the stainless-steel island. Though Grandma's health limited her in many ways, Olivia strove to include her in as much of the business as possible. Grandma was the heart of this place, and being involved seemed to make Grandma happy, even if she didn't fully understand what was going on. Including her also helped Olivia keep an eye on the wandering woman.

Olivia turned down the radio and raised her voice to be heard by all seven employees. "When you reach a good stopping point, I'd like to have a few minutes of your time." She went to grab paperwork from the office. By the time she returned to the kitchen, the giant mixers had stopped humming, two cakes were on the cooling cart, and the employees were clustered by the time clock. She took a deep breath. "To be successful, we must adapt to our customers' needs. Grandma and I have discussed this"—*several times*—"and we've decided to update the menu. We'll keep staple items, of course—breads, cookies, brownies. But now we'll offer new and seasonal desserts on a rotating schedule. My goal is to not only bring in new customers, but also to satisfy our local ones as well."

Darlene crossed her arms.

"Change can be a good thing." *Or not.* She'd had her share of both kinds. "During the peak of this bakery's success it offered a variety of goodies so delicious and unique they beckoned food critics and travel magazine writers. Unfortunately, the menu has gone stale. Let me prove it to you." Olivia handed a packet to each employee. "On page one, you'll see that the new items we've offered the last couple months have lifted sales by twenty-five percent."

Darlene's lips puckered like a grape left out in the Texas sun.

"We'll also start offering our customers specialty cake options—birthday, wedding, anniversary, graduation. These will require a consultation, to get a vision of what the customer wants, and a down payment."

Amelia's green eyes smiled along with her mouth. "Like the *Cake Boss*?"

Olivia chuckled. "I doubt we'll ever become that popular, but, yeah, that's the general idea."

Grandma splayed her fingers, palms up. "That takes hands."

"Yes," Olivia continued, "that will take extra time and hands. If you're interested in joining the cake decorating team, let me know. We'll also be hiring two additional employees."

Darlene's arms fell to her sides. "We don't need to hire more. We can handle this just fine."

Why did this woman oppose her at every turn? "The decision stands. If you have any further suggestions or concerns, I'll be in my office." Staccato voices and laughter floated through the doorway as Olivia retreated to her tiny haven. Confident these changes would take the bakery in the right direction, she inhaled a cleansing breath, closed her eyes, and massaged the knot in her right shoulder.

The office door slammed. Olivia jumped, heart pounding.

Darlene stormed toward the desk. "We're barely staying in operation as it is. If you go adding fancy things and more employees, you're going to bankrupt us."

For at least five seconds Olivia couldn't speak, stunned by the woman's brashness. She'd been nothing but kind to Darlene since her arrival, despite Darlene's crusade to make Olivia look like a fool.

Everyone had a breaking point.

"I'm not some inexperienced teenager giving orders. This place is my grandma's legacy, and I have everyone's best interests at heart. Including yours."

Darlene's fists settled on her ample hips. "I've worked here since the day this place opened twenty-three years ago. *I'm* the one who's stayed faithful to Elizabeth during good economies and bad. *I'm* the one who's managed this place in Elizabeth's mental absence. Then you come in and take over everything as if I haven't worked hard to keep this place going. What makes you more qualified?"

So that's what this was about. Olivia cleared her throat and tried for gentle. "Grandma and I appreciate all of your help. You've proved your loyalty, and are a valued and respected employee." Her comment earned an un-ladylike snort. "We no longer need you to make management decisions for the bakery. I can, however, offer you the position as head of the new cake department. This would include paid off-site training as well as a raise."

Darlene reared back as if Olivia had slapped her. "I decline. You've no legal grounds to demote me."

Olivia hated confrontation with every cell in her body. As a therapist, her job had been to analyze confrontation, not become embroiled in it. She was a peacemaker, not a pot-stirrer. "Actually, I do." Olivia reached into her stack of mail for the official document then handed it to Darlene for inspection. "As Grandma's legal Durable Power of Attorney, the bakery and everything that goes along with it falls under my care. Please, take some time to think about what I've offered and let me know by the end of the week."

The skin around Darlene's eye twitched as her face turned from pink to red to an unhealthy purple. Darlene tossed the papers on the desk and left in the same manner she'd arrived.

Much the same reaction Olivia's father had as well, according to his contesting the judge's decision.

So much for hope.

7

If Blake had a dollar for every time he'd told himself this was a bad idea—he'd be dead broke. His boots thumped across the bakery's wooden platform to the entrance, which had been built to resemble a pier. The paint had peeled, and the nautical lanterns on each side of the door were rusting. The sign read Closed, but Olivia had promised to leave it unlocked.

Should he slow down for once and consider the ramifications? He tended to do stupid things based on impulsive decisions now and again—because he was a man, as his mother liked to say. Blake knew his strong attraction to a practical stranger fell into this category, but did that stop him? No. He opened the door and went in anyway. Because if he had a dollar…

And what awaited him inside? Something more enticing than sugary dough. A yellow apron with tiny white flowers pinched around Olivia's waist, the apron strings swaying along with her ponytail and every swipe of her cleaning rag.

Her gaze met his and looked him over good before she blushed and turned away. She'd best watch herself or he'd think she'd finally warmed up to him.

"I know you're closed, ma'am, but I heard this is the best place around to get some pecan pie."

She turned, a smile lifting her mouth at his terrible attempt at a southern accent. At least now he knew there was a sense of humor behind that ice house she liked to hide in.

Olivia snapped her fingers. "Darn, I just sold the last piece. I can, however, offer you something new to the menu. On the house in exchange for an honest review."

"Best offer I've had all day."

She left for the kitchen, and Blake moved to the nearest table. His mom would go crazy in here. The room was styled like the front cover of one of those coastal home decorating magazines she always left lying around. The table seemed to shrink now that he was sitting at it, but he didn't mind getting cozy if Olivia was willing.

A moment later, the swinging kitchen doors opened, and Olivia presented a fancy bouquet-thing. She placed it on the table, cupped her hands on her hips, and smiled as if she were enjoying this way too much. Blake looked from the vase to her, then back again. Where was the pie?

"They're cake pops." She pulled out the chair across from him and sat.

Those glitter-coated puffballs were cake?

She pointed to each one. "Strawberry swirl, orange dreamsicle, cinnamon bun, and devil's food coated in chocolate ganache. If you like rich dessert, that's the one to try."

"Devil's food, it is." He turned his head from side to side. But how?

Raising a brow, she reached into the bouquet and yanked on a stick. "Surely, a big flannel man like you isn't intimidated by a little bite of cake?"

"Of course not." It was just the sissiest dessert he'd ever eaten. He took the stick from her hand and frowned at what looked like a little girl's magic wand with all the sprinkles and bling.

"The glitter is edible, if that's what you're worried about." Olivia rested her chin in her palm, waiting.

Blake wasn't worried, he was intimidated. Since he'd never let that stop him before, he leaned forward and bit into the flashy circle. And actually moaned.

Olivia smirked. "Glad you like it. Have as many as you want."

Like it? Good thing his mouth was full or he might propose marriage. He finished that cake ball and started on another.

Olivia went behind the counter and returned with a notebook, pen, and two foam cups of black coffee. "You seem like a basic coffee drinker to me, but if you need cream and sugar I can get them."

"Your perception is correct." He looked into her cup. "Hmm."

"What does 'hmm' mean?"

"Seems to me you could use some sugar and cream. You're a little tart."

The blue of her eyes sharpened, and her mouth fell open.

Blake laughed.

She slid the vase to the end of the table with a frown, proving his point. "Where do we start? Seaside Books or the winery?"

All business, that one. Did she ever have fun?

Blake wiped his mouth on a napkin and placed the empty stick on top. "I think we should start with the B&B. Glenda's already contacting past guests to offer them a forty percent discount if they stay before October twenty-fifth. Her sister is helping update their website, and Caleb Dugan is installing a bike rack to help transition the rental end of things."

Her pen scratched across the paper. "I talked to Hugh, my friend in marketing. He thinks he can get a generic version of the town website up and running within the next two weeks, including links to the different businesses. Then he can revamp as the new photographs come in. As for the Maine Tourism ad, he said he'll email a few different mock-ups we can vote on at our next meeting."

"That's a lot of work to do for free." Blake hated his curiosity.

She fidgeted with her pen. "It's an exchange of talents."

Blake leaned forward, prodding her to continue.

Olivia sighed. "His teenage daughter has Down Syndrome. Baking is her passion. I taught her what I know."

"And you wouldn't accept payment."

She concentrated on something outside the window. "The fun we had together and what she taught me far outweighed money." She went back to scribbling on her paper. "He told me if I ever needed help with marketing or web design to give him a call."

Blake leaned back in his chair. All he really knew about this woman was that she'd taken responsibility for her grandma with Alzheimer's, she gave free baking classes to kids with chromosomal handicaps, and she called in favors to help an entire town. He knew nothing else about her, but she had one of the biggest hearts he'd ever seen. The million dollar question was: why did she seem so miserable?

"We need to brainstorm ways we can incorporate the art gallery into our plans." She made another notation. "Oh, and Glenda told me some retired New

York hotshot is inquiring about the empty building on the east end of Main. Something about homemade soaps and essential oils."

"Where did you attend cooking school?"

She stilled. "Why?"

"Curiosity."

Olivia's slender fingers folded in front of her. "Le Cordon Bleu."

He was a weak man to let three little French words send him reeling.

Olivia placed her hands on top of her notebook. "If Marcy agrees, what do you think about each business taking a painting from her gallery and hanging it in their establishment for sale? That way her work is exposed to people who may not visit the gallery."

"Great idea. Did you work in a bakery before you moved here?"

"No."

"What's your favorite thing to make?"

"Peanut butter and jelly. Now, about the winery."

Blake chuckled. "You don't like talking about yourself, do you?"

Her lips flattened. "It's irrelevant."

"Not to me."

She stared at him, her bottom lip pressed between her teeth. "If I satisfy your curiosity, can we please get back to this meeting?"

"Yes." And then he could get back into the spring air and warm up.

"Despite the put-together woman you see before you, I was a very rebellious teenager." She looked at her lap and blushed. "My parents were about to crack when my counselor suggested I throw that energy into extracurricular courses. My father agreed to pay for Le

Cordon Bleu if I would agree to bake whenever I felt the impulse to be reckless. It worked. I settled down and became a contributing member of society. That's all the juice you're getting for today, so on with the meeting."

Olivia, rebellious? Reckless? *Interesting.*

"All right. What about the winery?" He wouldn't point out she'd said the words "for today."

She relaxed against her chair. "Mandy and Austin are already booking reservations for wine-making classes. Mandy said they draw quite a crowd during tourist season since they're right off the highway, and they'd like to help route that traffic to us as well as Kristport. They've suggested we put together a tour or trail from the winery to Stone Harbor."

"What do you mean?"

"Something that lists each business, like a flier or booklet, and when a person visits a business, they get a stamp. Once they receive all the stamps, they win a prize or something. I don't know. An incentive to get people's attention that we're still here."

We're. She said it as if she'd decided she was one of them and was settling in for the long haul. Blake sipped his coffee. "It could work. Where will they redeem their prize?"

"The last place they get a stamp?"

"What'll they win?"

Olivia propped her chin on her fist and looked up at the ceiling, thinking. "What if each business prints coupons for a free item? I could offer one dessert of choice. Then we combine the coupons in a bowl or something and the winner can randomly choose one. What they draw is what they get."

"And each business has one of these bowls?"

She nodded.

Blake shrugged. "We'd have to come up with a way to void their stamps once they've been redeemed. But if you think it'll work, go for it."

"I think it'll work." Her pen raced across the paper.

Blake looked around the shop. "Is that the space you're wanting to remodel?" He pointed to the corner behind him.

Her gaze followed his finger. "Yes."

She rose and walked to that side of the dining room. His chair scraped against the floor as he moved to follow. She explained her vision for a built-in book shelf, comfortable seating, Wi-Fi, and a small area for kids with a sand table, shovels, and buckets. A family atmosphere.

Blake tucked his hands into his pockets. "I'm not an artist, but I'll sketch it up after some measurements and get started if you approve."

Olivia crossed her arms. "All of us are benefiting from these changes, except you."

"You're buying my blueberries."

"We both know I'm not buying enough to compensate for all this work. What else can I do?"

Blake refrained from suggesting she go on a date with him. She'd probably deck him. "Help pick blueberries during harvest."

"That might be feasible for a day or two, but I have a business to run. What else?"

She really didn't want to be indebted to him, did she?

"I believe you mentioned you attended cooking school?"

Deadpan.

"A home-cooked meal is a great bargaining chip to a single guy."

The familiar seasick hue crept back into her face. She crossed her arms. Shifted. "Oh, I..."

When it was apparent she wasn't going to finish the sentence, he took over. "I'm not asking you to eat the meal with me, Livi."

She swallowed. "Only my parents call me Livi."

He hadn't meant to, it'd just come out. But Blake liked the way it sounded. "What do you say? A home-cooked meal once a week for a while?"

"All right. It still doesn't seem like a fair exchange."

Blake patted his gut. "Trust me. It is."

Her gaze lingered in the place his hand had just been. As soon as he noticed, she looked away. "Do Saturdays work?"

"Perfect."

Olivia hugged herself tighter. "I'll see you Saturday then."

8

Heat from the foil pan permeated Olivia's oven mitts as she soaked in every detail of Blake's Victorian farmhouse: the intricate gingerbreading, the baroque porch spindles, the stained-glass transom above the entrance. Though tattered in places, the house possessed an old-era charm, beckoning her inside.

"Where are we?" Grandma asked from the passenger seat.

"Paradise." Beyond the manicured ground surrounding the home and barn, blueberry bushes stretched every inch as far as her eyes could see. Dotted white, like a canopy of freshly fallen snow, the fields gently rolled, broken only by an occasional stack of yellow boxes. Had Olivia ever seen such an amazing sight?

"Where are we?" Grandma fiddled with the button of her seatbelt.

Olivia had explained the agreement between herself and Blake before they'd left the house, but Grandma continued to ask questions as if Olivia hadn't. "We're dropping this food off to a...friend, then we'll go back home. Would you mind carrying the basket in the backseat, please?"

Olivia bumped the car door with her hip and walked around to the other side. Once Grandma had the basket secured in the crook of her arm, they made their way to the front door. The closer they got, the more stunned Olivia was that Blake didn't live in a log cabin or a pole-barn with attached living quarters. This delicate restoration-in-progress didn't match his earthy, rugged aura.

Blake rounded the corner of the house and raised a hand in greeting. The brown-and-cream flannel he wore over a chocolate T-shirt conceded her last thought.

"Welcome." He gestured for them to climb the porch steps, then reached for the pan.

Olivia stepped back. "It's hot."

He glanced at her oven mitts and turned to Grandma with a smile. "It's good to see you again, Mrs. Hudson. May I help you inside?"

His smile and the gentleness of his words made Olivia's heart speed. Even her normally cautious grandmother couldn't resist him, for Grandma gripped his offered elbow. The trek up the porch steps took patience, but Blake didn't seem to mind. So far, the man was as sickeningly perfect as Sheriff Miller—and every other person in Stone Harbor—had described him.

The screen door, as intricately designed as the gingerbreading, squealed when Blake opened it. Olivia crossed the threshold onto a solid oak floor. To her left, a long staircase led to the second story, the railing made of vintage, stained boat oars.

"The kitchen's to your right." Blake's deep timbre, so close behind her, sent a zing up her spine.

Olivia followed his directions, and when she stepped into the big room beyond the hall, all air escaped her lungs. What appeared to be the original cabinets ran the length of one wall, adorned by unique knobs and latches. Modern granite countertops had been added on both sides of the hammered copper farmhouse sink. But what captivated her more than anything was the treasure tucked in the rear corner. "A Mayflower cook stove," she breathed.

Blake scratched his head. "Is that what that thing is?"

Was he serious? Olivia set the pan on the counter and removed the oven mitts. She practically ran to the cast-iron relic and rubbed her hand over the smooth surface, amazed at its near pristine condition. "Does it work?"

Blake approached. "I don't know, haven't tried it. I took it apart, piece by piece. It cleaned up pretty well."

Olivia swallowed. She was in love.

With the cook stove, of course. These were the things turn-of-the-century baking dreams were made of. And she was jealous it didn't belong to her. If she had her own place, she'd offer to buy it. But she didn't and...*oh, my goodness I have to have this stove.*

Grandma joined them, and together she and Olivia opened every door and warming compartment. Turned every knob. It wasn't until after they'd explored every inch that Olivia realized how rude she'd been in taking liberties with Blake's things. Her cheeks warmed. "Sorry to lose my head, but she's gorgeous."

Blake chuckled, rich and deep. "And to think I almost hauled her out of here when I bought the place."

"You can't get rid of this." She blinked at her bossy tone and softened her voice. "I mean, you *shouldn't* get rid of it. A Victorian-era cook stove of this caliber is rare. You should definitely keep it." *Or give it to me.*

A corner of his mouth twisted upward. Dark eyes studied her with interest and a fiery spark of attraction. Shoot. She'd been doing so well, keeping distant so he wouldn't get any ideas. Then she had to go and fawn over his kitchen appliances.

Blake tucked his hands in his pockets. "I guess I'll keep it then."

Because it was valuable or because she adored it? Her gut clenched. She was torn between wanting to scout the house for more antiques and wanting to flee his heated gaze. She was flattered. What woman in her right mind wouldn't be? Then again, she hadn't exactly been in her right mind for a while.

Blake glanced down at his boots, and when their gazes met again, the spark was gone. "I remember you saying you loved old houses. You're welcome to look around."

"Oh, we should probably get going. I don't want your dinner to get cold." Olivia took the basket still resting on Grandma's arm and unloaded the breadsticks and salad next to the foil pan of lasagna. Next came the pecan pie, which had seemed like a good idea this morning, since that's what he'd been after at the bakery the day of their meeting.

No, it didn't go with the Italian theme and, yes, she'd made it special to honor their deal. Now she couldn't shake the awkward vibe in the room. Was it suffocating everyone else, or just her?

Blake ushered them into the hallway that led to the living room. "Dinner will keep. You know you're dying to see it. Go on."

Was she that transparent? Either way, Blake was right. She desperately wanted to explore every inch of this house.

Brown leather furniture rested against two walls adjacent to each other separated by a floor lamp. A lovely, well-worn rug covered most of the wood flooring. Logs waited in the fireplace for the next chilly night. No shelves, pictures, or knick-knacks. Only the big screen television for a focal point.

Blake cupped Grandma's elbow. "Watch your step on the rug."

Grandma glowed under his attention. It was hard not to. Blake possessed the kind of charm that sneaked up on a girl, spoiled her, made her feel like the most important person in the world.

Since Olivia refused to be captivated, she walked to the fireplace and imagined how cozy this room would be with a few pillar candles and framed photos adorning the mantel.

"I tackled this last fall." Blake tapped the mantel, startling her from her decorating daydream.

"What a nightmare," he said. "Part of the chimney's lining had crumbled and had to be completely reconstructed. It's great to have around in the winter though. That first year here, I thought I was going to freeze to death. Not much insulation in these old places."

"That explains your obsession with flannel."

His deep rumble escaped again, wrapping around Olivia like a warm blanket. She'd always enjoyed a good spar but hadn't had it in her for a long time. Something about Blake managed to resurrect her feisty attitude.

"Live here long enough, and it'll become your best friend."

"Not likely. What room is the balcony attached

to?"

"The master bedroom. It's got a great view. You're welcome to go upstairs if you want. Don't mind the mess. I've been expecting an email, so I'm gonna check my messages. Take your time."

Before Olivia could confer with Grandma, the woman picked up a copy of *Co-Op Weekly*, dropped onto the couch's middle cushion, and stretched her legs in front of her. Olivia glanced at Blake. He winked his approval, sending another round of aggravating warmth into Olivia's cheeks.

She climbed the stairs, determined to relax and enjoy the tour since this would be the only time she'd allow herself to stay and visit. From here on out, she'd drop his food off at the door and leave.

No sparring. No winking. No flirting.

The house enchanted her more with every room she explored. The spare bedrooms were cold and had yet to be tackled. Decades-old wallpaper still clung to the plaster walls she wished could reveal their secrets.

Justin, amazing architect that he was, could design a place like this, but he'd never be able to build it. In fact, she doubted if he'd ever picked up a hammer. Maybe that's why he'd run at the first sign of difficulty. He could design his idea of marriage but wasn't capable of building it on a strong foundation, of restoring the broken pieces.

Blake, however, made a living with his hands, farming and building. And whether she wanted to admit it or not, there was something extremely appealing about such qualities. Of course, that didn't mean Blake used them in his relationships. After all, the man was single. There was probably a good reason why.

The next door opened to a finished bathroom restored to a perfect combination of white walls, slate floor tiles, and gray-stained trim. Keeping with the bachelor theme, the only objects in the room were simple lighting, a mirror, a laundry hamper, and a towel hanging from the wall hook. The replicated claw-foot tub held shower plumbing as well, and she suspected the tub had only been added for a touch of authenticity.

The last room was Blake's. She hesitated in the doorway. Going in seemed intimate somehow, which was silly since he was downstairs. It was just a room. The balcony view he'd boasted about eventually won out, and she stepped inside.

The scent of his cologne wrapped around her—sunshine, ocean water, and man. Ignoring the trigger it pulled in her brain, she flipped the light switch and covered her mouth to keep from laughing.

Flannel bedsheets. The man had a serious obsession.

If she hadn't experienced the mind-numbing cold of a Maine winter herself, she might question the man's faculties. However, the fabric served a purpose and combined with the fireplace across the room, no doubt he stayed warmer at night than she did.

A set of heavy French doors offered access to the balcony. She opened them to a vision of blueberry bushes stretching to the edge of the plateau, beyond which a sliver of ocean was visible in the distance. A strange sensation flooded her body—a tingle, like circulation flowing through a once-pinched limb.

This house. It whispered to her. The idea of lovingly restoring an object that was once vibrant but had fallen into shambles filled her with yearning so strong it brought tears to her eyes. Was it possible for a person to feel a connection to a house that wasn't hers? Maybe she was crazier than she thought.

A dog barked.

Olivia shook away the complicated feelings, realizing that for the first time in a long time, the numbness had faded and she was feeling. In some ways, it was almost painful. She stepped off the balcony, closed the doors, crossed the room, and rushed down the stairs, afraid if she took any longer, Blake would think she'd decided to move in.

Olivia found Blake and Grandma on the front porch.

A decrepit golden retriever lumbered up the steps and sat next to Grandma's feet.

"Dog," Grandma said.

Blake smiled, his white teeth contrasting against his five-o-clock shadow. "This is Scooby."

Olivia reached out so the dog could sniff her hand. "As in the cartoon mystery crime-fighter?"

He nodded. "I had Velma, too, but she passed away five years ago. The old boy hasn't been the same since."

"How old is he?"

"Eighteen."

Methuselah, in dog years.

"Hey, Scoob." Olivia patted his head.

Grandma smiled like a kid on Christmas and joined in the dog loving.

Scooby dropped to his side for a belly rub and moaned.

"Now he'll expect you to do that every time you come over." Blake leaned against the porch railing, crossing his arms and ankles.

Her next visit would go much differently. "We should get going." Olivia stood. "We've kept you from dinner long enough."

Blake's smile dimmed.

"Come on, Grandma." Olivia helped her up, linked their arms, and they slowly made their way down the steps.

When their feet hit grass, Grandma turned and waved. Not to Blake, but to Scooby.

Blake raised a hand and watched them all the way to the car.

Olivia knew this because she was also watching him from her peripheral vision. Once inside the car, Olivia checked Grandma's seatbelt then started the engine. Hand poised over the shifter, Olivia stopped when Grandma grabbed her wrist. "That man."

The same words Grandma had used to describe Blake the night he'd found her walking. Only this time her eyes were absent of fear.

Olivia stared at Blake through the windshield. He hadn't moved from his spot on the porch, arms and ankles crossed. That man, indeed.

9

Blake waved as Olivia's car angled toward the road and drove away. Minus the crickets warming up for their nightly symphony, a depressing silence hovered over him. He wasn't sure how long he stood there staring at the barren driveway. The thump of Scooby's tail against the floor reined him in. Blake knelt and rubbed the dog's thick neck. "Hey, boy."

Scooby sneezed, shooting dog spray on Blake's hand. Just as well. He needed to wash up and eat his dinner before it turned cold. It smelled amazing, and Blake had wanted to dive in as soon as Olivia arrived, but female company took precedence over food. Blake stood, and Scooby padded to his bed by the swing, eased down, and sighed.

With one last look toward the road, Blake noted the dry, dead stalks of rose bushes that lined the porch. The ones he'd planted for Madison. The ones she'd never tended. The ones that had never bloomed. Why hadn't he yanked them up before now? Why was he still hanging on to a dead idea two years later? Madison wasn't coming back. He didn't want her back. He wanted to move on, find the right woman to marry, and share this big house. Enough time had passed.

No woman since had captured his interest the way Olivia had in the last month. He knew virtually nothing about her except that she could go from a day at the beach to a blizzard in two point five seconds. Something about her tugged at his heart. It was clear as the blue of her eyes she'd been wounded. Deeply. Blake was determined to find out how and see if there was anything real in that spark between them.

First, dinner.

He went indoors, fetched a plate from the cabinet, and dished out man-sized portions of lasagna, salad, and garlic bread. He entered the living room, where he ate every night. For the first time, the room felt empty. The recliner sank with his weight. There was nothing good on TV, so he forced himself to concentrate on a show set on the Alaskan landscape, where a group was searching for gold. An episode he'd seen three times already. By the time the show ended, his mouth and belly were satisfied. His heart was not.

Oh, yeah, Olivia had brought dessert.

Hoping it would counteract his restlessness, Blake got a fresh plate and peeled back the foil. Pecan pie.

He smiled. Was there meaning behind this gesture? He'd like to think so. After cutting a slice big enough for two, he stood against the counter and forked his first bite as he watched darkness swallow the last sliver of daylight out the window. A nutty sweetness melted on his tongue. With each bite, Blake's motivation to know Olivia grew. Why would a woman with such talent abandon her life and move fifteen-hundred miles away to care for her grandmother?

He fetched a pencil and paper and got to work sketching the remodel she'd detailed for him. In order to start building, he'd have to take measurements. And measurements gave him an excuse to stop by the bakery.

~*~

Lightning flashed across the harbor toward Seal Island. Thunderheads rolled toward the bakery. Olivia quickened her pace sweeping the outdoor patio. The sky was painted a despairing gray, and the ocean matched her mood. Dark blue and churning with turmoil.

Her colleagues had assured her on this morning's video chat that all of Olivia's patients were progressing under their care and the practice would be waiting when she returned.

Did she want to go home? After her recovery and Justin's declaration they should take some time apart to regroup, Stone Harbor had been a temporary solution to her desire to get away. The longer she stayed and invested in the bakery, in Grandma's care, in this town, the more the term temporary gained its way to permanency.

In some ways, a new life appealed to Olivia. In other ways, she knew parts of herself had died, and she'd never get them back. And that wasn't OK with her.

The wind skidded over the water and whipped around her. Goosebumps covered her body. The oncoming storm reminded her of last summer when Justin had driven them to southern Indiana for a picnic in the country. The downpour had been an unexpected but welcome interruption, as they'd sought shelter in a nearby barn. The way he'd held her, the longing in his eyes. Then he'd lowered to one knee. It was by far the happiest day of her life.

Followed by the worst.

Now Justin was as lost to her as a leaf caught in a tornado. Another temporary solution that was quickly gaining permanency.

"Are you trying to get soaked?"

Olivia startled at the familiar tenor. Prickles aggravated her skin again for an entirely different reason. She propped the broom against the railing and rubbed the sensation away.

"You scared me."

"You were deep in thought."

Blake watched her with such intensity she almost bared her soul. A gust of wind blew the broom sideways, and it smacked the deck with a jarring clank.

He picked it up just as rain started to fall. He placed a palm on her upper back and led her inside the bakery at a jog. Nothing intimate. Something a relative or a friend might do. But it struck a place inside her that started to ache. She'd long forgotten the comfort of human contact. The simple squeeze of a hand for encouragement. A hug on a rotten day.

He severed his touch as soon as the door closed. "It always smells good in here."

"That's the point." She grinned, reaching for the broom in his hand.

Blake looked as if he'd forgotten he was holding it. He thrust it toward her.

"Thanks. What brings you in on such a fine day?"

The place was empty except for the two of them and Grandma and Brittany, who were in the kitchen. The morning had been steady, but late afternoon with this weather promised an early quitting time.

He pulled a folded paper from his coat pocket. "This."

She perused the sketch, amazed at how well he'd remembered all the details she'd mentioned.

"If I forgot something, let me know. Otherwise, I'll

take some measurements and work on getting materials."

Olivia studied it again, checking the sketch against the space. "Looks like you've got it covered. Thank you."

He took the offered paper. "Thank you for the lasagna Saturday. Much better than frozen."

The air crackled between them, causing another round of goosebumps.

Blake cleared his throat. "Maybe next time I can convince you to stay and eat with me."

Her insides tumbled. Adrenaline rushed. She knew Blake was attracted to her. He'd not tried to hide it. She was attracted to him, too. But things between them couldn't go any further than that.

"I...well, Saturdays are our busiest days and Grandma, she...tires easy, and it's hard to—"

"I understand. Doesn't hurt to ask." Blake winked and pulled a measuring tape from his coat pocket. His face revealed nothing, but she was familiar with the cold slap of rejection.

Maybe the Italian crème cake she'd planned to make him this Saturday would make up for it.

Blake set to work measuring the length and height of the wall.

From her vantage point behind the counter, she was aware of every move he made. Even if she wasn't looking. She scrubbed the counter until it shined. Separated the bread and rolls to be sold at discount the following day. Wiped smudges from the glass display case. Emptied the coffee pots. Closed out the register. She couldn't take another minute of the awkward tension.

Blake inched toward the door. "I think I've got

everything I need. We'll talk later." He turned the knob.

"Wait. About Saturday." She exhaled a breath full of angst and guilt.

"No worries, Livi." He opened the door, stepped through, then poked his head back in. "I'll ask again next week."

That wicked grin was so boyish and adorable, she couldn't tamp down her smile. In fact, she was still wearing it when she walked into the kitchen.

"What's got you beaming?" Brittany dunked the mop into the wheeled bucket. A cloud of lemon-scented bubbles floated to the floor.

"What are you talking about?" Olivia checked the ovens to make sure they'd been turned off.

"The womanly glow brought on from a flirty, hot guy."

"There was a hot guy here?"

Water whooshed as Brittany pulled the bucket handle to squeeze the mop. "Nice try. I saw Blake through the window." She pointed to the circular windows in the swinging doors. "If you really hadn't noticed him, your face wouldn't be as red as that cake." Now Brittany indicated the red velvet discs cooling on the rack.

Olivia pressed a hand to her cheek. Flaming.

Brittany giggled and worked the mop beneath the work tables.

Olivia transferred the cakes to the walk-in freezer then turned out the office lights. "Here." Olivia took the mop from Brittany. "I'll finish up. Go spend time with your fiancé."

Now Brittany was beaming. "Thanks. It's Aaron's birthday. We've got reservations in Bangor."

"Drive safely."

The bathroom door down the hall opened, then closed. Grandma entered the kitchen, drying her hands on a paper towel.

"Careful, Grandma, the floor is wet."

Grandma patted Olivia's shoulder in response and handed her the paper towel. She shuffled to the CD player and turned it on. Billie Holiday's *The Very Thought of You* flowed through the speakers. Grandma closed her eyes and swayed to the bluesy rhythm.

Olivia wrapped her hands around the mop handle and rested her chin on top. The nostalgic tones filled the room with magic from a bygone era. A time of simplicity, though every generation had their troubles.

In that moment, in the middle of a struggling bakery with half-mopped floors, Olivia witnessed her grandma drift to another time and place. If only Olivia could let go of her sorrow and dance freely.

~*~

Valentine's Day, 1950

The Tennessee Waltz by Patti Page. That's the song we were dancing to at Moe's when tears began running down your cheeks. You'd lost your father right after Christmas, and I had to practically drag you out with me that night. You'd not only lost the first man you'd ever loved, but also your protector. After the song was over, I sank to one knee and asked you to marry me. I wanted to take over as your protector. Become the last man you'd ever love.

Look at that smile on your face, Elizabeth! Tears and all. I told Brian Lueken not to capture the moment unless he saw that smile. You've always had the most beautiful smile.

"They that sow in tears shall reap in joy." Psalm 126:5. Show me your smile again, my dear. You've been sowing long enough.

10

Blake yawned into his fist. "Thanks for dinner, Mom."

"You're welcome, sweetheart. Are you sure you got enough to eat?"

He patted his full gut. "And then some." He kissed her cheek, breathing in the citrusy scent of her perfume.

"There's a bag of leftovers by the door. Take them with you." She fluffed the puff of blonde curls pinned to her head.

"Thanks." He looked around the corner into the living room where his dad was reclined, watching basketball. "Bye, Dad."

No reply. Blake chuckled.

"Kenneth! Blake's leaving."

The chair rocked forward. Dad approached him, arm outstretched, his gaze never leaving the big screen. "Bye, son. Drive safe."

Blake clasped his hand. Lines fanned out from around the man's eyes and mouth, though he still looked younger than his fifty-nine years. The older Blake got, the more he noticed their similarities in the mirror.

This room held so many memories. Worn carpet from wrestling matches, indoor camp outs, and family movie nights. Nothing had been updated except for the television and the computer in the corner. Same curtains, same furniture, same framed photos lining the mantel. He avoided those snapshots during visits.

Too painful.

Blake turned to the door. "Thanks again for the food."

"There's a bag of chocolate chip cookies in there. From the bakery."

Blake stilled, his hand wrapped around the doorknob. Oh, no. She had that I-have-something-to-say-but-I'm-trying-to-be-sneaky-about-it look. *Must tread carefully.* "Sounds good. 'Night, Mom." He picked up the bag and twisted the doorknob.

"I ran into Glenda at the market." Mom casually tucked her hands into her pants pockets. "She said you were working with the bakery's new manager, Olivia, on the *Mayberry of Maine* project."

He'd almost made it through the door. Blake closed it once again, blocking the chilly air. Cleared his throat. "And out of curiosity you went by the bakery to meet Olivia?"

Mom lifted a bony shoulder. "Well, naturally, I was interested."

"Meddling."

"Researching."

"Ah." Blake nodded, dreading where this conversation was going. "And what did you learn?"

She stepped closer. "Olivia's sweet. And very cute."

"Is she?"

Mom squinted. "As if you didn't notice."

Blake scratched his cheek. "What are you getting at?"

"Oh…just that you're single…she's single…you're around the same age."

"You asked her if she was single?"

"Not outright."

"Leave the boy alone, Rita," Dad called from his recliner.

She threw her hands out. "I just want to see my son happy again."

"I'm happy, Mom." He patted her cheek and tried again for the door.

"I talked to your brother yesterday."

Blake's chin dropped to his chest. The noise from the TV silenced. He inhaled through his nose, trying to damper his smoldering temper. "I have a brother?" He regretted the wince he caused her.

"Honey, I know you're still upset—and rightfully so—but he's still your brother."

"Brotherhood doesn't mean a thing to him. He's the one who betrayed me, remember?"

Mom nodded. "I haven't forgotten. You weren't the only one hurt." She blinked rapidly. "He said Madison is well."

"Oh, good. I've been worried about that."

Dad entered the hall, cold steel in his gaze. Three or thirty, it was meant to put Blake in his place.

Blake released a long breath. "I don't mean to be disrespectful. I just don't understand the point of this conversation."

Mom swallowed. "They're engaged."

Her words were a mammoth bowling ball, and Blake the only pin.

Engaged.

Wouldn't that make family holidays awkward? Especially once they had kids.

"I'm so sorry, honey." Her voice trembled. "I know this isn't easy for you to hear. You're our sons, and we love you both very much. Even if we're not happy with your brother's decisions. They're able to live with what they've done, and…" she sighed, "they love each other. It's been almost three years. Forgive your brother, Blake. Open your heart to someone else again."

This time Blake escaped. The night air rolled across his heated skin as he stormed to his truck. Engaged. *Engaged.* The word tumbled inside his brain like an avalanche. The next thing he knew, he was pulling into his own driveway. Gravel popped beneath the tires. He killed the heat pooling at his feet and ran both hands along his face, remembering the mix of regret and surety on Madison's face the day she confessed she was leaving Blake for his brother. The urge to punch something roared inside him. His forehead tightened, and he rubbed the tension pounding behind his brows.

Lucas always had a way of getting what he wanted—The older brother, sure of what he wanted in life and determined to get it no matter whom he had to bulldoze. Blake had figured one day Lucas would hit the limit of his selfishness, but that day was yet to come.

The truck door slammed shut behind Blake. His boots devoured the distance to the porch. He paced the length of the railing.

He didn't want Madison back. Still, all this time, he kept expecting the day when their relationship would crumble and Lucas would admit how stupid he'd been. How wrong. Not that their relationship would ever be the same, but it would've brought some comfort to know his brother regretted his behavior. Blake leaned his elbows on the railing and fought to steady his breath, slow his racing pulse.

Scooby whimpered and pressed the side of his wet

nose to Blake's leg. The porch light revealed the dog's questioning brown eyes.

Blake rubbed Scooby's head. He'd been rude to his mother tonight, and he felt bad for that. Mom was as torn up about it as Blake was, though in a different way. He hated that for her. As a mother, her position couldn't be easy. But forgiveness was asking more than Blake could give.

Two years—almost three as Mom had reminded him—had a way of numbing the pain. Until tonight. He was ready to move on, find the woman God had created for him. Build a life together on this land. Raise a family. But he couldn't get over his brother's betrayal.

An image of Olivia materialized in his mind. Mom had brought her up, which was most likely why she was there. Like him, Olivia had been the victim of some situation, not the perpetrator. She wore it as tangibly as a winter coat.

Was that what intrigued him? Some invisible common bond? No, it was more than that. Something Blake couldn't decipher but wanted to. Desperately.

~*~

Olivia glanced at Grandma asleep in the passenger seat, mouth open, snores escaping with every inhale. Grandma had wandered the first floor most of the night. She'd insisted on cooking breakfast at two in the morning, and then had vacuumed the already vacuumed rugs. Grandma was getting her nights and days confused, one of the more difficult stages for a caregiver to cope with. Especially a caregiver with a bakery to run.

The road blurred before her, and Olivia blinked. It'd been a long day with a visit to Grandma's doctor, work, and cooking Blake's dinner. She was grateful she'd prepped the night before. A hot bath and ten hours of sleep were calling her name. Hopefully, the doctor's suggestion of a nighttime routine with soft music, gentle massages, and no television would help Grandma sleep better at night.

The Hartford Farms sign appeared in the distance. She tapped the brake and slowed the car to make the right turn into Blake's driveway. She'd gone all out, making fried chicken, buttery mashed potatoes, green beans, and Italian crème cake for him to enjoy. Alone. The niggling guilt hadn't ceased since he'd asked her to join him, and she'd refused. Ridiculous, since him dining alone was part of their agreement in the first place.

Still, Blake was a great guy, and he'd managed to weasel more smiles out of her since they'd met than in the entire past year. She was beginning to enjoy his company. Or maybe it was her lack of Zs talking.

She parked, unbuckled her seatbelt, and got out of the car, deciding it best not to wake Grandma. The temperature was finally warm enough to make Olivia believe spring was close, which gave her spirit a little energy. She shouldn't be long, but she draped a throw blanket they kept in the backseat over Grandma and collected the food, bumping the door closed with her hip.

Blake was kneeling in the mulched pad in front of his porch, yanking up what she suspected were rosebushes. With gloved hands, he yanked and tore, ripping up the ground, sending thorny branches sailing into the air. The muscles in his back and arms rolled with every angry strike at the plants.

"I have your dinner."

Blake jumped and spun to face her, dark eyes narrowed, sweat beading his forehead. A thin line of red smeared his arm where he'd rolled up his sleeves and a thorn had gotten revenge.

Fierce. And handsome. Olivia stepped back, weak-kneed.

Blake swallowed. His features relaxed. "I didn't hear you pull up." His voice was deeper than usual. Strained.

"I'm sorry." Why she apologized, she didn't know.

He frowned. Was he mad that she'd turned him down?

The weight of the food sent Olivia into motion. "Grandma's sleeping in the car, so I need to get going. I'll put this in the kitchen where I did last time, if that's all right. Unless you don't plan on eating soon. If not, I can put it in the fridge."

His gaze pierced her. Not in a threatening manner, but full of intensity. This brooding Blake was not the guy she knew.

He yanked off his work gloves. "Fridge is fine. I'll get the door."

Holding her elbow in the slightest of touches, he guided her up the steps and opened the screen door.

Scooby stood from his bed in the corner, tail wagging, nose sniffing in the air.

Olivia tried not to gawk at the Mayflower stove on her way to the fridge, but she failed. The smooth cast iron was begging to be touched.

"Thanks for the food." Blake stepped to the sink and washed his hands. Olivia couldn't help but stare at them, whitened with suds. There wasn't anything extraordinary about them. They were average in length with short, squared nails on each finger. An equal combination of soft skin and callouses. They were capable hands. Capable of hard work and gentle caressing. Capable of fighting off danger or cradling a baby.

Whoa. Where had that come from?

Olivia turned away, mentally slapping herself. She had to get some sleep tonight before she completely lost her faculties. "Uh, you're welcome. See you around."

Another mental slap for a squeaky voice. The screen door clapped behind her, followed by the thump of Blake's boots and another clap.

Scooby waited at the stairs, whining for attention.

Olivia bent to rub his neck before fleeing to the car. The guilt of disappointing Blake ate her alive. Just past the steps, she turned around, continuing her walk backwards. "The mock website is up. You should check it out. If you don't have Internet, you're welcome to stop by and use ours." Her face heated. Why was she tripping all over herself because a guy washed his hands? Stupid.

Blake nodded.

Olivia turned and finished her trek to the car. She didn't have to look at Blake to know he was watching her. She could feel his eyes on her.

Thrilling.

Disturbing.

She was certifiably crazy. Blake was entitled to a bad mood. Why should a little brooding—even if it was dark and a little sexy—twist her insides? Jet her pulse?

More importantly, what happened to cause Blake to turn inside out and act completely out of character? He wasn't one of her clients, and they were barely friends. She shouldn't care. Couldn't care.

Oh, but care she did.

11

If punctuality was the politeness of kings, Arianne Anderson was a queen.

Olivia looked from her friend to the clock then back again. Every Thursday, like clockwork.

Arianne's polka-dot rain boots squeaked on the linoleum as she shed her coat, hung it on a hook by the bakery's entrance, and walked to a barstool. "I'm here for an appointment with Ms. Hudson."

Olivia smirked. "You're six hours early."

"And you look like a dewy flower. What's up?" Arianne raised her elbows on the counter to see Olivia's entire outfit.

"A dewy flower. Can't say I've ever been called that before."

"Looks to me like you purposefully matched your blush and lipstick to your pink blouse. Who's the bee?" Arianne wiggled her eyebrows.

"I'm confused."

"You're the flower, so—"

"Who's the bee, I gotcha." Olivia leaned one arm on the counter and propped the other her hip. "Can't a girl just feel like dressing up?"

"Of course, but usually, at your age, said feeling is caused by a man."

"Are you calling me old?"

"Old enough."

"Pick your poison."

"Surprise me." Arianne clasped her hands in front of her. "I'm loving the retro apron, by the way. Very strategic."

With a playful scowl, Olivia slipped on poly gloves and reached into the display case. The local women's club was meeting in the back corner. Several members clustered around a woman with a tablet, all dressed in red and purple with large hats and feather boas. They cackled and howled over something on the screen, making Olivia smile. She was glad the locals were using the bakery to fellowship.

Olivia set a plate and fork in front of Arianne. "Lemon-raspberry wedding cake with marzipan frosting."

"Mmm. You're the best."

"I know." Olivia went for a napkin. "How are things in the world of wedded bliss?"

"Business is good. In my personal life, we had a scare in the emergency room last weekend." Arianne took a bite. "This is amazing."

Olivia grabbed a cleaning rag. "What happened?"

"Emma came home from school sick. Pneumococcal pneumonia. She'd been feeling puny for a few days, but we never suspected anything that serious."

"How's she doing?"

"Better. She's on a long-term antibiotic and is only going to school half-days. It'll be a slow recovery, but she's a strong girl. I think Huck's blaming himself."

Olivia held up a finger and filled a to-go order for a customer. She waited until the woman left before continuing the conversation. "Why would Huck feel responsible?"

Arianne swallowed her bite of cake and pointed to the coffee machine. "I'm a terrible wife who freaked out because this illness is a huge deal for a transplant patient." She sighed. "And because my downfall is blaming others when unexpected events happen in my life."

Olivia poured her coffee. "You're a control freak."

Arianne sucked in a breath. "I am not."

Olivia raised the foam cup in the air to emphasize her point.

"OK, maybe I am."

The women's club were clustered by the door, grabbing their umbrellas and coats from the hooks.

Olivia raised a hand. "Bye, ladies. Thanks for coming in."

Fingers wiggled back before they filed out the door, bringing in a rush of cool, damp air.

Olivia leaned her elbows on the counter, grateful they could have this conversation alone. "You're afraid of falling apart, so you micromanage to bind anxiety." She smiled at her friend to soften the blow.

Arianne's forehead knotted. "I don't like surprises."

"Not the bad ones anyway."

"I know I do this, so why do I keep doing it?"

Olivia took a seat next to her friend. "A lot of adult control issues stem from childhood. A chaotic home, early abandonment, a parent who abuses drugs or alcohol."

"My mom died from leukemia when I was seven. My dad was never the same after that. I became mother hen to my little sister."

"There you have it."

"How do I stop?"

"Unfortunately, you'll probably carry those tendencies the rest of your life. They're branded on you. It'll take work, but you'll have to train yourself to function differently. Start by relinquishing your hold on little things—chores, planning an event, petty arguments. Remind yourself if things don't go *your* way, the world will keep spinning. Then work your way up to the big things." Olivia laid her hand on Arianne's arm and softened her voice. "Like getting pregnant."

Arianne inhaled, as if Olivia had punched her in the stomach. She nodded. "Let go, and let God." She exhaled. "I *know* He's in control and His plans are perfect. I hate that I struggle believing it sometimes."

Olivia turned away before Arianne could see the sheen in her own eyes. She was such a hypocrite.

"What did you do before you moved here? Career wise?"

Olivia froze. "I...kept busy."

Silence reined for a few moments.

"Like the way you're keeping busy rearranging the desserts in the display case to avoid answering?"

"Maybe."

"Eat a cookie."

"That was random."

"When I eat here, I spill my secrets. Have a cookie."

Olivia shrugged. "I'm immune to my own charms."

Arianne stood and perused the case, eyes squinted. "That one right there." She pointed to a thick cookie the size of her hand. "If I have to walk back there and get it myself, I will. You have no customers besides me at the moment, so take a break, grab a snack, and sit."

"Control freak."

Arianne returned to her cake. "So I am. But I know there's more to you than vanilla frosting, and I have a feeling you're going at things alone. Talk to me."

Olivia obeyed. Not because she wanted to confess her life story, but because it had been a really long time since someone had looked at her deep enough to notice her needs. And actually care.

"I'm worn out. Grandma's been keeping me up most nights. I'm helping on the town project, working long hours…"

"Have you considered live-in help?"

"As much as I hate to, I guess I'm going to have to consider that possibility." Olivia nibbled the cookie.

"That's good." She took a bigger bite.

"What kind is it?"

"Chocolate chip coconut."

"I'll take two for the road."

Olivia's stomach growled. She pressed a hand against it. "I didn't even realize I was hungry."

"You're overworked." Arianne pointed at her. "Self-inflicted." She cocked her head. "Are you trying to stay so busy you forget your troubles?"

Olivia twisted her lips.

"Been there. Done that. Now, back to my earlier question. What was your career back in Indiana?"

Rats.

Olivia opened her mouth. Closed it.

Arianne nudged Olivia's knee with her own.

"I'm a certified mental health therapist."

"I knew it!" Arianne looked around and lowered her voice. "You're too good at helping others to be anything else. What brought you here?" Arianne patted the counter. "Wait, let me guess. You…fell in love with one of your patients."

"Gack." Olivia chuckled. "Don't buy into the stigma of the job. That rarely happens." She took another bite. "I reached a dead end in my life and needed to go another direction. Baking has always been therapeutic for me, and Grandma needed help. Here I am."

Arianne ate the last of her cake and pushed her plate away. "A dead end street is a great place to turn around." She caressed Olivia's arm. "I'm glad you ended up here."

Emotion rose in Olivia's chest. "Please don't share my secret. The customers might stop buying if they think the magic isn't in my desserts."

Arianne moved her thumb and pointer finger over her mouth like a zipper. "When life gives you nuts, make trail mix."

They laughed.

The door to the bakery blew open and a man stepped through, bringing a spray of rain inside with him and interrupting their conversation.

Olivia's body went on full alert.

The door closed, and Blake swept the hood from his head. "It's a lot sunnier in here than it is out there." He stood on the mat and removed his jacket, then hung it on the rack. His dark blue shirt, a muted southwestern pattern, was tucked in, revealing a leather belt.

Olivia squelched the desire to run her fingertips on his sleeve to see if the material was flannel, even if the pattern was not. "Hey." That was not her breathy voice. Well, it was, but only from the dry cookie. Except her cookies weren't dry.

He wiped his boots on the rug. "I brought you some samples to look over if you have a minute."

"Sure." Olivia popped up off the stool and threw the remaining cookie into the trash.

"Blake?" Arianne stood and slung her purse strap over her shoulder.

"Oh, hey, Arianne." Blake threw up a hand. "How's Emma?"

"Doing better. She's back home."

Olivia fiddled with her apron strings. "You two know each other?"

Arianne opened her purse and pulled out her wallet. "Blake used to own the building my bridal boutique is in. He gave Huck a good deal on it."

Of course he did, because Blake had yet to have any flaws. "Whatcha got?" Olivia indicated the small bag in his hands.

Mist clung to the dark hair at his forehead where the wind had blown it under his hood. Even with a foot between them she could feel the heat radiating off his body. And, my goodness, the man smelled better than her kitchen. Heat flushed her insides. Where had this sudden and unwanted attraction come from?

Arianne gave a knowing smirk and took her precious time sliding the cash across the counter.

"You said you wanted the bookshelf to be white." Blake pulled out three paint sample squares. "You wouldn't believe how many shades of white there are. Anyway, if you want to keep it simple you can pick from matte, semi-gloss, or glossy." He handed Olivia the samples.

"Um…" These decisions were too hard with him hovering over her, and a romance-addict analyzing her every move. "Glossy is fine."

"Great." He tucked that card in his back pocket. "As for trim," he dug around in the bag and pulled out several small pieces of wood about two inches long. "This will go at the top and bottom of the bookcase. There's crown molding," he lined two strips on the counter, "cove," one more, "and ornamental."

Three choices on the ornamental alone. Six in all. And why did Arianne have that goofy grin on her face? "I like this one." Olivia held up a strip of crown molding. Simple. Easy to clean.

"Renovations?" Arianne dropped her wallet back into her purse and reached for her coat.

Olivia busied herself putting Arianne's money into the register. "Every business in town is making changes in hopes to draw in tourists. We're reinventing ourselves. Blake is helping me here."

"Good move. I hear Blake is very talented with his hands."

He shrugged. "I enjoy making things."

Modest. And ignorant to innuendos, thank heavens.

"Aren't you meeting with a client in twenty minutes?" Olivia handed Arianne a bag with three cookies and widened her eyes in a please-agree-and-leave look.

Arianne glanced at her watch. "Thanks for reminding me. Good to see you, Blake."

"Bye, Arianne. Take care."

Arianne slipped her arms into her coat, covered her head with her hood, and stepped halfway out the door. "The roads are slick." Arianne winked at Olivia. "*Bee* careful."

Flowers. Bees. Hilarious.

Blake's brow knotted.

"Where were we?" Olivia joined him and held her hand out for the bag.

"The sand table. But, now that she's gone, I need to say something." Feet shoulder width apart, one hand in his pocket, Blake ran his other hand over the back of his head.

Oh, boy.

"I'm sorry for my gruff behavior Saturday."

Whew.

"I'd gotten some bad news that, well, put me in a foul mood. I'm sorry."

Then it wasn't her rejection of his dinner offer? Good. "I understand. No worries." She smiled to solidify their truce. And got a little lost in his eyes. What kind of news could've rattled such an easy-going guy?

The corner of Blake's mouth curled. His fingertips brushed her forearm.

"Sand tables." Olivia jerked away, the spell broken. "Let's talk sand tables."

Because that was a much safer topic than where her mind had been heading. Everyone had problems. That didn't mean she had to fix them. She was a baker now. Not a therapist. And certainly not a relationship expert.

13

Olivia pulled into the garage, peering at the empty black sports car parked next to the house. She didn't recognize the vehicle and couldn't make out the license plate from this angle. "Were you expecting company?"

Grandma stopped humming and opened her eyes. "We have company."

Yes, they did. Leery of who would stop by unannounced at dusk, and where they were on the property, Olivia turned off the engine, secured her pepper spray, and readied her cell phone to dial 911. Her measures might be extreme for this remote area, but the habits of a single woman living and working in a big city die hard.

They got out of the car, and Olivia scouted the perimeter of the house. The outdoor lights were on, something Olivia was positive she'd turned off this morning. Whoever was here had to be inside.

A chill ran the length of her spine. Who else would have access to the house?

Pepper spray at the ready, she turned the knob. Unlocked.

"Stay behind me," Olivia whispered, wedging herself between Grandma and the door.

How would she ever get Grandma to safety if this visitor was a threat? The woman wasn't physically able to run, and her slow reaction time might cost them precious seconds.

Arm raised in the air, Olivia flung open the door and lunged inside. The sight of the tall, barrel-chested man stopped her cold. "Dad?" She dropped her arm to her side, dreading their visitor for an entirely different reason now.

Dad pointed to her pepper spray. "This is Stone Harbor, Livi, not the inner-city."

Her father was so good at warm and fuzzy. She dropped the pepper spray back into her purse, closed the front door, and slipped off her shoes.

"Mom." Dad leaned in to kiss Grandma's cheek. He assessed her from head to toe. His brows knotted with each pass.

Grandma shrank into herself, keeping close to Olivia. Olivia put her arm around Grandma's waist. "It's all right, Grandma. This is my dad. Your son."

Dad tugged at the beltline of his khakis.

Grandma frowned, deepening the lines around her mouth. "My son?"

"Your son," Olivia and her dad said in unison.

Grandma cocked her head, and after a moment her eyes glossed over with tears. "Jacob?"

Dad stiffened and backed away, his face like granite. "Jonathan. I'm John."

Grandma stared at him, her head tilting from side to side. "You're my son?"

"Yes. John." Olivia didn't expect Grandma to recognize him, but where had the name Jacob come from? And why was her father so bristled by it?

Dad shook his head and turned back to Olivia with that flat-lipped, chin-raised, hands-in-pockets stance that said he had something on his mind, and he was preparing to unload. So much for that hot bath and relaxation she'd planned. "I thought you were in Hawaii?"

"I was." He leaned in to kiss her cheek as well. An obvious afterthought to their entrance.

The spicy scent of his aftershave brought back memories of sitting in his lap while he read *Frog and Toad* aloud, and snuggling on the couch while she watched Saturday morning cartoons and he read the newspaper. The man had been her hero for years, only to turn in his title so he could chase a woman half his age. A woman barely older than Olivia. Bored with his wife, his house, and the overall direction his life had taken—he left for something he'd deemed better.

Had it ever been real? Or had she lived an illusion most of her life? That cold, dark room in the corner of her mind she retreated to whenever her mind asked such questions opened its creaky door. "I didn't know you were coming." Her voice sounded tinny in her own ears. She felt small beside him. The helpless little girl she'd tried to lock away was crawling her way out.

"I figured it was best not to say anything, considering the circumstances."

"I don't want to fight with you, Dad." Olivia checked on Grandma who'd gone to the living room and settled in front of the TV. After handing Grandma the remote and reminding her which button to use when she wanted to change the channel—something Olivia went through on a daily basis—she stormed right past Dad still standing in the hallway and went to the kitchen. Dad's heavy footfalls echoed in the hall behind her. He hadn't even taken off his shoes.

"If you don't feel like arguing, then stop this nonsense and go home."

One hand on the open cabinet door, Olivia whirled

around. "I'm working to keep a business out of bankruptcy and to support myself and my grandmother. Which nonsense are you referring to?"

"All of it. You're life isn't here. Stop pretending it is." He rubbed the bridge of his nose with his forefinger and thumb.

Her glass clinked against the countertop. She closed the cabinet door with more force than she intended to and headed for the fridge. "I'm pretending? You're the one who left your family to pretend you're still in your twenties." Heat scalded her face, relieved by the open refrigerator door. She hadn't spoken to him like this since she was a rebellious teenager. After realizing her father was not the man she'd always known, and that her life was based on a complete lie, she'd been too stricken for harsh words.

She busied herself with pouring a glass of juice while she waited for the whip of his next remark. It didn't come. Instead, he wiped a hand down his face. A face she now noticed had aged ten years in the last one.

"I'm sorry for hurting you...and your mother. You've no idea how sorry. But I've made my bed, and I can't change what I've done. All I can do is move forward. And I'm moving forward with Marilyn. You need to move on with your life, too."

The woman's name churned bile up Olivia's throat. "Why do you think I'm here?"

"That's what I came to find out." He reached into the cabinet above her for a glass of his own and poured the juice she'd left sitting on the counter. He leaned against the sink, took a sip, and then swirled the glass as if it were wine instead of orange juice. "You have a life in Indy. A successful practice you've worked hard for, a fiancé."

"Justin left me." Her voice quivered. "Left. Me."

"He just needs time. You guys were swimming through some heavy stuff."

"How much time do I give a man who left me when I needed him most? Two men who did, in fact? Huh? If Justin runs during adversity now, what'll he do when it comes and we're married?"

He'll leave you like your father did your mother.

She'd counseled over a hundred women in the last few years who wanted freedom from the psychological hold their fathers had on them so they could find and keep a healthy relationship. To break the pattern of physical or emotional abuse. Olivia refused to become a statistic.

Dad swiped at a drop of juice marring his blue-and-white striped button-down. "Justin asked for time. He didn't abandon you. He put your wedding on hold so you could both take a breather. To let you heal and regroup."

"Then why haven't I heard from him in the last four months? Not an email, a text, or a call. Nothing. That constitutes a break-up to me."

"Your plan is to move here, inherit your grandmother's assets when she dies, and then what?"

The air thickened to a smothering fog. Her lungs struggled to keep up. "Now it makes sense. You're fighting me in court for power-of-attorney because you're afraid I'll steal your rightful inheritance as Grandma's only child." The room swayed. Olivia cupped her forehead to still the nausea. Her dad's selfishness had no bounds. Inhaling a deep breath, she steadied herself and her voice. "I'm not here for *things*. I'm here to care for Grandma since you won't do it."

Dad rinsed his glass and put it in the sink as casually as he would at a dinner party.

Olivia's blood simmered even hotter.

"What she needs is round-the-clock care in a facility from staff trained to handle her."

She sucked in a breath. "A nursing home?"

"They'll take good care of her." He produced three pamphlets from his back pocket and dropped them on the counter.

Bangor Senior Living. Downeast Living Center. Washington County Nursing Home. Olivia's stomach turned. Yes, there would be a day when that was her only option, but today was not that day.

Dad leaned his elbows on the counter and clasped his hands. "Let's check into these places. Together. We'll find one you feel comfortable with, sell the house, and you can go back to your life."

She couldn't take her eyes off the pictures of the facilities designed to look homey and safe. Buildings like her father and Justin drafted, made into blueprints, and contracted to build. But Olivia had learned that what happened inside a home made it what it was, not the pretty exterior.

She swiped a stray tear. "You sure this is about me? Or are you wanting to wrap everything up with a pretty bow so you can live guilt-free with your mistress?"

He rose to his full height, hands at his sides, disapproval tightening the skin around his eyes. "I won't let you talk about Marilyn like that. Now, if you don't cease this power-of-attorney idea, we'll have our day in court."

And just like that, Olivia lost her importance in his heart to a home wrecker, despite the agony he knew he'd caused. Tears rose from deep inside and spilled over her cheeks, threatening to choke her. The black hand of despair which she knew better than her father clamped its icy fingers around her mind. "What happened to my Daddy?" she whispered.

He blinked. Then left the room.

Leaving her to sink into the pit of depression she'd barely escaped last time.

~*~

Niagara Falls
July 1951

Our first vacation together was certainly a memorable one. We set off at dawn in your dad's old 1940 Plymouth, the world and a thousand adventures stretching out ahead of us. Adventure was exactly what we got, though it wasn't the kind we expected.

It all started with a flat tire on MA-2 W not far into Massachusetts. We pulled over, only to find there was no spare, and you told me kicking the car would not fix it. An hour later, we walked into the tiny town of Bellmont, paid for a tow, and arranged to stay the night at the Bellmont Inn, a plantation-style house converted to a motel.

The repair and the extra night's hotel cost more than we'd bargained for, which cut into our already tight budget.

Then what started out as a beautiful day turned into rain in Amsterdam and your window refused to roll up. You had to hold up your raincoat for three hours until the weather subsided.

Between traffic and pulling into the gas station on fumes, we were both frustrated and exhausted by the time we reached Niagara. Right after I had taken this amazing shot of the falls with you by my side, you kissed my cheek and whispered, "It was all worth it."

God is for you, not against you, Elizabeth. Like all the obstacles we had to endure to reach the magnificence of our final destination, so with life. One day we'll see the entire picture. One day, we'll understand.

14

The bee hives were healthy, the blueberries pollinated, and the predicted late frost guaranteed to hurt farmers hadn't come. Blake sat straight on the resting four-wheeler and admired God's handiwork.

"Nature was kind this year." Huck lifted his bee smoker from the ground and walked to his ATV parked beside Blake's.

"We both know who controls nature."

"Amen." Huck opened the smoker's lid to let the rest of the kindling burn out, and then set it by the passenger side wheel. Smart move. There'd been enough arson fires in the area lately. They didn't need any accidents.

"I saw Arianne the other day." Blake opened his water bottle and took a sip. "At the bakery in Stone Harbor."

Huck nodded. "If she didn't come home tasting like chocolate every Thursday, I'd start to worry."

Blake chuckled. "Livi mentioned that Arianne's her best customer."

Huck raised a brow.

"Olivia, the new manager."

"On a pet name basis with the same woman who earlier accused you of preying on little old ladies. Interesting."

Blake capped his water. "The one and only."

Huck rolled his eyes. "You have a dorky grin on your face right now."

Blake reached into the cooler and threw a water bottle at Huck, football style.

The action took Huck by surprise, and he caught it with an *oomph*.

"Glad to hear Emma's doing better."

"Thanks. Breaks my heart to see her like that. Little girls should be worried about who they're going to play with at recess, not if that kid is going to make them sick."

The conversation turned cold as they prepared to leave this end of the property.

Huck's silence was different than usual, his movements lethargic. It was clear his attention had drifted elsewhere, to a place too dark for this beautiful day.

Blake started to inquire but thought better of it. He wasn't one to pry. If Huck wanted to talk it out, he would.

Once the ashes had cooled, they started the ATVs.

Blake led the way around the outskirts of the blueberry bushes toward the barn. Though the temp was above fifty, the wind bit at his face. He'd love to bring Olivia out here sometime, show her the property, maybe share a four-wheeler. See if she appreciated what Madison never had.

Comparing the two women was like comparing apples and oranges except one was rotten. And it was a waste of time. Madison was out of his life for good, and he really wanted to see what possibilities a relationship with Olivia might hold.

~*~

Olivia blinked at the seventy-ish woman dressed in black sitting across the bakery counter.

Mrs. Campbell sobbed, her lacy, white handkerchief pressed to her nose. "He kidnapped Harrison."

"Did you call the police?" Olivia's heart sank, unable to fathom how scared the Campbell family must be.

The woman blew her nose with enough force to slick the lid off a canning jar. She inhaled a deep breath and released it. She opened her large and very shiny red purse and dropped the hankie inside. "They said there's nothing they can do." Sniff. "It's 'just a cat'. They've obviously never lost a close member of their family."

Olivia leaned closer. "Harrison's a cat?"

Mrs. Campbell's mouth dropped open. "Harrison is *not* just a cat. He's my baby." Her face crumpled. "And now he's gone."

The waterworks started again. Olivia cleared her throat, relieved that Harrison wasn't the woman's grandson as she'd first suspected. "Just to clarify — your eighty-year-old boyfriend seduced you for your cat?"

The woman blinked. "That's what I said."

Wow. Olivia thought teenagers were mean. Apparently senior citizens had discovered how to take bullying to a whole other level.

Mrs. Campbell retrieved her hanky and blew another round of gale-force winds across the counter.

Olivia squeezed her hands into fists to keep from sanitizing the surface in front of the woman. "And how can I help you?"

"I've come because I've heard you solve people's problems through your desserts."

This had to stop. Olivia would have to put an ad in the paper letting everyone know she was a certified mental health therapist and the fact that customers came here, spilled their guts, and left feeling better had nothing to do with food. Of course, then she might acquire another practice she wasn't worthy of running. Which she was kind of doing anyway. An hour session that included dessert. Maybe she was on to something there. "Mrs. Campbell, I can't—"

The woman slashed the air with her hand. "No need for humility, dear. I've heard the stories, and I believe you're the only person who can help me."

"What is it you think I can do?"

"I need a box of walnut brownies, extra fudge, delivered to Arthur Greene. He'll exchange my Harrison for them. Guaranteed."

"Mr. Greene? As in the guy who owns Seaside Books?"

He was the pet terrorist?

Mrs. Campbell nodded. "They're his favorite. But don't hand them over until you have Harrison safely in your arms."

"The bakery doesn't deliver." Thank goodness because Olivia wanted no part of this hostage negotiation.

"Please, dear." Mrs. Campbell, once again, reached into her purse, pulled out a one-hundred-dollar bill and pushed it across the counter. "You're my only hope."

Hope. Why did that word keep coming up in conversation like a constant poke in the forehead? Olivia sighed. She'd come here to un-complicate her life, not make it worse. So how did she keep getting involved in other people's lives? She needed to stop by Arthur's shop anyway to deliver the packet she and Glenda had prepared for the merchants participating in this year's first annual Fourth of July celebration. Olivia supposed she could take a box of extra fudge walnut brownies and discuss a certain cat named Harrison. After all, Mrs. Campbell was one of Grandma's dearest friends. "Keep your money, Mrs. Campbell. I'll talk to Arthur within the next couple of days."

The woman stretched her aged hand to cover Olivia's. "You, dear, are a treasure. I hope your young fella realizes how special you are."

No fella. No hope.

~*~

Why was she attempting to save a stranger's cat again? Olivia's logic had made sense up until she swung the gold knocker attached to Arthur Greene's blue door. Now every rational thought she'd had about the situation fled.

Grandma eyed the brick stoop much like a young child would take in a museum, curious but unattached.

Olivia knocked again, harder. "This is Arthur Greene's house. Remember him? I need to drop this off"—she tapped a manila folder against her palm—"and discuss some things." Olivia's stomach knotted.

"Cookies." Grandma raised the book-sized box in her hands.

"Walnut brownies. Extra fudge. You think it'll sway him?" She'd filled Grandma in on the situation, as she did with all the town news to keep her involved, though Grandma never retained the information for long.

"Don't worry. Be happy."

Easier said from a woman who had no idea what was going on.

A muffled clack beat in rhythm behind the door, growing louder as it approached. One inch at a time, the door opened to Mr. Greene leaning on his walker. "Well, isn't this a pleasant surprise."

"Sorry to drop by without warning. Glenda finished the packets for the Fourth of July festival, and we brought left over treats." Leftover from the large tray she'd made specifically for this purpose. Hopefully six brownies for a single bookstore owner was enough.

He reached up and tapped the device in his ear. "Beautiful women are welcome in my home anytime." The cat-napping Casanova opened the door wider. "Come in."

Olivia helped Grandma cross the stoop, and it was then that Arthur's bright green and yellow plaid pants caught Olivia's attention. What a way to live up to one's last name. The man looked like he belonged on a PGA world tour. Or a box of cereal.

They followed Arthur to his living room, slippers shuffling, walker clacking. "I hate this blasted piece of metal. I try not to use it if I don't have to. My arthritis is determined to get me down today." He sank onto a couch that screamed 1970s. "Make yourselves comfortable."

Olivia lifted the lid and scooted the box across the end table to Mr. Greene. "These should help your arthritis."

Liar!

Arthur's eyes rounded. He grinned at the contents.

Olivia searched the room for a black-and-white feline.

"Extra fudge?" he asked.

"Extra fudge."

With a bony hand, he reached in and took one. His groan melded with the TV audience cheering on a game show contestant. An audience whose volume was turned up entirely too loud.

He licked his lips then took a sip of the diet cherry soda sitting on a coaster, sweating.

Olivia was too. It had to be a hundred degrees in here.

And Arthur was wearing a sweater.

"How did you know these were my favorite? Did you remember, Elizabeth?" He took another bite.

A furry friend trotted from the hall and into Grandma's lap. Grandma startled, her attention shifting from the rowdy game show to the cat. "Oh." Grandma smiled and stroked Harrison as carefully as if he were made of porcelain.

Perfect timing. Olivia cleared her throat. "Eugenia Campbell told me."

Arthur stopped mid-chew. Frowned.

"I came to drop off the packet, but I also came to discuss—"

"Harrison," he finished, around a mouthful. Mr. Greene looked everywhere but at her. His cheeks turned a blotchy magenta.

"Why are you holding the cat hostage?" Olivia shifted on the coffee-brown cushion and placed her hand over Mr. Greene's to soften the sting of her words.

He sighed and returned what was left of the brownie to the box. "I'm not holding him hostage." He rubbed his hands together to rid the traces of chocolate. "GiGi's welcome to come and get him whenever she pleases."

GiGi? "You mean she hasn't tried that already?"

He hung his head. "Haven't seen her in almost a month."

Olivia sank against the couch. She hadn't thought to ask Mrs. Campbell if she'd tried going to Arthur's house to retrieve the cat herself. She'd assumed that had been the woman's first move. Now, here Olivia was, stuck in a love triangle between two old people and a cat. "Why did you take Harrison in the first place?"

Arthur ran his finger along the seam of the couch. "So she couldn't cut me completely out her life again."

Again? This was worse than a soap opera.

Her thoughts must've shown on her face because Arthur continued before she could respond.

"Summer, 1955. The age of Elvis, Chuck Berry, and the best looking car Chevy ever created. I'd just taken GiGi to see *East of Eden* with James Dean and Julie Harris. The day had been perfect." He sighed, his eyes glazing over with faraway memories. "We strolled along the harbor, hand in hand, enjoying each other's company and the double-dipped cones I'd bought at Schweenie's Ice Cream parlor." A grin lifted the folds of his cheeks. "She let me try her orange creamsicle. When I offered mine, she leaned in too close and smeared butter pecan on the side of her mouth. I'd forgotten to grab napkins, so I—" Arthur cleared his throat. "Anyway, I knew she'd be disappointed when I told her I'd joined the Army, but I never expected she'd get mad enough to marry another man."

Oh. "She didn't know you wanted to join the military?"

"She didn't understand my need to do my part. Things were heating up in Vietnam. There were rumors that Eisenhower might send in combat troops at any time. I was young, strong. Capable of helping my fellow men end the conflict within a few short months." Arthur shook his head at his own naïvety.

Harrison purred from his position cradled in Grandma's arms. She rocked him like a newborn, his tail swishing from side to side.

Olivia scratched between Harrison's ears. "What happened?"

"Her letters became scarcer each passing month. A year after boot camp, I received the final one letting me know she was getting married. I didn't think she'd go through with it. Not after I begged her not to. I eventually got deployed and then returned home after an oxygen tank fell and crushed my left foot." He tapped it against his walker. "After fighting in Vietnam, all I had waiting for me at home was years of physical difficulty and dreams that would never come true."

Olivia looked around the room. No pictures adorned the walls. No knick-knacks. Not the slightest feminine touch appeared to have ever lived here. "Did you ever marry?"

He swallowed. "No."

Fat tears blurred her vision. Unconditional love.

"When Jerry passed away two years ago—God rest his soul, he was a good man—I was ready to pick up where GiGi and I had left off. Even if our dates took us to the pharmacy instead of the drive-in."

Olivia smiled. "What happened?"

"I asked her when she was going to take off Jerry's ring and start wearing mine. She nearly exploded."

"That was a rather backhanded proposal."

"It wasn't my words. It's me. She started ranting about the past, waving her little arms in the air. The next thing I know, I'm on the sidewalk staring at the slammed door with only my walker for comfort. She refused my calls, my visits. So I stole her cat."

"Why?"

"So she'd have to come over to get him. Then she'd have to talk to me. Look me in the eyes and tell me why she was throwing me away again."

Hostage-for-ransom. Not too unlike the criminal version, where the kidnapper holds someone hostage based on emotional upheaval. Arthur Greene didn't fit the threatening profile so there was no need to alert the authorities. The situation did need resolved, however.

Question was, how deep into the lives of the residents of Stone Harbor was Olivia willing to wade?

15

Blake grunted as the screw slipped off the drywall and plinked to the floor. He should've taken Dad up on his offer to help after they'd torn out the old plaster in the spare bedroom yesterday. The man's pinched lips and the tight skin around his eyes told Blake that Dad had pushed his old back injury too far. Stubborn man. He bent and picked up the screw when a faint voice hit his ears. He stood and cocked his head toward the open bedroom door.

"Blake? Are you home?"

Olivia. With dinner. Was it really five o'clock already? "Be right down." Dropping the screw into a pocket of his tool belt, he inhaled the aroma of something delicious wafting up the stairs. He detached the battery from his cordless drill and plugged it in to charge. Before he had time to remove his tool belt, Olivia entered the room.

"I brought dinner." The last word plunged. Her gaze roamed his unshaven face, his shirt, the tools hanging from his waist. By the time she made it back to his face, her creamy skin had toasted with a beautiful flush.

She must've noticed his amusement because the heat instantly doused to irritation. "Flannel again? It's a hundred degrees up here."

As if the temperature had anything to do with it.

He smoothed a hand down his shirt. "Yep. It's not above seventy outside yet."

Her eyes narrowed. "What do you do then? Have flannel tank tops specially made?"

"Nah. I just cut off the sleeves." He chucked his elbow out.

"You don't."

"Chicks dig it."

"No, we don't."

"Wait and see, sweetheart." He winked, barely able to contain his laughter over her curled upper lip and lowered brows.

"No thank you." She nodded her head at the hallway. "I left Grandma on the porch with Scooby. Dinner is in the kitchen."

"I appreciate it."

He followed her downstairs. Halfway down, his nose caught something spicy. He sniffed again. "Is that—?"

"Buffalo chicken wings with homemade bleu cheese dressing."

He almost missed the last step.

Olivia turned, arms crossed. "I notice you've about worn out that baseball cap." She flicked a hand at his head. "They play tonight at six. I figured you for the type to never miss a game."

Homemade wings. With baseball. This woman would make the perfect girlfriend. She giggled, and that's when he noticed he'd been rubbing the warm sensation on his chest.

"There's also celery and carrot slices, focaccia bread, and peanut butter cupcakes—after the wings have settled."

"Eat with me."

"I've already eaten."

"Stay for dessert then. Watch the game with me. Please."

The battle warred behind irises that darkened from sky blue to stormy. "As nice as that sounds, Flannel Man, I can't." She turned and stepped onto the porch, the screen door slapping shut just like his opportunity to impress her.

He'd wear her down. Eventually. The way she looked at him these days proved she was softening toward him. Blake followed her out.

Mrs. Hudson sat on the top step, Scooby half-laying in her lap. She hummed, stroking the dog with a tenderness only a grandma possessed.

The evening sun cast a golden glow on the side of Olivia's smiling face, making Blake desire more than ever to scale the wall she hid behind. Earn the right to touch her soft cheek. He pointed at the dog. "Now he'll expect me to hold him."

Olivia set that smile on Blake, and he had to force himself not to beg her to stay. "Grandma's whole personality changes around animals," she whispered. "Of all the things she's lost, she still possesses the instinct to love and nurture."

"Have you thought about getting her a pet?"

She shrugged. "Not really. Maybe I should. I just don't know that I could handle one more thing to take care of."

"You could get a low-maintenance pet like a goldfish or a cat. Just not both."

She laughed. "A cat might not be bad. Other than a litter box they generally take care of themselves. And she did enjoy spoiling Harrison yesterday."

"Harrison?"

"Oh." She rubbed her fingertips along her forehead. "That's another mess I've gotten myself into."

Blake shifted his weight to the other foot and tucked his hands in his pockets. "What do you mean?"

"Eugenia Campbell came in Wednesday, upset because her boyfriend had stolen her cat, Harrison. Turns out the boyfriend is—"

"Arthur Greene."

"You know this?"

"Everyone knows."

"Well, I didn't." She sighed. "Anyway, she begged me to take him a box of brownies and talk him into returning her cat he's holding for ransom in exchange for a viable reason why she'd dumped him. I had to drop off the itinerary for the Fourth of July festival anyway, so..."

"You felt sorry for Mrs. Campbell and talked to Arthur."

The corner of her mouth twisted. "Guilty."

Olivia might portray a cold, independent woman, but her heart was softer than sifted sugar. "How'd it go?"

"He'll return Harrison when she comes herself to get him—which I thought she'd already tried. He's basically forcing her to hear him out."

"Lover's quarrel."

"Part of me just wanted to snatch the cat and return him to his rightful owner so it would all be over. But considering their history...I couldn't do it."

Blake nodded. "Arthur told you about the summer of 1955."

Her mouth dropped open. "You knew that too?"

He chuckled. "He tells that story to anyone who'll

listen. As many times as they'll let him tell it."

"Sounds as though you need to be on the Case of the Hostage Cat."

Blake threw his palms out and backed up a step. "Sorry, I'm no expert at matters of the heart."

She studied him a moment. A shadow crossed over her features. Olivia gazed at the pasture. "Apparently, I'm not either," she mumbled.

Her tone implied the comment wasn't based on Arthur and Eugenia's situation.

"Most of us aren't, I'd say." Blake spread his feet wide, prepared to investigate as far as she'd allow him. "When I was a kid, my mom had this flowery picture on our living room wall, a paraphrased printing of First Corinthians, thirteen. 'Love is patient, love is kind. It is not jealous. Love is not pompous, inflated, or rude. It does not seek its own interests, is not quick-tempered, does not brood over injury. It does not rejoice over wrongdoing but rejoices in the truth. It bears all things, believes all things, hopes all things, endures all things." He shook his head. "I can't believe I remember that. Whenever my brother and I would fight as kids, Mom would make us copy it in cursive like ten times. And it had to be legible." That heavy cloak of fury that smothered Blake whenever he thought of Lucas settled over him. Why had he mentioned his brother?

After a few moments of silence, Olivia looked at him, a sad smile curling one side of her mouth. "I think only dogs are capable of that kind of affection." She looked at Scooby.

As if recognizing he was the topic of discussion, Scooby flopped over on his side so Mrs. Hudson could rub his belly, and let out an I'm-in-doggie-heaven moan.

Blake knew Olivia was deflecting the topic by turning her attention to the dog, but the ache in her voice made him think she believed her words. "Dogs and Jesus." She blinked at him. Swallowed. Gave a slight nod.

If Olivia believed anything, Blake hoped she believed that.

A shiver rocked her body, and she rubbed her arms. "We should probably go, Grandma. Blake's putting up new drywall."

"It can wait." The mention of Jesus had obviously affected her enough to retreat. She descended the steps until she stood in front of Mrs. Hudson.

The woman ignored Olivia and continued stroking the dog. "I love peaches."

"His name is Scooby." Olivia patted the mutt's head.

Oh, she was calling the dog Peaches.

"I love Peaches." Mrs. Hudson's words grew louder.

Olivia closed her eyes for a few seconds, then looked to Blake for help. He snapped his fingers at the dog, and Scooby slowly raised his arthritic body and padded to his side.

"Peaches…" Hurt laced Mrs. Hudson's words.

Blake felt like a jerk.

Olivia helped her grandma stand. "How about we go to the shelter next week and get you a pet of your very own. A cat maybe? You can name her Peaches if you want."

"Peaches?" Mrs. Hudson nodded.

"We'll go Monday." Olivia turned to Blake and mouthed *Thank you*.

He lifted his hand in a wave. "There's another game on next Saturday. I'll save you a seat in front of the big screen."

"You don't give up easily, do you?" Olivia said over her shoulder.

Not when it was something important.

16

A Stone's Throw Beauty Shop was located two blocks from the bakery, across from what used to be Hammond's Shrimp House. Olivia had to squint to read the faded letters on the sign. Shame the place wasn't still around. The building held a coastal ruggedness that would appeal to tourists.

Many of the current businesses were nearing the completion of their makeovers, while the bakery was just today getting started. They closed early on Wednesday afternoons, and she'd promised Blake her help as soon as Grandma got her hair done.

Olivia parked on the curb and walked around to the passenger side to Grandma's door. "How do you want her to do your hair this time?"

Grandma took her offered hand and stepped onto the sidewalk. "Braids."

While braids would be much easier for Olivia to handle every morning than Grandma's short bob shellacked with hair spray, it wasn't feasible. "We'll see what she can do. Would you like her to add some color? Dark gray, maybe? Blue, purple?"

Grandma made a disgusted face.

"My thoughts exactly." Olivia shut the door and clicked the lock button on her key fob.

The pungent odor of perm solution assaulted them as they stepped inside the salon. With today's technology, why couldn't someone invent a liquid that didn't make a person cringe?

Six women, all around Grandma's age, sat beneath ancient bulbous hairdryers.

"Hello, Elizabeth." Wanda Russelburg tossed her magazine aside and stood from her swivel chair. "I'm ready whenever you are."

Grandma clutched Olivia's arm and pulled her closer, shrinking away from the hairdresser. Wanda had been doing Grandma's hair for fifteen years.

"She's a nice lady," Olivia whispered. "She's going to trim your hair so it's easier for me to style. She's done this for you lots of times. I'll make sure she treats you right." She patted Grandma's hand.

Reluctant, Grandma moved forward at Olivia's prodding. The stylist's chair presented a bit of a challenge for Grandma this time, but within a few minutes she was seated with a smock covering her body.

Wanda grabbed the comb and scissors and looked at Grandma in the mirror. "What can I do for you today?"

"Braids." Grandma raised her chin much the same way she had as a child, Olivia was certain.

Wanda raised a questioning brow.

"I was thinking something in the way of this." Olivia pulled out her phone and showed Wanda a picture of an older, classy actress. "I like the dark gray lowlights."

"Ooh, I love it." Wanda took the phone and showed Grandma, who curled her lip.

"She's old."

"She's *mature*. Like we are." Wanda, at least twenty years Grandma's junior, patted Grandma's shoulder and returned the phone. "I think you'll look fabulous. What do you say?"

"Braids."

Olivia leaned down to Grandma's eye level. "That's the great thing about this style—it can be braided because it's longer without the perm. If you approve, I promise to braid your hair every night before bed."

Grandma's eyes narrowed. She glared at Olivia for a long time before finally nodding her agreement. "Braids."

Olivia held up her hand. "Deal."

Wanda winked and left to mix the hair color. Olivia fetched Grandma's book from her purse. The title indicated a murder mystery in a flower shop. She wondered, not for the first time, if such books were healthy for an Alzheimer's patient. The genre had always been Grandma's favorite though, and reading kept her mind active while she still possessed the ability.

Olivia settled in a chair of her own and skimmed through the pamphlet they'd gotten at the animal shelter. Grandma had been crushed when they'd pulled into an empty parking lot to find the shelter was closed on Mondays. She'd thrown a fit to rival any toddler. The bakery had been swamped with two birthday cake orders, and an order for six dozen yeast donuts for the American Legion breakfast, so a return trip yesterday was out. The security company was installing a wireless monitoring system at home this evening. Olivia's promise of a pet would have to wait until the weekend. Thankfully, Grandma hadn't brought it up again.

Olivia was strongly leaning toward a cat. An

online newspaper source had written about a nursing home in Connecticut that had brought abandoned newborn kittens to dementia patients for bottle feedings. Studies showed the loving, nurturing instinct was one of the last traits lost in the majority of patients. Not only did the kittens thrive, but so did the patients.

A young stylist with blonde streaks in her black hair, or vice versa, sashayed to the hair dryers and turned one of them off. "All right, 'Genia, you're all done."

Eugenia Campbell set her magazine on the vacant chair beside her, then pushed on the chair's arms to steady her ascent. She fluffed her new do with a shaky hand, grabbed her large red purse, and gave the stylist a fifty.

Olivia had been trying to get ahold of the woman for almost a week. Here was her opportunity to convince the woman to act rationally and talk to Mr. Greene.

As Eugenia headed for the door, she noticed Olivia and paused. The woman's slumped posture straightened, and her mouth turned down in a frown.

Olivia stood. "I've tried calling several times, but I haven't been able to reach you."

"You didn't get Harrison back. What's left to say?" She continued shuffling to the exit.

"It's a little more complicated than that." Olivia moved past and held the door open for Mrs. Campbell. This conversation was best out of earshot of the parlor gossips anyway.

"A little?"

"Mr. Greene is willing to give the cat back if you'll pick it up and hear what he has to say."

"Harrison. He's not an *it*. Furthermore, I have

nothing to say to Arthur Greene." She dug for her car keys.

"He loves you." Not that Mr. Greene had confided that to Olivia, but it was obvious. "He doesn't want you to talk. He wants you to listen."

Keys rattled together as Eugenia unlocked her Cadillac. "I'm through listening to that man. It's not as if I get a say in what he decides anyway." Bitterness oozed from her words. The acidic kind that resulted from years of fermentation.

"Does that comment have to do with him joining the Army?"

Eugenia froze. Her entire body wilted. "What do you know of that?"

"Arthur told me everything. You've reconnected after years apart. What did he do now that's made you angry?"

"He proposed," she whispered, tears springing in her blue eyes.

Fear. The four letter word that kept so many people from living a full life. The life this woman had envisioned with her fiancé hadn't worked out any better than Olivia's had. It changed a person when they gave their heart to someone who'd mistreated it— friend, fiancé, or parent.

"What is it you're afraid of, Mrs. Campbell?"

Eugenia opened her door and dropped her suitcase of a purse in the seat. She thought for a moment, rolling her tongue along her top teeth. "Losing him again."

"I don't think you have to worry about that this time."

"But I do. We're not twenty anymore. I don't want to become widowed a second time."

Oh. That.

Eugenia moved her purse and eased onto the seat. Olivia held the door to keep it from closing. "You love Arthur, whether you remain a couple or whether you marry. If he passes, you'll mourn him either way. Why not let go of your fear and let yourself be happy?"

The engine started. "Easy to say, harder to do. Thank you for trying."

Olivia let her go, watching her drive away until she disappeared onto Main Street. Who was she to tell someone to let go of their fear and be happy when that very fear had prompted her to quit her job and move across the country? And refuse a perfectly good dinner invitation from a perfectly wonderful man.

~*~

Blake had bent to sweep chunks of drywall and splinters of paneling littering the floor when a car door sounded from the bakery's parking lot. He turned toward the window. Olivia was helping Mrs. Hudson from the car. He propped the broom against the wall and met them outside.

Arms propped against his tailgate, Olivia stood on tiptoe to see inside. Her fitted jeans were cuffed, revealing the curve of muscular calves. "What's the damage?"

He gazed at her over studs too long for the bed, which stuck out with a little orange flag attached. "Not much. A friend of mine opened his own mill a few years ago. That's where I get what I need for the house. Any business I bring his way comes with a discount."

Blake handed her the receipt. She glanced at it

then lowered her shoes back to the ground. "Thanks. I'll cut you a check." She tucked the receipt in her pocket. "What can I do to help?"

"You should've brought work clothes."

Her forehead wrinkled. "These are my work clothes." She tugged at the bottom of her blue shirt. "See, a paint spot."

No, he didn't see. But he noticed how beautiful she could make a simple T-shirt look.

Mrs. Hudson joined them. "Brian."

Olivia opened her mouth to correct her grandma, but Blake put up a hand. "Beautiful day, isn't it, Mrs. Hudson. How about we go for a walk around the harbor once the work is done?"

Mrs. Hudson wrinkled her nose. "I'm married."

Blake chuckled at how quickly Olivia's face turned from rosy peach to deep red. "Just a walk, nothing more." He leaned in and whispered, "Besides, I'm sweet on your granddaughter."

The woman's face brightened. Olivia cocked her head to the side. "What are you conspiring?"

"Don't worry. Be happy." Mrs. Hudson slipped her arm in Blake's. The woman looked different somehow, younger maybe, though Blake couldn't pinpoint why.

They went inside the bakery.

Olivia tucked her hands in her back pockets as she observed his progress. "Wow, you've already gotten a lot done." She grabbed the broom and began sweeping his mess into the dustpan.

"I can get that." He reached for the broom.

Olivia jerked it away. "I can too. I'm good for more than food, you know."

Heat climbed up the back of his neck. He didn't

doubt that one bit. He set up his circular-saw stand on the sidewalk, then snapped on his tool belt. The sun beat down on his shoulders, but the breeze off the water made the day too nice for working indoors. According to Glenda, the bed and breakfast had acquired several new reservations, and he wanted to get this finished before the projected influx of tourists arrived.

"Help."

He turned, expecting to see Mrs. Hudson hurt. Instead, she was staring at the boards he'd stacked next to the saw. He pulled a pair of work gloves from his tool belt and handed them to her. "I'll cut the boards if you'll hold them steady." She nodded. He hoisted a board onto the saw stand, measured the length he needed, and marked it with a pencil. He lowered his safety glasses, realized he didn't have an extra pair, then took them off and gave them to Mrs. Hudson. "Ready?"

"Ready."

Olivia stood in the doorway watching them, a faint smile teasing her lips. The saw spun to life and bit into the wood with ease. High quality Maine pine.

They cut four more boards before Blake turned off the machine. "Thank you, Mrs. Hudson."

"Thank you."

He was pretty sure she meant to say you're welcome.

She tugged off the glasses, messing up her hair.

"That's what's different today. Your hair. It looks nice."

Mrs. Hudson fingered the ends.

Olivia joined them on the sidewalk. "You do look fantastic, Grandma." Olivia's hair, so dark it was almost black, framed her face with little pieces she'd failed to secure in her ponytail. "There's sliced fruit on the table, along with chocolate dipped nuts. Help yourself."

Always thinking of his belly. "Peanuts?"

"Of course."

"I'll let you stay and help me then." He winked, lifted all four cut boards and carried them inside.

"You're so kind."

He lowered the boards to the linoleum.

"I appreciate you covering the display case and counter." Olivia held out the platter of goodies.

"I think the construction zone is far enough away from the food it would've been fine, but I didn't want to take any chances." He removed his gloves and took a strawberry and a handful of chocolate covered peanuts. That's when he noticed a tinge of purple beneath her eyes. "You look worn out. Still not sleeping?"

He nodded his head at Mrs. Hudson, who'd sat at a corner table to eat a cup of yogurt.

"Not really. There's a guy coming at five to install a wireless alarm system so I'll know whenever she tries to leave the house. I've been leaning toward getting her a cat but maybe a trained dog is the better option."

"You could always say yes and eat with me. Let her spend more time with Scooby before you make a decision."

She reached for a peanut and popped it into her mouth. "We're eating together right now."

Her defiant smile flamed his competitive nature. "Doesn't count. It's not a meal unless there's meat." Blake stepped closer until their toes touched. He lowered his voice. "What is it you're afraid of, Olivia?"

"Afraid?" Her voice squeaked, and she cleared her throat. "I'm not afraid."

"Then why won't you look at me?"

Her gaze darted around the room before finally settling on him. The spark of attraction, which he'd convinced himself he'd misread before, blazed along with her cheeks. He fought the urge to fist pump the air. "Cincinnati's playing Saturday night."

"I'm not a fan. Besides, I promised Grandma we'd go to the shelter. I'll need to drop off your dinner early that day."

"How about a live game then? Friday night. Little League practice. You can help me coach."

"I don't know the first thing about coaching baseball."

Blake leaned a little closer. "Don't need to. You can follow my lead."

She just stared at him with those amazing eyes, clutching the tray of snacks like a lifeline. Without moving away, he took the tray and set it on a nearby table. "It'll be fun. I'll put your name on the shirts as a sponsor and everything." He made a circle on his shirt. "Harbor Town Bakery, with a picture of a growling cupcake slapping a bat in its palm."

Her gaze followed his finger as he demonstrated on his torso.

"Will the shirts be flannel?"

"And sleeveless."

She rolled her eyes and backed away. "You seriously better be joking about that." She plucked a few grapes off the platter and walked to the stack of cut boards. The heated tension between them snapped like a stretched rubber band.

Blake lifted a board and positioned it at a ninety-degree angle from the one that served as the bottom stud of the new wall. "I'll bring Scooby. He can hang out with Grams while we play. I'll even take you both out for pizza afterward."

"Grams?"

He shrugged.

Her lips closed around a grape. She studied him as she chewed.

And he studied her lips.

"Are you trying to wear me down?"

"Is it working?"

"Yes."

"Friday, then?"

She shook her head, as if she couldn't believe she'd agreed to live on the same planet as he did. "Friday, it is, Flannel Man."

17

Had she just agreed to a date? A bead of sweat trickled down Olivia's temple. She swiped it away with the back of her hand. Surely not. It didn't classify as a date if they were accompanied by a grandma and a dog, right?

The board she was holding in place for Blake shuddered with the force of the drill. He was right. She was afraid of him. Blake was selfless, handsome, and had talent to spare. When he'd leaned in to whisper, she'd had to stop herself from closing the remaining distance.

She couldn't handle anything serious with him now—she'd been un-engaged for barely six months. But she couldn't ignore her attraction to him any longer, either. He'd made his intentions clear. And she liked it. In fact, it caused a crack in her heart to let in what felt like…sunshine. A glimpse of light in her darkened life.

Blake pulled another screw from his tool belt, and they moved on to the next board. Stubble covered his chin and cheeks. The hair on his upper lip was slightly darker, and surrounded very kissable lips.

Wow. She'd never been the head-in-the-clouds, sit and daydream like a hopeless romantic type. She liked everything in her life to have order, make sense. For things to be planned in a monthly calendar with a sharp, number two pencil. No surprises.

Desiring the company of a man when every other man in her life had let her down was not logical. Not in her plan.

Blake drove the screw enough to get it started, then stopped and looked her way, hand braced against the board. She tried to say something, come up with some lame excuse as to why she'd been staring at him, but there was no point. He winked and zipped the rest of the screw into the wood.

She enjoyed those winks, too. Wondered if he saved them just for her.

Metal clinked as he fished for another screw. "Tell me more about the teenage girl you taught to cook. The one with Down Syndrome."

It took a moment for her brain to register one of their first conversations. "Oh, you mean Cassie." The warmth of affection bloomed in her chest every time she thought of the girl.

"Her dad did a great job with the website." Blake knelt to screw into the bottom of the board.

"I thought so too. They started going to our church my junior year of college. She loved helping in the kitchen during fellowship meals and prayer breakfasts. When her mom was diagnosed with cancer, Cassie started acting out. She was seventeen. The same age I was when cooking replaced my unruly behavior. Church members took turns keeping her occupied while her mom endured chemo treatments. Cooking was her favorite. We had a great time together."

"I thought you went to cooking school."

"I did."

"At a four-year college?"

"No."

Blake set down the drill. An arm draped casually over his knee as one brow arched up at her. She searched for words to evade the truth yet not tell a lie. His scrutiny made her efforts useless. Olivia sucked in a deep breath and released it, defeated. "You can farm, you can build, and you can save a town, but can you keep a secret?"

Three of his fingers raised in a Scout's Honor pledge while his other hand made an X over his heart.

"I have a master's in psychology."

He blinked. "Huh."

Blake returned to his drill as if she'd never said a thing.

When the drill stopped, she said, "What do you mean, 'huh'?"

He shrugged. "Impressive. You're here, though, baking cupcakes in Stone Harbor. Judging by the way your eyes are clouded over, I'm guessing there's a story behind that."

It would be easy to reveal herself to this man. To seek refuge in his trustworthy kindness. Blake was safe. Then again, she'd been wrong before. "A heavy tale for another day."

Blake nodded and together they raised the wall frame. "Until then, if you start feeling rebellious, I'll gladly eat anything that results from it."

She grinned, grateful he hadn't pressed her for answers. "What do you do when you feel rebellious?"

He looked up at the ceiling and squinted. "I wear an extra layer of flannel."

"Ugh. I'll introduce you to my friend, polyester."

"Is she single?"

Olivia gave him a playful kick.

He dodged her foot, laughing.

"What about the rest of the Hartfords? Are you all one big happy flannel family?"

The light in his eyes dimmed. His mouth fell into a grim line as he stared at something behind her.

She instantly regretted her remark. Apparently, she wasn't the only one with a story to tell. "I'm sorry. I shouldn't have asked."

He went to work, securing the frame to the existing wall. Once finished, he slapped it to test its sturdiness. "Don't be sorry for asking. I'm close with my parents."

"Are you an only child?" Olivia was so used to prying into people's lives that it was a hard habit to break.

He dropped the drill in the loop of his tool belt. "I have an older brother. Lucas. I haven't seen or spoken to him in almost three years." He double-checked his work using a level.

"Can I ask what happened?"

His jaw worked. "He took off with something very important to me."

So, it was Blake's choice not to speak to his brother. The action was a paradox to his character. She should stop asking questions, but her curious nature wanted to know the backstory of this too-good-to-be-true farmer. "He won't give it back?"

Blake's face turned to granite. "It was my fiancée. They can have each other."

Air escaped Olivia's lungs so quickly she went dizzy. "Oh, Blake. I'm sorry."

He grabbed another board to start a new frame on the other side. "I should've learned to cook."

"Instead, you started restoring a Victorian home."

His gaze bored through hers. Understanding

dawned like the sunrise. "Yeah. I guess I did."

A home that had probably been intended for a wife and family that wasn't to be. The woman was an idiot, whoever she was. A hot, ugly sensation crept under Olivia's skin. She knew the crushing weight of broken dreams all too well. How could that woman hurt such a wonderful man? Tears pricked her eyes, and she blinked them away. "Maybe I'll teach you how to cook."

"Doctor's orders?"

She nodded.

"I accept."

~*~

Olivia assisted Grandma across the gravel lot to the baseball diamond, feeling a hundred kinds of silly. She didn't know the first thing about coaching sports. She wasn't athletic, no matter how much she'd wanted to be.

"Where we at?" Grandma asked.

"I promised Blake I'd help him with his Little League team tonight." The answer she'd given Grandma the last ten times she'd asked.

Scooby lumbered around the dugout, wriggling his backside. A rush of kids followed him out and ran onto the field. The air was sticky with the brunt of the day's heat clinging to the last few hours of daylight.

She dropped the small cooler she was carrying onto the bleachers. "If you want to rest here, I'll find Blake's dog for you. He can keep you company while we practice."

"Where we at?" Grandma frowned.

Olivia took a deep breath. "I'm helping Blake coach his Little League team." She fished two cold bottled waters from the cooler and handed one to Grandma. "Stay here. I'll bring the dog to you."

Pop flies and practice swings ensued on the field.

She hadn't thought to ask Blake what age group he coached, but the kids appeared to be around eight or nine. She stepped into the shade of the dugout.

At the other end of the small building, Blake knelt, facing away from her, in front of a boy with a pouty lip gripping his bat and glove in one hand. Her gaze traveled across the boy's small chest to where a glimpse of flesh peeked from beneath his sleeve.

"Don't get down, buddy. You can do this." Blake's warm tenor filled the small space. "You're just as good a player as they are. Even more so with what you have to overcome. Your batting average is spot on. We can't win this tournament without you."

The boy gave Blake an unsteady smile. Then his brown eyes drifted over Blake's head and fixed on Olivia. Blake swiveled to see what had caught the boy's attention, and then he rose to his feet.

Scooby padded over and pressed his wet nose on Olivia's hand.

"You head on out there." Blake slapped the boy's shoulder. "We'll talk later."

The kid avoided further eye contact as he hurried past her to the field.

"Sorry to interrupt your pep talk."

Blake shrugged. "No worries. Have you seen Olivia?"

She cocked her head.

"Baggy T-shirt, ratty cut-offs, beat-up hat. Did you mug an unsuspecting hobo on your way?"

"Very funny. I almost didn't recognize you either without your flannel."

He rubbed a palm over his dry-fit T-shirt, flattening it to his carved chest and abs. "You don't approve?"

Air turned to dust in her lungs. Oh, she approved all right. She coughed to distract him from seeing the extent of her approval at the way his shirt clung to his rather nice form.

"You OK?" He held out his sports drink.

"Fine." She uncapped her water and took a sip. "Thanks, though. The dust rolling off home base choked me up." So did the way her body reacted to him every time they were together.

He pressed a hand to her back and rubbed. "Ready to play some ball?"

Olivia nearly jumped out of her skin. "Yep. Let's do this."

Blake walked Scooby over to Grandma and commanded the canine to stay by pressing down his palm. The dog flopped down and laid his head in Grandma's lap. From the other side of the fence, Olivia could hear Grandma cooing.

Blake put his thumb and forefinger between his lips and whistled, then motioned the players into a huddle. "This is Olivia Hudson. She's my assistant tonight. Now—"

"Coach," a husky-sized boy interrupted. He glanced at Olivia then leaned into Blake. "She's a girl," he whispered.

"Yes, she is."

"But you said that girls—"

"Never mind what I said." Blake clapped his hands once, his face tinging pink. "We're gonna split up into two teams and play a five inning game. With the adults included, we'll have enough players. I'll give you each a number. Ones are on my team, twos are on Livi's team. Any questions?"

She'd always hated being called that by anyone other than her parents. Blake's use of the nickname, however, didn't bother her so much.

Blake split the group and claimed the outfield.

Olivia's team moped all the way to the dugout. Poor kids. Nothing like getting stuck with a girl coach who knew little about baseball. No one said a word as they donned helmets and grabbed bats.

"I'll do my best not to let you down. I'm very competitive, and I used to play softball." In third grade, the year she'd discovered she wasn't athletic in the least, but they didn't need the details.

A few shoulders perked up.

"Think of how fun it'll be to rub it in their faces when we win." She was smack-talking big dreams now. Olivia stretched out her hand and waited. The boys looked at one another. None of them wanted to be the first to join the pact. They probably thought she had cooties.

Finally, number five gave in and inched his hand toward hers—hovering but not touching—then the rest followed.

Olivia held up her hand to high-five the first boy up to bat.

He tugged on his earlobe. "Uh…people don't do that anymore." He created a fist and bumped it off hers. "Fist bump instead."

She was officially uncool. "Got it."

The kid took a couple of practice swings then stepped inside the box. Blake pitched. The boy didn't move. Too high.

"Good eye, kid." She leaned against the fence.

Another pitch. Too low.

Olivia cupped her hands around her mouth. "We want a pitcher…" Her team finished the chant for her.

"OK, OK." Blake slapped his mitt with the ball and fired again.

Crack! The ball soared through the air. Number twelve sprinted to first base while the team cheered.

The next three innings passed with each team scoring, keeping the game neck and neck.

Olivia checked on Grandma periodically. With the shade of the roof over the bleachers and Scooby's company, Grandma seemed to be enjoying the game.

Blake called for a break and sent the kids to the water jug.

Olivia rested on the bench and chugged the rest of her water, then started on a sports drink Blake passed to her.

"Tired, city girl?" Blake dropped onto the bench beside her. Legs outstretched, he rested his head against the concrete wall.

"Me? I could go for days."

He chuckled. "Maybe you should start coaching then."

"After we win this game, they'll be begging me to."

"Are you trash talking?"

"The teams are tied, you know."

He tipped his cup and chugged the last of his water. "Pride goes before a fall."

She narrowed her eyes. "I refuse to let you win. For their sake."

"Care to make a wager then?"

"Depends on what you have in mind. I'm not shaving my head or eating anything weird."

A bead of sweat trailed down his unshaven cheek. He twisted his hat backwards and shifted. She couldn't help but notice his long legs. His nylon pants fit him oh, so perfectly. The heat of his body infused with the scent of soap and sweat clung to his skin. "If you win, I'll let you fan me with a palm leaf and feed me grapes."

"Ha! That's fair."

"I think so." He leaned closer. "How about I feed you grapes, then."

She hit his knee with hers. "No thanks."

"Your call, then."

Olivia gave the matter some thought. "My grandpa was a photographer. Not long after I moved here I found a photo journal he'd made Grandma. It starts with pictures of them while dating and goes through most of their marriage. I don't know much about their history and thought it'd be nice to find those places, tell Grandma the stories behind them according to what I know from the journal, and see if it jogs any of her memories. If I win, you help me go through the journal and mark those places on a map so I can take her."

Blake stared at her hand splayed on the bench. His own twitched as if wanting to entwine their fingers. "Deal."

That was too easy. "If you win?" Oh, those eyes. The message they spoke made her heart race.

"Eat dinner with me Saturday. I'd like a chance to better know you, Olivia."

Her chest squeezed. "Like a date?"

"You don't have to call it that if it scares you. We

can talk about dessert and blueberries and call it a business meeting if you want. Write it off on taxes." He nudged her elbow with his.

She wanted to agree, but her tongue wouldn't utter the word. They just stared at each other while she battled the anxiety that kept her life from moving forward. She was tired of being idle.

"You don't have to worry about following through," he said. "Your team's a shoe-in anyway, right?"

The smile lines around his eyes had relaxed into something much like disappointment. She couldn't do that to him. Not after he'd rescued Grandma from a storm, endured her insults, befriended her when she wasn't friendly, and constantly found ways to help her out and make sure she fit in.

Above all, something about Blake Hartford awakened a part of her she thought she'd lost forever. Belonging.

She drank the rest of the purple liquid to loosen up her vocal chords. "Deal."

Blake took her offered hand. Shook it. Caressed her wrist with his fingertips. Despite the heat and sweat, she shivered.

"Coach?" Two boys were taking in the spectacle, their fingers wrapped around the chain-link fence.

Blake released her. "We're coming. Take your bases."

Blake followed the boys from the dugout, only to return a moment later. "By the way, I'm partial to the green grapes."

He tapped the fence twice and then jogged to the pitcher's mound.

She would not let her mind go there.

Bats hung on a rack beside the exit. Olivia examined them, testing a few to see if any were heavier than the one she'd used last. She needed to win this game. For her heart's sake.

18

Blake stepped onto the pitcher's mound feeling as if he'd climbed a mountain. He'd finally broken through Olivia's defenses. Their mutual attraction was evident, and she was slowly giving in to it.

He glanced at Mrs. Hudson, who was standing at the fence, watching.

Olivia swung the bat twice and then stepped up to home plate. She hunkered down, elbow up, one eye half-closed. The tough act was a ruse, but she sure looked cute.

Blake curved his fingers around the dusty, worn cowhide until his knuckles turned white. He could let her win. He should let her win. To erase the anxiety on her face.

What would be the fun in that?

He fired the ball toward home plate.

Olivia swung. Missed.

"Strike one!" Buddy yelled and sailed the ball back to Blake.

Olivia's lips twisted in a pout. She tapped the bat against the plate and regained her stance.

He pitched again.

"Strike two!"

Blake opened his mitt for the incoming ball. "I think we've got a whiffle-bat somewhere, if that'd work better for you."

Olivia yanked off her hat and sailed it like a Frisbee toward the dugout. Placing the bat between her knees, she tightened the band on her ponytail. "Try again, hot shot."

She glared.

He pulled back, contracting every muscle in his upper body, and threw the heat, confident he'd have a date tomorrow night.

Crack!

The ball soared above him. He jumped, mitt open, and missed. Olivia pumped her arms and legs, tagging first base and angling to second.

"Come on, boys, get it in!" Blake yelled.

As she rounded second base, the ball returned from the outfield. He ran at it, arresting the ball in the hollow of his glove. He went to throw it but stopped. Where was the baseman?

Blake raced toward her, glove out. She saw him coming, squealed, and ran faster. He lunged. She dodged. Blake regained his footing and tried again. Her foot slipped on dirt, rammed into his, and they both tripped in a tangle of legs.

Pain split Blake's forehead as the ground rose to meet him. A few seconds later, when the stun of impact had settled, Blake became aware of the soft body beneath his. He lifted the bulk of his weight. "Livi, are you OK?"

Nothing. Her closed eyelids didn't even flutter.

"Livi?" *Oh, God, let her be all right.*

She groaned. Blake eased his hand behind her head to cushion her skull, praying he wouldn't find a pool of sticky blood.

"Livi, can you hear me?" No blood. "Does anything hurt?"

Her eyelids peeled open. It took a moment for the fog in them to clear. "I win."

Laughter, laced with relief, bubbled out of him. He kissed the red knot on her forehead before he realized what he'd done. She seemed oblivious, no doubt her world still spinning. Every nerve in his body took notice, however, as he became achingly aware of her curvy hip pressed against his leg. Instinctively, his fingers curled around the back of her head, gently tangling in her soft hair. She held him in a trance he never wanted to escape. His attention honed on her full, pink lips. Shadows covered them, breaking his concentration.

"Coach, is she dead?"

Oh, yeah. They were in the middle of a game. "No. She's fine."

Stuffing down his disappointment at having company, Blake eased himself up and helped Olivia to her feet.

She took a deep breath, her hand covering the angry red circle on her head, and swayed. "Did we win?"

Blake steadied her. He didn't have the heart to tell her he'd tagged her out. Not when she was trying to be brave. While she focused on the boys standing around her, he rolled the ball through the grass behind her. "You won."

The boys on her team started cheering. A few from his team rebuffed. "Sorry I let you down, guys."

They stomped toward the dugout, verbally replaying the event, trying to find proof the other team had lost.

Blake turned his attention back to Olivia. "No breaks? How's your stomach, ribs?"

"I'm fine. Really. Tomorrow will be a different story."

He snaked an arm around her waist and walked her to the dugout. After a short celebration with cookies provided by Bobby's mom, everyone collected their gear and cleared the dugout. Olivia fist-bumped the players, who agreed she could practice with them anytime.

After informing the parents about the next practice, Blake hoisted his bat bag on his shoulder and picked up the bucket of balls. Olivia offered to carry the empty water jug. They walked toward the bleachers on the other side of the dugout. The lump near her hairline was quarter-sized and angry. "I'm sorry I hurt you."

"It was an accident." Her gaze flickered up to the spot where his head had hit hers and she pointed to the lump above his left eye. "You're heavier than a grand piano."

"I can't carry a tune, though." He reached out and removed the bottom half of her ponytail that had stuck under the collar of her shirt.

She frowned at him. Then she gave a little sigh and leaned into his side. After making sure he hadn't hit his head harder than he'd thought, Blake slipped his arm around her back and pulled her close.

Halfway to the bleachers, she froze and pointed to the empty seats. "She's gone."

A small cooler sat on the ground beside a paperback. "Is that your stuff?"

Olivia nodded. "She was just here a few minutes ago."

"Maybe she went to the restroom. Or the car. Check there. I'll bring your things."

She took off at a jog the other direction. He maneuvered the items to make them easier to carry and hurried to the parking lot. He met her at her car.

"I can't find her. Or Scooby."

"If Scooby's with her, she'll be fine. We'll find her." He put the cooler and book in her backseat, then dumped his equipment in the bed of his truck. They asked the few remaining parents in the parking lot if they'd seen any sign of her.

Bobby's dad, Mike, asked what Mrs. Hudson had been wearing.

Olivia closed her eyes, thinking. "Um, khaki-colored linen pants and a white blouse."

Mike palmed his keys and moved toward his car. "Bobby, get in." He turned back to Blake. "We'll search the roads and let you know if we find her."

"Thanks, Mike." Blake turned, searching the area for clues. Where should they start?

He yelled for Scooby in hopes the dog would appear.

Olivia raced to the tree line.

Blake caught up to her.

She swiped tears from her eyes. "Where did she go? I have to find her."

He tugged her to a stop. Cupping her face in both hands, he leaned down until they were at eye level. "We'll find her. I promise."

19

Where could Grandma have gone? She'd disappeared so quickly. Or had she?

Olivia had noticed Grandma's fidgeting but the game had been almost over. Then she'd hit her head and...Olivia hadn't paid attention after that. Between the buzzing in her head and the buzzing her body had started with Blake pressed against her, she'd been too distracted. "Grandma?" Olivia yelled as she rounded the side of the school.

She blew a long, shaky breath. Between the bakery, juggling the finances, the town project, counseling an elderly couple, and Blake, tracking Grandma's every move was getting harder each day. Olivia needed to give up some things. She didn't want Blake to be one of them, but anything more than friendship—and even that, at times—wasn't feasible right now.

Her heartbeat pounded in her ears. Why was reaching the shore of her dreams like paddling across the Atlantic in a rowboat during a hurricane?

Blake sprinted past her up the school steps and yanked on the doors. Locked.

Grandma could be anywhere by now. *Please, Lord, let us find her safe and unharmed.* Olivia looked to the sky, surprised she'd uttered a full prayer after months of trying and failing.

"Come on." Blake grabbed her hand and they

raced to the edge of the school property where a dirt path veered to the left into the trees.

A wadded tissue on the dirt caught her eye. Grandma had asked for a tissue when they'd pulled into the ball field's lot. Olivia jerked Blake to a stop. "I think she's this way."

They may be trailing a dead end, but it was worth a try.

Sweat dripped down the sides of her face, creating a cocktail of dust and grime that suffocated the pores of her skin.

A dog barked.

Blake and Olivia looked at each other and then sprinted toward the sound. Grandma's white shirt winked from behind a copse of trees. Olivia's body emptied a flash flood of adrenaline, causing her legs to nearly collapse.

Scooby trudged from Grandma's side over to Blake, ready to be rewarded for keeping his new friend safe. However, Grandma's hollow gray eyes and tear-stained cheeks confessed her compromised mental state.

"Grandma, it's me, Olivia. You're safe now, we've found you." She rubbed circles on Grandma's back.

Grandma's mind didn't seem to want to return from its detour. "Jacob. Hurt." Grandma grasped Olivia's hands, both trembling. "My boy."

Olivia cradled Grandma's bony frame. She'd called Olivia's father Jacob once before. "Your boy is grown up now. He's in Indianapolis. Safe." Or so she assumed.

"But...Jacob."

Blake approached slowly, tucking his phone in his pocket. "Mrs. Hudson, it's me Blake. I don't know about you, but I'm starving. How about I take you girls out for some pizza?"

Grandma shied away from him.

Blake stepped back.

What could she do to ease Grandma's fears? Olivia leaned close. "Don't worry. Be happy."

After a few more minutes of gentle coaxing, Grandma agreed to return to the car. Their shoes crunched the sticks and debris as they made their way out of the woods.

When they reached Olivia's vehicle, Blake held open Grandma's door. "Are we still on for pizza?"

They couldn't go out like this. Olivia was a mess, inside and out. Grandma was calmer, but looked as if she could collapse at any moment. "We need to go home. I'm sorry."

Blake opened his mouth as if to protest, then closed it. His brows pulled in disappointment. "I understand. Will you be all right?"

"I think so." Even she didn't believe her words over the tremble in her voice.

He came around to her side and pulled her into a hug. She stiffened, but then melted into it. It felt good to know she wasn't alone. "If you need anything, call me."

Oh, how easy it would be to let him lead for a while. To rest in the comfort of his arms. She was tired. Olivia nodded, not trusting her words. She pulled away first.

He didn't let go. Keeping one hand on her back, he touched the bump on her forehead with the other. "Get some rest. Don't worry about bringing me food tomorrow. I'll manage."

She nodded, pain radiating in her skull now that

she'd remembered her injury. "Good night."

"'Night." Blake let her go, one slow inch at a time.

Overwhelmed in a thousand different ways, Olivia sank onto the driver's seat.

Blake shut her door. All the way home Grandma murmured about a boy named Jacob.

And Olivia tried to forget the masculine heat of Blake's touch.

20

Blake carried two glasses of tea and weaved through the idle vehicles parked next to his barn. Ice cubes clinked against the sides, already melting in the afternoon heat. His eyes adjusted to the dim light of the barn where his dad sat at a picnic table full of pens and IRS forms for hiring seasonal help.

He loved this part. Meeting new people, welcoming past employees, getting to know the migrant workers and their families. Their cultures. Everyone coming together to get the job done.

Blake set his dad's drink on the table in front of him.

"Thanks, son. Abejundio says he's worked for you the last two years." Dad pointed to the dark-skinned, stocky man in the corner who was using a support beam as a writing surface.

"Abe." Blake wiped his wet fingers on his pant leg and approached the man, arm outstretched.

Transferring pen and paper to his left hand, Abe extended his right. "Nice see you, Blake."

The man's English had improved since last summer. "Thanks for coming back. Is your family with you?"

"Catalina with child. It's me and Fausto this year."

"Congratulations. I look forward to working with you both again." Blake clamped the man's shoulder.

Huck and his wife walked in.

Arianne smiled. "Got room for a couple more?"

"Absolutely." Blake took a swig of tea to quench his parched throat and to wash down envy for the life Huck had. "Are you signing up for harvest, or are you helping this guy collect the honey?"

She slipped her arm through Huck's, gripping the bend of his elbow. "As much as I love him, he can have his bees. I'm here for the blueberries. And the vitamin D. Plus, Olivia mentioned she planned to help, so I thought I'd join her."

The mention of Olivia's name brought back the image of her in his arms, the feel of her against him. How close he'd been to kissing her senseless. Tea. He needed more tea. Blake downed half the glass. "Welcome aboard. There's paperwork over there, if you've got a minute."

Blake had texted Olivia this morning to see how they were doing after yesterday's scare. She hadn't replied. He'd gotten so close, and now she was running like a frightened animal. If she'd simply trust him, he'd show her how good they'd be together. Like chicken wings and a baseball game.

Except he wouldn't get his Saturday dose of her today. That bothered him more than watching the game alone. Again. "Would you mind helping me move another table out here?"

Huck followed him to the tack room, where the scent of oil and leather hung in the air from Blake's grandfather's old saddle. Blake moved a can of nails and the blueprints of his last hobby off the dusty table. Removing a clean hanky from his back pocket, Blake wiped away the dust.

Huck braced his hands under one side while Blake took the other. "How are things in the world of baking?"

"Stale."

"I hear ya."

They guided the table through the doorway. "Arianne seems to think the baker has a thing for you. Then again, she's a hopeless romantic who won't stop matchmaking until love has rued the day. Be careful, my friend."

"I sell weddings for a living." At the sound of Arianne's voice, Huck's end fell, stopping Blake short. "I can't help it," she said.

Huck leaned over and kissed her cheek. "Have I told you how pretty you look today?"

One hand found her hip. "No, you haven't."

"You look beautiful today."

"Nice try."

This. This was what Blake wanted. A wife to love, to tease. To keep warm at night. A wife who'd stick by him no matter how stupid or pig-headed he was.

Arianne shrugged. "She thinks highly of you, Blake. Give her time. She's been through a lot." She looked at her husband. "Sometimes love takes time."

Love is patient. Was this love? They hadn't even had a date yet. But what he felt for Olivia was a whole lot closer to the target than not.

Arianne turned to walk out of the barn, but stopped and called over her shoulder. "And when you both set a date, you know where my shop is."

Huck's head craned heavenward, eyes rolling.

Seemed Blake had a lot of work to do.

~*~

The animal shelter's doors opened to a cacophony of dogs—large and small—barking for attention. A Chihuahua growled from its little cage, warning Olivia it would eat her ankles if given the opportunity. A collie with sad, brown eyes begged for affection. The woof of what appeared to be a beagle and pug mix tore at Olivia's heart. It stood on back legs, its front paws gripping the chain-link gate, tail wagging like a metronome on high speed. She could no more pick a favorite canine than she could a new purse. If only she could take them all home. "If you find one you want to pet, let me know and we can take it for a walk."

Grandma didn't respond, only bent to look at each one before moving to the next cage.

They walked up and down all the aisles twice before Grandma's interest settled on a tiny gray kitten with patches of white on her upper lip and paws. "Home."

"Remember, we talked about a dog and how much fun it would be to take it with us when we go places." A trained dog that could help keep Grandma out of trouble.

Grandma tried to open the cage. "Home."

"He's awfully little. Let's look at all the animals before we decide."

"Home." Grandma stamped her foot.

Mood swings were getting as hard to deal with as wandering off and not sleeping.

The uniformed woman who had let them in came around the corner. "Find one you want to see closer?"

"Home." Grandma stuck her fingers through the bars as far as the cage would allow. The tiny ball of fuzz rubbed its head on her finger then raised its back end as it rubbed the rest of itself.

"We'd come in search of a dog." Olivia whispered to the woman. "One we could train to stay by her side, alert someone if she tries to wander off."

The woman placed her hand on Olivia's arm and squeezed. "I understand. My mother had dementia before she died. However, a cat makes just as good a companion as a dog. Especially one like Smokey. I'm Jackie, by the way." The woman unlatched the cage, reached inside, and tucked the feline against her ample breasts. "It's about feeding time. I've got a small bottle in the back. Let's see how your grandma does."

They followed the woman to a small cubicle with rubber benches. Once Grandma was seated, Jackie placed the kitten in Grandma's lap. "I'll go get the bottle."

Grandma lifted the kitten to her chin and cooed. It purred and meowed, as if torn between wanting snuggled and wanting to eat.

Jackie returned with an odd-looking bottle and handed it to Grandma. Like a pro, she turned the kitten upside down in her arm like an infant and stuck the bottle between its tiny, sharp teeth. Sucking noises filled the space.

"Huh." Olivia leaned forward and rested her chin against her fist.

Jackie smiled and joined Olivia on the bench.

"She seems pretty happy." Olivia pointed at Grandma, who was gazing proudly at the kitten as if she'd given birth to it herself.

Olivia leaned her elbows on her knees. "Thing is, I run a business. Between that and Grandma's care, I don't think we can keep up with regular feedings."

"Smokey needs to be fed every three to four hours. It'll still be a few weeks before she's ready for wet food. Plus, she'll need to be cleaned several times a day to stimulate healthy bladder and bowel function."

The suckling stopped. Milk dripped down the side of the kitten's mouth. It meowed, hooked it claws into Grandma's hand, and proceeded to climb up her arm. "Ouch!"

Jackie stood and removed the kitten.

Grandma scowled at the feline.

Olivia stood as well. "Do you know if cats help with sleeping habits?"

"I can't answer that. However, if you're willing to consider a dog, I have the perfect companion."

After spending some time with a Tricolour Cavalier King Charles Spaniel, a purebred female rescued from a puppy mill two years prior, they all agreed they'd found the one. Sydney would stimulate nurturing with less maintenance.

Olivia ran her fingers over the dog's silky ears. "Sold."

Jackie tugged her pants up her thick waist. "I'll draw up the paperwork."

Two hours later, after purchasing Sydney and stopping by the store for the necessary supplies, they settled on the couch under a large quilt with chamomile tea and their new friend. Jackie had assured them the breed was patient, sociable, and adapted well to any environment—perfect for children or the elderly.

Olivia was flipping through the TV channels in search of something to watch when a baseball game made her pause. Her mind traveled to yesterday, to Blake's firm hand cushioning her head, the weight of his torso on hers, one hand curled on her hip. Handsome and strong and good. The way he always put her first. She missed seeing him today. More than she'd even realized, until now.

21

The only thing more perfect than the temperature for Stone Harbor's First Annual July Fourth Festival was the way Olivia looked in her frilly apron, standing under the shade of a canopy and serving cupcakes. She hadn't yet spotted Blake, which provided him the opportunity to look his fill.

She grinned at a toddler wearing a bright yellow dress. Reddish curls twisted at the end of her pigtails. Lips pressed together, her little cheeks puffed out to propel the petals of her red, white, and blue pinwheel. The girl said something to her mother, then wrapped her arms around the woman's leg and squeezed. Laughter, then the exchange of money, followed by Olivia handing over two cupcakes.

A block over, the roar of a marching band tuning instruments warned the crowd the parade would start soon. Now to coax Olivia from her booth long enough to watch it with him.

Olivia waved to the little girl. "Happy Fourth of July!"

The tot skipped backwards. "Happy Forwf."

Olivia pinned that smile on Blake as he approached. "Here comes Uncle Sam himself."

"Huh, uh. I passed that duty to Bob Thatcher last week."

"Why?"

"He's tall, skinny, and already has a white

goatee."

She frowned, though the mirth never left her eyes. "I was looking forward to seeing you in patriotic flannel."

He tapped the table with his knuckle. "That's it, Olivia Hudson. I vow right now that I'll have you wearing flannel this next winter or I'll…"

"Eat it?"

He made a face.

"Until then, have a cupcake." She plucked one out of a pink box, set it on a napkin, and passed it to him. "A hummingbird cupcake made with Huck's honey, which we're now selling at the bakery."

He went for his wallet.

"It's on the house. I happen to know the owner."

"Your cheeks are glowing."

"I'm…happy." Her head tipped to the side, as if surprised by her confession. She slipped her hands in her apron pockets. "My father and I reached an understanding. I've officially taken over financial responsibility for the business, so when he receives his inheritance, the bakery will fall to me."

Her father. Blake ran this new information through his mind slowly. He started to ask, but decided to focus on the most important clue. "Sounds like you're putting down roots."

"I am."

Blake's heart kicked up speed. Best news he'd heard in three years.

The church bells sounded the top of the hour.

"Will you watch the parade with me?"

"I can't."

"Yes, you can." Brittany, one of Olivia's employees, and a woman Blake had dated a few times, walked up to the table and shooed Olivia away. "I've got this covered, boss. Take a break." Brittany winked at Olivia—the way women do when sharing a secret—and showcased her dimples.

"Thanks. Let me get Grandma."

Blake followed Olivia into the bakery, doing his best not to stare at the hollow of her back where she was clumsily untying her apron strings. Instead, he focused on the miniature American flags decorating the edges of the sidewalk leading to the entrance. He counted twelve.

Black-and-white pictures of old war ships, poster style, covered most of the walls. A huge banner hid the bookshelves in the still-in-progress nook where patrons could write a thank-you message to veterans for delivery to the nearest VA hospital. Even the desserts on display commemorated the holiday.

Olivia weaved through the line of customers to the kitchen.

Blake peeled off a section of wrapper and bit into the cupcake while he waited. An explosion of southern flavors burst in his mouth, followed by the sweetness of honey. The woman sure had talent for mixing stuff in a bowl and making it delicious.

A few minutes later, the ladies joined him. He stuffed the last bite into his mouth, tossed the wrapper in the trashcan, and held the door while they exited.

The sun hit Olivia's face at just the right angle to start a golden fire in those blue eyes. "What'd'ya think?"

Blake licked the stickiness off his lips then pressed them together. "Definitely a keeper."

Drums pounded down the alley while trumpets and tubas signaled the band's approach. They'd need to find an open spot soon or they'd miss the whole thing. Mrs. Hudson hunkered over and covered her ears. He hadn't figured on the noise bothering her. He glanced around for a solution.

"Here." Blake led them to a concrete bench away from the people lining the street. He hopped up and then helped them stand on it as well. From this vantage point, they could still see the parade without having to endure the sharp sounds of the instruments.

Firemen threw candy from shiny red trucks, followed by the local high school cheerleaders waving pom-poms to the beat of the school's fight song. Uncle Sam was next. Bob fit the role perfectly in a tailored, striped suit and stilts for effect. Pointing at the spectators, he mimicked Uncle Sam's "I want you" campaign from World War II.

A Chihuahua broke free from its owner and nipped at the icon's heels. Bob stumbled. "Oh, no!" Olivia grabbed Blake's arm, her mouth open, watching for disaster.

Bob leaned and took several steps to the left, then to the right, and turned in a perfect circle, twice, before someone ran into the street and snatched up the dog. Bob regained his footing, wiped his brow, and then waved his flag in victory. Cheers momentarily muted the band.

With a hand to her chest, Olivia looked up at Blake and laughed. "That was close."

Blake would've eaten pavement. "Now I feel bad pawning the job off on him."

Jerry Rizzo, the bank manager, led the line of classic vehicles in his red convertible.

Olivia pointed to the street. "Look!" she yelled, waving hysterically. "It's Arianne."

Arianne leaned out the window of Huck's 1959 truck, her hand splayed above the Summerville Honey Farm logo. Sunlight glared off the teal paint, accentuating the spots that had been painted to look like rust. She spotted Olivia, and her face lit up as she waved back.

Emma, their eight-year-old daughter, sat in the bed dressed in a yellow-and-black striped costume with shimmery wings attached. The girl waved like Miss America. She looked healthy compared to the last time he'd seen her. The little sweetheart deserved a normal life.

The last of the parade went by, and the crowd dispersed. Kids gathered the few pieces of leftover candy abandoned in the street.

Blake jumped off the bench and helped Mrs. Hudson down first. Then he held up his hand for Olivia.

She grasped it but stayed in place. "Want to grab some lunch?"

He blinked. Did he imagine the words, or had the band affected his hearing?

She stepped onto the grass and looked up at him. "Unless you've eaten already."

"No, let's do it. But you have to let me buy." He released her hand against his will.

"That sounds like a date."

"If you're not comfortable with that, we'll say it's a celebration of your new position. Or a town board member officially welcoming you as a permanent resident."

They walked toward the food vendors. "Very slick. I'll take you up on it, however, since I owe you a date after the baseball practice fiasco."

Blake palmed the small of her back. "You don't owe me anything. I understand." The unplanned gesture felt completely right and didn't seem to bother Olivia, so he went with it. All the way to the vendor offering giant tenderloins and loaded nachos.

They ordered and Blake paid while the women secured a table.

Blake met up with them and dug into his sandwich. "How's your barbecue, Mrs. Hudson?"

Sauce coated the woman's fingers. Blake handed her a napkin and grinned when she refused it and licked her fingers instead. "Cliff makes better."

Now Mrs. Hudson reached for the napkin.

"Who's Cliff?"

"My grandpa," Olivia said. "According to the journal I told you about, they used to camp a lot. Grandpa would slow cook barbecue over a fire. He made his own special sauce."

Mrs. Hudson gazed into the distance, her eyes unfocused. Remembering. Or trying to, it seemed.

"Sounds good. Wish I'd have had the opportunity to sample it."

Olivia sipped her soda. "Me, too."

Fifteen minutes later, when he and Olivia were down to the last few bites of their meal, Mrs. Hudson still hadn't come out of her daze. Olivia placed her hand over her grandma's and gave it a little shake. "Grandma, are you going to finish your sandwich?"

Mrs. Hudson blinked. Then she turned toward Olivia with the saddest eyes Blake had ever seen. She pushed her food away.

Olivia's forehead wrinkled. She reached across the table and tucked the sandwich back inside its foil wrapper. "We'll save it for later."

Blake unfolded his legs from under the picnic table and gathered his trash. "Are you going to the fireworks tonight? They're setting them off at Middle River."

She looked at Mrs. Hudson. "I don't know. I think I'll take her home for a nap and see how she is later."

Blake dropped his mess into the trashcan. "I'll be there if you decide to come. I'll save you ladies a spot."

Olivia nodded. She helped Mrs. Hudson up from the table, steadied her, and threw away their trash. "I'll text if we decide to come."

The women started to walk away. Blake still had no idea why Olivia had left her former life to start a new one here, but he was grateful she had. Stone Harbor was better with her in it. He was better.

"Livi?" he called.

She turned, one hand still wrapped around her grandma's arm.

Blake swallowed a lump of emotion he wasn't about to name. "Welcome home."

22

We're here.

Olivia sent the text and stepped from her car into the humid evening air. They still had at least thirty minutes before the sky would be dark enough to see fireworks. She smoothed the silky yellow shirt hugging her waist, brushed her fingers through her hair. An awful lot of fuss for a guy she wasn't interested in being more than friends with. She met Grandma by the trunk. "Ready?"

"My purse."

Olivia lifted the tote of drinks Grandma called a purse. "I'll get it." She rested the strap on her shoulder.

Her phone buzzed with an incoming message.

Meet me at the shelter house.

Olivia could make out the roofline in the distance. The challenge would be to get through the sea of strangers all scrambling for a good spot. Grandma didn't like crowds, but Blake had promised to save them an area away from the mass.

They maneuvered around a group of cyclists walking their bikes on the path, taking them closer to the cart selling florescent necklaces. Grandma angled toward the merchandise. "Have."

Olivia followed. "We need to find Blake before the fireworks start."

"Have."

Biting back a groan, Olivia fished in her purse for

cash. Three families stood in line ahead of them. She craned her neck around a dad with a toddler on his shoulders and scanned the merchandise list. Four-ninety-nine! For one necklace? She looked around the darkening landscape. Neon necklaces everywhere.

The line moved quickly, but when it came Grandma's turn to choose which color she wanted it was like trying to pick a favorite scent in a candle store—she had to examine each one.

"The pink would look nice on you." Olivia handed the vendor a ten-dollar bill, ready to be on their way.

"Two." Grandma plucked another pink necklace from the container.

"I think one is sufficient."

"Two. You." Grandma handed the other necklace to Olivia.

The vendor smiled.

"Keep the change," Olivia grumbled.

They continued to the shelter house. The soft glow from inside lit Blake's familiar form standing by the water spigot, hands in his shorts pockets, handsome as ever in a gray T-shirt that rested flawlessly over farm-sculpted brawn. Stubble that hadn't covered his cheeks that morning shadowed his face as he smiled. "I was about to send out a search party."

She willed her hormones to calm down. "Sorry, we had a detour." She held up the necklace.

Blake's gaze flicked to Grandma, who was proudly wearing her new purchase. "Ah. I found a place further down from the blast site. Hopefully, the noise won't bother her as much. You think she's up for walking?" He glanced at his watch.

"We'll manage."

He led them to a little knoll facing the bank. As

promised, the area wasn't nearly as congested. Hundreds of blankets spread across the grass below them, occupied by families and couples.

Blake stopped at a spread of quilts. A can of bug spray and an empty cup rested on the grass beside them. He unfolded a lawn chair and set it beside the quilt. "I brought this for Mrs. Hudson. Thought it might be easier on her than the hard ground."

Warmth spread through her chest. Even she hadn't thought of that. "Thank you."

He guided Grandma onto it. Grandma patted his hand. "Bradley."

Blake winked.

With two blankets, Olivia didn't need to sit right next to Blake, but after slipping off her sandals, she did anyway, curling her knees to her chest and folding her arms around them. At the bottom of the hill, sparklers flashed in a circle of children chasing each other.

Blake bumped his elbow with hers. "How'd you do today?"

"We brought in more revenue than we have on a single day in the last five years. We still have a lot of catching up to do, but the new cake service is going well. And once I get the Wi-Fi and furniture in the nook, I think more locals will spend time there."

"I have a truck. Let me know when you're ready to pick up your furniture."

"You've done so much for us already, Blake. I can't keep relying on you."

"Yes, you can." The deep timbre of his voice dropped on his last word.

She shivered. There was no end to the man's kindness, and she often found herself wanting to curl up in it like a heated blanket. She leaned a little closer.

"Why didn't you have a booth today?"

"Nothing's ready yet. I'll start harvesting in about a month. I have a booth saved at the Machias Blueberry Festival in August."

"That sounds like fun."

"It is. You should come with me."

Maybe she would. Though it was hard to plan ahead when she was still living from one day to the next. Each day brought its own challenges. Not only with Grandma's care, but with taking her life back. Loneliness was a hard enemy to beat. She'd not only lost her family and her home, but she'd also lost her future. A murdered dream with someone she'd thought loved her.

Being with Justin was nothing like being with Blake. Justin had always been content in their relationship, which had not been digressing but hadn't grown either. Justin had never pushed her, never challenged her, never expected much from her at all. Blake nudged her, in his quiet and good way, to expand.

She'd loved Justin. Had since childhood. It was only natural that when they'd started dating their senior year and continued throughout their four years of college that they marry. But practicality didn't equal love. Now she wondered if what they'd shared had ever amounted to real love at all.

Spending time with Blake both eased her smothering loneliness and made it worse.

A loud boom rent the air. Multi-colored fireworks burst into the night sky. They sizzled away, and others took their place. The water on Middle River lay smooth as glass, reflecting a mirror image of the pyrotechnics.

She and Blake stretched their legs in front of them.

The night heat brought out the scent of his cologne, the same sea spray and sunshine aroma she'd detected in his room the day she'd toured his house. She was comfortable with Blake now that they'd spent so much time together. However, fireworks on a hot summer night brought a level of intimacy to their relationship that made her pulse rush, despite telling herself—repeatedly—to remain on firm ground.

Blasts of white filled the sky. A dog barked in the distance to her right, drawing her attention to the elderly couple sitting not ten feet away. "Is that Mrs. Campbell and Arthur Greene?"

Blake followed her finger and smiled. "It is."

Olivia sat, stunned. The couple sat side by side in lawn chairs, Eugenia's head nestled on Arthur's shoulder. Olivia hadn't seen either one since the day at the beauty shop. When had the couple reconciled? Who had made the first move? The sky's display no longer held Olivia's attention. She stared at the couple, dumbfounded.

Love endureth all things.

Maybe somehow, some way, it did.

A warm touch, calloused yet gentle, skimmed the top of her hand. Though she couldn't pull her teary gaze off the older couple, she turned over her palm to meet Blake's. He linked their fingers together. Her chest burned with an unfamiliar sensation. Painful. Yet awakening. She glanced down at their entwined hands, terrified and in complete awe. His thumb rubbed hers. She swallowed.

Hopeth all things.

~*~

October 1955

The day our Jonathan was born. Headstrong, opinionated, and independent from the moment he took his first breath. Look at those ruddy cheeks. The set of his jaw. Oh, but I was a proud papa. Despite all your fears, the ones that had you apprehensive about having babies at all, you were a proud mama.

Fear is debilitating. It keeps us from experiencing so many things. We cling to fear because we think it keeps us safe, when what it really does is robs us of possibilities. Blessings.

See what you would've missed if you'd have continued believing you'd be a terrible mother? "For God hath not given us a spirit of fear; but of power, and of love, and of a sound mind." II Timothy 1:7

You're a great mother, Elizabeth. I know you're in a dark place right now, hurting and scared. I am too. But let fear go. I need you. Jonathan needs you. What happened isn't his fault. He needs his mother. Needs to know you love him.

Let fear go.

23

Olivia couldn't put it off any longer. It was time she called her mother.

Curling her legs behind her on the couch, she covered them with a blanket. The only light in the room came from the muted television where *Mr. Smith Goes to Washington* played in silence. Sheer curtains rustled from the breeze of the open window. At eight o'clock, Grandma and her new companion, Sydney, were tucked in bed, allowing Olivia at least an hour of free time before she made her way upstairs.

She scrolled through her phone contacts and tapped on her mother's name, pressing a hand to her stomach. This shouldn't be difficult. The two of them had rarely agreed on anything in the past—clothes, friends, careers. Olivia doubted her decision to remain in Stone Harbor would be any different.

The muffled hum of several voices bled through the line. "You mean I get to talk, actually talk, to my daughter? No emails? No texting?"

Here it was. The familiar disapproval. "I know it's been a while. I'm sorry for that."

"You've called three times in six months. Counting this one."

True. And each time, Mom had spent at least an hour relaying every ugly detail of her father's infidelity, every argument between them, and every possession they were fighting over in court. Each time when Olivia hung up the phone, she sat in stunned silence as the walls closed in around her, the security of her life slipping further away.

"I've had a lot going on, Mom. Grandma's stroke complicated things. I've had to work hard to keep the bakery from going bankrupt. Grandma had appointments, and I'm working with the other merchants to boost tourism." Why was she defending herself? She'd done nothing wrong.

"That's a lot for someone who's only there temporarily..."

The last word hung in the air like the blade of a guillotine.

Olivia closed her eyes, as if that would lessen the blow. "I'm staying. Permanently."

A pause. "I wondered how long it would take you to tell me."

Olivia pulled the blanket up to her chest, the comfortable breeze suddenly becoming chilly. "You knew?"

"Of course, I did. Your father and I still talk. It's just a lot louder and usually includes our lawyers."

How did a man and woman married for thirty years wake up one day and decide they weren't in love anymore? How was it easy to abandon the very principles on which they'd founded their lives? Branded on their daughter?

How was that daughter supposed to sort those shattered pieces for signs of truth?

How could she not feel as though her whole life was based on a lie?

Olivia curled her fingers into the chenille blanket. "I found a scrapbook journal Grandpa made for Grandma. I've been reading it, and it sounds as if something devastating happened when Dad was little. Do you know anything about it?"

Mom sighed. "For years I've suspected something haunts that man, but I've never been able to get him to open up about his childhood. He's too focused on the future, on cushioning his bank account. And now his bed."

For the next twenty minutes, Olivia sat, numb, watching the movie while her mother ranted over who should get the house, the vehicles, and Dad's retirement fund.

Why didn't Olivia, who'd been trained and paid well to put people's broken lives back together, have the power to fix her parents?

Because she wasn't God.

Her mother hadn't asked to be cheated on, to be tossed aside for a younger, more voluptuous version. It wasn't fair. A marriage took two to make it work, and both her parents were guilty of letting the marriage fizzle out. But in order for Olivia to function, to move on with some semblance of her life, she couldn't be stuck in the middle of all the ugliness.

"Four-thirty comes quickly, Mom. I need to get to bed. If you need anything, call. Try and hang in there."

"I'm hanging in just fine." Her fake enthusiasm proved it. "I'm out with a few girlfriends, having cocktails. All is good!"

Cocktails? Her mother didn't drink.

At least she didn't used to.

Another wholesome part of Olivia's life scrambled like liquid in a blender. Tears pricked her eyes. "Love you, Mom. Call you soon."

After ending the call and tossing her phone aside, Olivia curled into a ball in the corner of the couch and rested her head against the arm. A soft whine sounded from the floor. Olivia lifted Sydney beside her and rubbed her chin against the dog's silky fur.

Olivia loved her mother with all her heart, but she'd always been a daddy's girl. What had made him think just because she was grown she didn't need him anymore? As thoughts of this faceless woman, days older than Olivia, tortured her mind, she buried her face in Sydney's neck and wept.

24

Warm house. Full fields. Empty life. Though, a pretty little baker had let Blake hold her hand the other night. As middle school as that was, it was something. He'd finally scaled her wall of ice. Now to melt it down to expose all her layers.

Blake took the porch steps two at a time and went into the house. Scooby scratched at the screen door, wanting in, too. "Come on, old man."

Scooby trotted past him and into the living room without a glance. Tired pooch. He was just as beat and ready to cool off as Blake was.

He toed off his boots and climbed the stairs to his bedroom, peeling his shirt from his sticky skin. Shower, then food.

A ring echoed through the silent house. His landline. He jogged down the steps and snatched it from the base by the couch. "This is Blake."

"Hey, son. I'll make this quick. I only have a few minutes until your mom gets back in the car. I'm throwing her a surprise sixtieth birthday party."

"Um, great. Are you sure though? Women are funny about their age."

"I feel bad for ruining her fiftieth with a heart attack, so I thought I'd throw her one this year—invite everyone we know, make a big deal out of it."

"You had no control over the heart attack, and not celebrating her birthday was the least of her worries."

Then his father's words penetrated. Blake lowered onto the edge of the couch. "When you say you're inviting everyone, I assume you mean Lucas? As much as I love Mom, I won't be there if he's coming."

Dad sighed. Probably at how immature Blake's comment sounded. "Your brother can't make it. Madison has some fancy banquet she has to attend for work, and she wants your brother there."

Selfish as always. "When's the party?"

"Last minute, a week from tomorrow."

"Wow." Blake scratched the back of his head. "Let me know how I can help."

"We're going to need a cake."

Of course. Blake smiled at the excuse to stop by the bakery. Four days without seeing her was too long. "I'll take care of it."

"Thanks, son. Got to go."

Blake hung up and rubbed the bridge of his nose. Yawned. Saturday he was hauling new furniture for the bakery and helping Olivia arrange it in the new space. A whole day with her all to himself. He could get used to that.

~*~

"What do you think of this one?" Olivia gazed up at Blake from her spot on the white wicker settee. The gray-and-yellow cushion was plush yet firm, and the pattern would offset the solid accent chairs they'd purchased earlier.

Blake was doing his best to hide the glazed-over expression every man got when shopping. However, his best wasn't quite enough.

He lowered onto the space next to her. Their thighs brushed, causing her heart to speed. Then Blake's arm stretched along her shoulders. "Yep. This is definitely the one."

She elbowed his ribs. They'd flirted like a couple of kids all morning. He had a way of focusing his attention solely on her, making her feel special. Something she hadn't felt in a long time. "I think this settee and the chairs we bought earlier will go great with the antique travel trunk-turned-coffee table."

He nodded. "The only thing that would make this moment better is food."

"You're right." They'd searched every furniture and antique store in Bangor. Feeding him was the least she could do. Though she was nice and cozy.

He removed his arm. "You pay. I'll load."

She gripped his knee and used it as leverage to stand. "Lunch is on me."

"I don't think so."

"Payment for helping me."

"I don't want to be paid." Blake stood and inched closer until they stood toe to toe. His fingers skimmed the back of her hand, tying her stomach in delightful knots. "Consider this a date."

Olivia looked away. Those giddy knots were now stomach cramps. Oh, how she wanted to give in. "There's a lot of things you don't know about me and—"

"That's what dating is for, Livi." He touched her chin and guided her face around to meet his. "I'm not afraid of anything you have to tell me."

That's because he didn't know what she would say.

Blake bent his knees to meet her at eye level. "Will

you agree to get to know me?"

As if she could deny him when his gentle touch stirred a fire inside her belly that melted her insides like butter in a hot skillet. "When you put it like that, how can a girl say no?"

He grinned. "That's a yes?"

"Don't let it go to your head."

"Impossible."

They separated at the register. She paid while Blake drove the truck around the back to the warehouse. After the settee, the accent chairs, and the trunk were secured in Blake's truck bed, Olivia climbed in beside him, and they turned onto the highway.

The wind rushed through the open windows, lashing her hair around her face. She rested her head on the seatbelt and closed her eyes. The freedom of an entire day off from work and caregiving invigorated Olivia's spirit. As much as she loved her grandma, the break was welcome. Eugenia was a saint for staying with Grandma today.

The sun poured through the window and heated her legs. She stretched and opened her eyes. Blake took his gaze off the road long enough to watch her in that way a man did when he very much approved of a woman. That's when she noticed her feet on his dashboard. "Oh. Sorry."

She started to pull them away, but he put out a hand to stop her. "I don't mind. Go ahead and let your hair down, let the grass grow under your feet, or whatever you flatlanders say."

"I can honestly claim I've never used either one of those terms. What would you seafarers call it?"

"I'd say, for a city puke, you're wicked cunnin'."

"Ha! Is that code or something? What does that even mean?"

"It means for a Midwesterner, you're pretty amazing." He winked. "Very cute."

Blake had to be the only man on earth charming enough to make a girl blush after referring to her as a "city puke." That wink, a gesture she'd come to know as all Blake and innocent of anything sleazy, made her insides squirm with pleasure every time.

He reached for her hand. "What were you thinking all kicked back on my dashboard?"

"How nice it is to have a day away from…everything."

Blake squeezed her hand.

"That sounds terrible."

"No, it doesn't. No matter how much we love our jobs, or the people in our lives, it's nice to have a day off." He slowed and flicked on his turn signal. "How about we celebrate with a lobster roll?"

"I accept. I haven't had lobster since I moved here."

"I don't eat them very often, but you can't drive past the Seafood Shack without stopping for a lobster roll."

They turned off the highway and wound along the road for a couple miles before turning into a parking lot full of cars packed like sardines. Blake managed to find a narrow space part-way in the grass. She met him at the tailgate, where he linked his fingers with hers and they ascended the natural granite steps to a level plateau.

Blue-and-white gingham table cloths covered picnic tables filled with customers. The cerulean Atlantic rolled into the cliffs below, sending white puffs of sea spray over the rocks. Another set of steps, where the granite had worn into layers through time, angled down toward the water where a group of teenagers tested their courage.

The order line moved quickly. They both accepted a tray with their meal and turned to find a vacant table. "Let's eat down there," Blake said, nodding to where the granite layered down to the water. "We won't go too far."

Balancing his tray on one hand, he helped her navigate with the other. They sat far enough away from everyone else to have privacy. Olivia bit into her lobster roll, relishing the creamy sauce and delicate spices surrounding the fresh meat. "Mmm."

"Told yah."

They ate in silence. Waves crashed into the rocks, swirled, and churned before rejoining the open blue. Osprey circled overhead. This day was nothing short of peaceful.

She stacked her trash in one heap to keep it from dancing away. "How's the renovation going?"

Blake wiped his mouth with a napkin. "Slow. I don't get much time to work on it in the summer." He piled his trash as well. "Arianne signed up to harvest. She said you'd mentioned helping also."

"I'll be there at least one day. More, if I can. I'm confident leaving Brittany in charge at the bakery when I take time off, but finding someone to stay with Grandma is another matter."

"Have you considered in-home health care? Mrs. Hudson might be eligible, depending on her insurance."

Olivia stretched her legs in front of her and lay back on her elbows. "I've tried to put off the decision as long as I can, but…I feel guilty even thinking about it."

Blake swallowed his last bite and wiped his mouth with a napkin. "Having help can only benefit both of you."

"I know, I'm just…"

"Have trouble letting go?" He sipped the last of his drink and added the cup to the pile.

His words stung.

As a teenager, she'd struggled with letting go of her will to follow God's and obey her parents. After her mom and dad split, she'd fought letting go of a life that no longer existed. She didn't know how to let go. To accept things she didn't understand.

"I'm sorry, Livi. I shouldn't have said that."

She sat straight and wrapped her arms around her knees, keeping her attention trained on the Atlantic and not Blake's probing gaze. "Don't be sorry. You're right."

Now was the time to give answers to his questions, before they ventured any further into— whatever this was. Give him a chance to leave before she made the stupid mistake of giving him her heart.

"I was raised in a Christian home. I don't remember a time I wasn't in church. My parents were active members. They helped out with many things over the years. Taught Sunday school, lead music, cleaned and maintained the building—whatever was needed.

"They taught me to love my neighbor, serve God, stay pure until marriage. That a marriage commitment is forever. You know, the basic foundation of a Christian life. I made the decision to follow Christ when I was twelve."

Blake scooted closer and put his arm around her back. "I'm really glad to hear that."

That cold, dark cellar of her mind yawned wide. Blake propped her up as she leaned into him. His warm hand rubbed her upper arm, urging her to continue. That simple gesture of human kindness had her spewing pieces of her story into the air like a feather pillow that had ripped open.

"A little over a year ago, it came out that my dad was having an affair. It'd been going on for a couple of years actually. Still is. She's not that much older than I am."

Blake blew out a puff of air.

"Turns out my parents hadn't had a happy marriage for most of my life. I had no idea. All those principles they taught me, those rules they were determined I follow, suddenly didn't apply to them."

He pulled her closer. "I'm sorry."

A lump of despair rose in her throat, and she swallowed it back down. How could Blake be sorry when her parents weren't?

A single tear escaped. "They chose not to reconcile. Dad says it's time to do what makes him happy. Mom's decided to sow the wild oats she didn't sow when she was young because she'd chosen to become a wife and mother instead. Now I'm stuck trying to navigate a life based on deception with no map."

Blake cleared his throat. "That's when you came here."

She nodded. "Every day, I went to my office and helped people sort out their problems. Repair their marriages. Escape the pit of depression. Then I found myself in that very pit, except everything I used to help my patients didn't work for me. I cracked."

So did her voice.

Blake stiffened. "What do you mean?"

"I don't know how to explain it. I crawled deep inside myself to a place dark and ugly. I became detached. Like...like I wasn't inside of my body. I could see myself, could hear myself speaking, but I had no control."

"You...you didn't try to hurt yourself, did you?"

She met his gaze. "No, nothing like that. I didn't want to end my life, but I didn't know what to do with it, either. I spent a few days in a facility while they tried to pinpoint a cure. That's when I realized how broken our mental health care system is. I was put in the same ward with sobering addicts and people suffering with severe mental illness. The things I heard and saw... It was horrifying.

"After I got released, I knew I couldn't stick around and watch my parents destroy each other over money and possessions. I couldn't go through it all again. Grandma offered me a haven."

Olivia had never expected to tell a man she'd only known for four months the detailed extent of her pain. The confession lightened the weight of her heavy soul, somehow. She stared at the water and imagined dumping her turmoil into the foamy waves below. Watching it carry them far out to sea, never to return.

She laid her head on his shoulder. If she never shared an intimate moment with this man, she at least had in him a friend. "Now are you scared?"

Blake palmed her hip and pulled her so close she was practically on his lap. "Nope."

"It's gonna be mighty hard dating a girl with my issues."

He kissed the top of her head. "I know it's easy for me to say, but what your parents taught you were the right things, whether they're choosing to abide by those principles or not. As long as you keep going in the direction of Jesus, you'll be going the right way."

He hooked a finger under her chin and lifted her face. His dark eyes were earnest, full of honesty. "Besides, I'll be here. Turns out you and I are heading to the same place."

25

Blake had never read any of the classics, save for the ones required by his high school English teachers, but he could well imagine curling up with Olivia on the tiny couch she'd bought today and giving one a try. Or on his leather couch at home in front of the fireplace on a cold night.

Maybe he was getting a little ahead of himself with those thoughts, but after what she'd told him earlier, he wanted to tuck her away, wrap his arms around her and shield her from any more hurt. He couldn't imagine her pain.

Sure, he'd dealt with his own amount of deception and loss, but not on that level. His parents' love grew stronger with each passing year, and it showed. In fact, there were times even now when the two would act like newlyweds, and Blake would gladly excuse himself from the room. How devastating it must be to have that safe, nurturing blanket of love and trust ripped out from under you.

He gripped the last novel from the box and slid it onto the shelf with the others, while Olivia compressed the stack with a weathered mermaid bookend.

She stepped back to study the finished space. "It's perfect, Blake. Thank you."

"My pleasure." He removed the tag still clipped to the wicker with his pocketknife.

Olivia yawned. Her hyperactive energy had

depleted since their conversation at lunch, her mood settling into something in between sentimental and depressed. She glanced at her watch. "I should pick up Grandma and get home."

He threw away the tag. "Want me to drive you both home?"

"That's OK. Hopefully, Mrs. Campbell wore her out, and we'll both get a full night's sleep. Tomorrow, I'll start planning your mom's cake."

Her smile didn't quite reach her eyes. The scab she'd ripped off with her confession was still bleeding.

"Come here." Blake opened his arms and, to his surprise, she stepped into them. She circled his waist, and he pulled her close. The silky strands of her hair tickled the back of his hand.

"Instead of us picking up the cake, will you consider delivery? I'd like you to meet my parents."

She pulled back enough to see his face, eyes rounded. "After all I told you today, you want me to meet your family?"

"Absolutely." He moved his hand up her back. "You've nothing to be ashamed of."

Her head shook so slightly, he would've missed it had he not been absorbing every detail. She wasn't turning down his offer, simply having trouble believing it.

She swallowed. "All right."

Blake fought the desire to taste her lips and prove just how right he could make things for her. She wasn't whole again, yet, and he refused to take advantage of her vulnerability. "Text me when you get home and settled."

She pulled away in slow motion, almost as if she were as reluctant to break contact as he was. "I will."

Four hours later, he was turning off his bedroom lamp when his cell buzzed with an incoming text.

Home. Rough evening. Thanks again for your help today. Goodnight.

Blake wished he could do more to lighten her load. He turned his lamp back on and opened his Bible to the passage he'd highlighted earlier. He texted back.

Joel 2:25. Sleep well.

26

This cake was a disaster.

Olivia stepped back and crossed her arms, fighting tears. "Don't do this to me now."

July was ending with a humid ninety-five degrees, melting her three-tiered masterpiece into mush.

The bakery's ancient air-conditioning unit was straining to keep up with the temperature of the kitchen, which was nearly as hot as it was outside. And on the day of Blake's mom's birthday, no less.

Tears danced on the edges of her eyelids as a blob of buttercream slid down the side of the cake and plopped onto the bottom tier. She couldn't let Blake down. Not after all he'd done for her. Not after he'd stuck around after her heavy confession.

Brittany joined her at the table, cocking her head in the direction the cake leaned. "It's not...that bad."

Olivia smirked.

"OK, it is." Brittany snapped. "But there's a way to fix it. We can pipe little windows and arches and say it's the leaning Tower of Pisa."

Olivia buried her face in her hands, allowing tears to escape with a chuckle. "That's not funny."

Brittany gave her a side-arm hug. "Sure, it is. I'm hilarious."

Olivia wiped tears with the back of her hand and sighed. Brittany had filled the few orders for multitiered cakes they'd gotten since offering the service. Olivia should've put her in charge of this one too instead of insisting on doing it herself.

"I used to be good at this, but I haven't done one of this caliber in years. I thought it would be like riding a bike."

Susan passed, carrying a tray of orange cranberry muffins. "It looks like someone ran over it with a bike," she mumbled.

"Don't listen to her." Brittany elbowed Olivia's arm.

It should be Olivia encouraging her employees, instilling confidence and ensuring them she was capable enough to run this company. Instead, she was proving to the group what a mess she really was.

Olivia bit her lip. "I'm supposed to deliver this in three hours." She inhaled a deep breath, rubbed the back of her neck, and analyzed her predicament. The humidity was causing the layers to become unstable and the icing to melt. She needed to make the room cooler. But how? "I have to start over." She turned to Brittany and projected her voice. "I need you to whip up some more buttercream. I'll use the chilled layers of white and chocolate we've pre-baked for the Finecy wedding." She faced the ovens. "Amelia, I need you to re-fill that order. Emily, can you please get me the small card table out of the office? I'll be in the walk-in. Darlene, please keep an eye on Grandma."

Olivia picked up the sloppy cake and balanced it on one hand while she entered the walk-in refrigerator. She'd have to cut the new layers to size, but, if she worked quickly, she could pull this off. She might be a little late to the party, but better late than on time with a cake they could sip through a straw.

Once she had the card table in place and covered, Olivia measured and cut new cake layers, then stacked them with the leftover buttercream from the first attempt, which had firmed to a manageable consistency. She, however, was near hypothermic.

Once Brittany entered with the fresh icing, they swapped places so Olivia could warm up. Taking turns, they crumb-coated the layers, then frosted them with sunflower yellow-tinted buttercream. Within the hour, all three tiers were stacked and decorated with the white gum paste hydrangeas Olivia had pre-made, along with the chocolate monarch butterflies and a few strategically placed non-pareils.

"Olivia, this is stunning," Brittany said through chattering teeth.

"I couldn't have done it without you." Olivia would make sure Brittany was well compensated for her dedication. They left the walk-in into the blessed heat. "Now, I just have to get it there."

"Take my SUV." Brittany handed Olivia the keys. "I already have it cooling down. The cake will stay cooler in it than it will your trunk. We'll take care of Grandma."

Gratitude filled Olivia. "I don't know what I'd do without you."

Brittany smiled. "Me, either."

~*~

Blake studied the mantel clock. The party had started ten minutes ago, and Olivia still hadn't arrived. Even if meeting his parents was too overwhelming, she at least would've called or texted asking him to pick up the cake. Right? He checked his phone again. Nothing. Then again, cell reception was spotty on this side of the county.

"Great party, Blake."

Cindy. The girl who'd been crushing on him since second grade. He hated to acknowledge her, because each time he did, it produced a spark of hope in her eyes. But she was a nice person and didn't deserve rudeness either.

"Thanks. Glad you could come."

And there it was, the glow filling her face. The flame of attraction in her eyes.

Where was Olivia?

Cindy's mouth moved, but Blake caught only every other word. He was trying his best to listen. Really, he was. But his concern for Olivia and all the reasons she could be late took precedence. He nodded occasionally, concentrating on the driveway through the bay window.

At ten 'til, a compact, blue SUV rolled toward the house.

"Sorry to interrupt, but I think the cake is here." He weaved through all the guests to the kitchen door.

Olivia had made it to the front stoop. She knocked on the glass with her elbow, steadying the large box in her hands at the same time.

Blake opened the door to a disheveled, and very sexy, baker. "I was beginning to think you'd stood me up."

"Sorry, I'm late. We had an icing emergency."

Blake took the hefty box from her arms, and she followed him inside. He placed the box on the counter, since the kitchen table was now in the living room.

Olivia went to work removing the cake.

"That looks amazing."

She sighed. "I'm glad you like it."

"There's a table in the living room already set up with food. There's room for the cake. Mom's in there with the guests."

As if looking at him for the first time since arriving, her gaze raked over him. "You look really nice."

He glanced down at his denim dress shirt and khakis, not noticing anything special. In fact, he'd rolled up the sleeves to his elbows to keep from sweating to death from all the bodies crammed into the small house. But if Livi approved, he wouldn't complain.

She glanced at her own clothing. Her shoulders dropped as she opened her palms to reveal yellow stained fingers. She yanked the strings on her apron that was soiled with a kaleidoscope of colors. "I'm a mess."

He rather liked her tousled hair, clingy black shirt, and slightly wrinkled shorts. "You're beautiful." And he really liked making her cheeks turn pink.

"I can't meet your parents looking like this."

He reached out and wrapped his hand around her small one. "There are almost sixty people in there. It's a good opportunity for you to show them what you can do." He pointed to the cake. "Once they see that, you'll have customers lined out your door."

"I hope your mom likes it."

"She'll love it."

Together they carried the cake into the living room.

A few guests took that as their cue to sing Happy Birthday and, like the Red Sea parting, a path cleared to the table. Clapping erupted, along with a few whistles.

After setting her end of the cake on the table, Olivia turned and almost bumped noses with his mom. "Oh."

Blake cleared his throat. "Livi, this is my mom, Rita. Mom, this is Olivia from the bakery."

"I remember you." Mom pulled her into a signature Rita-hug—a tight squeeze with a little rocking side to side.

"Um, it's a pleasure to meet you." Olivia's hands dangled at her sides for a few moments and then rose in the air before they finally returned the hug. "Happy birthday."

Mom loosened her hold and stepped away. "Thank you, sweetheart. I've never had such a magnificent cake. Are these flowers real?" Mom fingered the white petals.

Olivia tucked her hands in her back pockets. "They're made of edible gum paste."

"I can eat these?"

Olivia curled her nose in that cute little way she did when something didn't suit. "I wouldn't suggest it. Gum paste isn't tasty."

Mom looked the cake over again, putting a hand to her chest. "It's breathtaking."

Livi tugged at her shirt and glanced around the room where dozens of stares were fixed on her.

Blake settled his hand in the small of her back and introduced her to the guests, many of them family or fellow church members. He ended with his dad, who had, within seconds, patted Blake's shoulder in silent approval.

"Olivia?" Mom weaseled between them. "Would

you do the honors of cutting the cake?"

Olivia placed a hand to her stomach. "Of course, Mrs. Hartford."

"Call me Rita."

When Olivia had walked far enough from earshot, his mother leaned over to Blake and whispered, "Or Mom."

Blake shook his head, though he didn't bother hiding his smile.

Once everyone else was served, he grabbed one of the few remaining pieces on the table and handed another to Livi. "She's having a great time." He glanced across the room at his mom and saw her laughing.

The back door opened, and Mom squealed, shoving her cake plate into Dad's hands.

The sweet dessert turned to dust on Blake's tongue.

Lucas.

Mom threw her arms around her son's neck.

Lucas hugged her back, careful of the white and yellow roses in his hand. He kissed her cheek. "Happy Birthday, Mom."

The too-familiar voice of his big brother made Blake's skin turn hot. The last time Blake had heard that voice, Lucas had declared he was leaving with Blake's fiancée.

Mom pulled away and glanced at Dad. "I thought you weren't coming? Madison had a work banquet or something, right?"

"I told her to go without me. I wasn't going to miss your birthday for anything."

The prodigal son returns. An anchor of bitterness dropped in Blake's gut. He'd rather hang than stick around for the praises and the slaughtering of the fatted calf. Blake put his cake on the table and turned to leave.

Lucas caught Blake's gaze over Dad's shoulder and nodded.

An inferno raged through Blake's veins. His hands curled into fists so tight it made his fingers ache. He took a step toward his brother when a hand wrapped around his elbow.

"Blake?" There was caution in Olivia's tone. A little fear in her eyes.

Blake ripped his arm from her gentle hold and stormed into the kitchen. How dare Lucas show up like that? How typical to never consider anyone else's feelings.

"Blake, are you all right?" Olivia's footsteps sounded behind him on the linoleum.

He couldn't look at her right now. He threw open the door.

"Blake." The plea came again, jabbing his heart.

He should respond. It wasn't Olivia's fault his louse of a brother ruined everything Blake did. This sweet, beautiful woman was as broken as he was. They needed each other. But not today. He wouldn't be good for anything today. Blake ate the distance to his truck. He threw open the door and slammed it behind him.

Olivia jumped onto the running board and hooked her elbow through the open window. "I understand you need to go." She put a cool palm to his cheek, searching him for answers he couldn't give. "Be careful."

Blake pressed his lips together to fight working his frustration out on hers. In the split second it took his brain to communicate his desires to his body, she'd jumped down and moved well out of his way. For the best. He had years of pent-up anger that would devour her in minutes. Blake started the engine and mashed the gas pedal so hard, gravel spewed behind his tires the entire length of the driveway.

27

Black vapor billowed from the smoke stack. Blake revved the tractor's engine. Four hundred horsepower rumbled beneath him. Not perfect, but it should last another year. He choked the engine and jumped down.

"Sounds good." Dad tossed him a rag.

"Thanks for your help." Blake wiped the grease from his hands. Dad had a gift with engine repair, something Blake hadn't fully inherited.

"A couple more weeks?"

Blake followed his dad's gaze to the blue-covered fields. "We'll harvest in ten days, max."

Dad swiped his forehead with the back of his wrist. "It's going to be a good year. You have plenty of help?"

"More than enough." Blake reached into the cooler for two bottled waters. He passed one to his dad.

"Your mom's already planning to raid your kitchen. Insists on cooking you breakfast every morning and enough freezer meals to last through September." Dad took a swig of water.

"She doesn't need to do that."

"You know your mother."

Blake nodded. He lowered onto his closed toolbox and downed half of his water.

"Speaking of your mom," Dad blew out a loud breath. "I'm sorry about Lucas showing up at the party."

"Dad."

"Hear me out." Dad looked off in the distance. "I love my boys. Both of you. But I also know how much Lucas hurt you, and it must've been quite a shock to see him there."

Blake's blood pressure spiked. Seeing his brother had been a staggering blow. But what rocked Blake more than anything was what had run through his mind the first second he'd seen Lucas. That he missed his brother. Who in their sane mind could miss a family member who had blatantly stolen their world from under them? The question brought thoughts of Olivia. Blake swallowed. "It's not your fault. Mom had a good day. That's what matters."

"It was good. She's still carrying on about that cake."

"Livi did a great job." She'd also given him space that had turned into three days, and he'd yet to apologize for his behavior.

Dad pulled a hankie from his back pocket. The action caused Blake to notice his dad had lost weight. "She seems like a nice girl."

"She is." Blake knew when Mom's prodding was behind his dad's words. He let it go.

"It's OK for you to move on." Dad blew his nose. Sniffed. Then tucked the square back into his pocket. "In fact, I encourage it."

Blake sighed. "We're going slow. She has a lot going on right now." Which was why he'd cornered Jennifer Wright after church yesterday.

She'd just received her RN certification, and the prayer list on the back of the bulletin said she was searching for a job. He suggested she talk to Olivia about in-home care for Mrs. Hudson. Jennifer was young and full of energy. Perfect for keeping up with the Hudson women's needs.

Dad leaned against the tractor tire. "It does your mom and me good to see the way you look at her. It's obvious your feelings run deep. A good excuse to forgive your brother."

Blake remained silent.

"Grace is a beautiful thing."

So was justice.

28

Heat stung Olivia's arms as she pulled trays of sourdough bread from the oven. Spongy loaves with a slight golden tinge—perfect. A sweet, yeasty aroma filled the kitchen. She transferred the trays onto a cooling rack and refilled the oven with pans of banana bread batter.

Teresa tapped her foot to the jazzy tune of Nat King Cole, dumping ingredients for buttercream into the floor-stand mixer. Darlene iced sugar cookies. Brittany stood at one of the stainless-steel tables, leveling sheet cakes for the retirement party order they'd received. One white, one chocolate, no disasters.

Tina entered the kitchen from the dining area. "We need more lemon cupcakes. The strawberry puree swirled into the frosting is a hit." She gave Olivia a thumbs-up and opened the walk-in refrigerator for more treats. On her way out, Tina said, "I love the new nook, by the way. It's exactly what the place needed. And the kids are loving that sand table." She disappeared through the swinging doors.

Brittany bumped her hip. "How was your shopping excursion?" she whispered.

"Good." Olivia fought the smile inching up her face.

"I'd say it was more than good, the way you're blushing."

"Sunburn."

"Your face was pale earlier."

"Hot flash." Olivia fanned her face with her hand.

"It's a hot flash all right."

Olivia nudged Brittany with her elbow. "Nosy."

No doubt, Olivia's face showed everything—her attraction to Blake, her admiration of his character, how his tenderness after her confession melted her heart, awakening her icy core. "Wash up and meet me in the office."

Grandma was seated on a corner stool, engrossed in the latest edition of *Professional Bakers Magazine*. The issue featured recipes for savory cupcakes, something Olivia had never attempted but was now inspired to try.

Brittany followed her into the small office and closed the door. "You're not firing me, are you?"

Olivia frowned. "Hardly. I'm promoting you."

She picked up an envelope off her desk and handed it to Brittany. "It's not huge in the way of bonuses, but I want you to know how impressed I am with your cake skills. You've really helped boost sales."

Brittany swatted a hand, brushing off the comment. "Oh...go on."

Olivia laughed. "You bring a smile to work every day, you have a great sense of humor, and the respect the other women have for you shows." She rested her backside on the edge of the desk. "I'd like to offer you a manager position."

Brittany was all perfect teeth and dimples.

"I need someone I trust to run the bakery when I can't be here. I don't know what the future holds as Grandma's condition gets worse, but I'm realizing I can't do this by myself. The position will involve a pay increase, of course. And time off for your upcoming honeymoon."

"Sign me up." Brittany slapped the envelope against her palm.

Olivia stood, relieved. Now she could take a day off or help Blake harvest his blueberries without a flood of worry or guilt. Funny how he'd crept into her future plans.

Brittany folded her check and tucked it into her back pocket. "I'm glad you're doing this. Not just for my sake but for yours, too. You need a break."

Olivia nodded. "Not everyone will be pleased with your promotion."

Brittany rolled her eyes. "I know."

They stood for a few awkward seconds before deciding to hug.

Brittany stepped away, curling her nose. "Ew, we're both sweaty."

The door opened. Darlene peered inside. Her gaze stretched from Olivia to Brittany, and her face puckered into a scowl. "Blake Hartford is here with a delivery."

Olivia examined her soiled apron, remembered Brittany's words, and realized just how unpresentable she was.

"Ooh," Brittany teased, "flowers? Candy?"

Darlene's lips flattened. "Fruit."

"Even better." Brittany moved to the door with a triumphant smile, forcing Darlene to return to the kitchen or get run over.

Olivia left the office and welcomed the sunshine as she stepped from the building into the parking lot.

Blake leaned against his downed tailgate, reached into the bed, and pulled boxes toward him.

Here came the real hot flash. Her body reacted in ten different ways just seeing him. The old adage was right; five days' absence had made her heart grow fonder.

"I brought you the first berries of the season." Two cardboard crates waited on his tailgate.

"I thought they wouldn't be ready to harvest until next week?"

"The majority won't."

Olivia plucked a fat blueberry and popped it into her mouth. "Mmm, thank you."

His face morphed into deep, serious lines, an expression unlike the Blake she'd come to know. The sight nagged at the problem-solving, situation-analyzing therapist inside her, and she wanted nothing more than to remove whatever burden weighed him down.

"I've got to get back to the farm. The acres for open-picking are in use, and my mom is running things until I get back." He stacked the crates and lifted them with ease. "Let me know where you want these, and I'll carry them in for you."

Even the tone of his voice was laced with melancholy.

He followed her to the walk-in fridge and placed the crate on a vacant shelf. "Will I see you Saturday?"

She searched his face, wanting to make him smile. "I'll be there."

"Good." A battle raged behind those dark eyes, one Olivia was all too familiar with. A war of wanting to shirk off the past and move forward, but the vice-like grip it held made that impossible.

Blake squeezed her hand and headed for his truck.

Olivia drummed her fingers on her leg. What

could she do to show she supported him?

Dessert.

She snatched a lemon cupcake from the last tray, closed the fridge behind her, and chased Blake to his truck. His diesel roared and then settled into a purr as he shifted into drive.

"Wait!"

He looked her way, then rolled down his window and moved the gear shift into park.

She gripped his outstretched hand and stepped onto the running board, hooking her elbow inside to keep her balance. Cold air blasted from the vents and blew his earthy cologne her direction.

Blake stared at their linked hands, making no effort to let go. "What's up?"

Your brooding is killing me with its attractiveness. She produced the cupcake. "To cheer you up."

One corner of his mouth lifted.

"What can I do to help you?"

His serious gaze settled on her lips with an intensity that stole her breath. She'd almost talked herself into giving in when he brought her hand to his mouth and kissed her fingers.

"This right here." Blake sighed. "I apologize for running out on you at the party. And for not calling. I just wasn't expecting...Lucas."

She gathered her courage to ask the question that had been nagging her for days. "Do you...still have feelings for her?" Her heart thrashed in her chest while she awaited his answer.

"No." Blake released the wheel and ran the calloused pad of his thumb along the dip above her chin. It grazed her lower lip, shooting lightning into her limbs. His morose gaze turned fierce. Intense.

Her insides warmed and desire rose in her chest like yeast in a ball of dough. "Good to know." From this point on, she could no longer deny she'd given this man a piece of her heart.

His fingers left her face and tangled into the hair at her nape. Oh, yeah. She was all in now. Whether she wanted to be or not.

On shaky legs, she lowered her feet to the pavement before either of them did anything too rash. Like make out right here in the parking lot. Because the heated way Blake was looking at her right now made that possibility all too real.

~*~

November 1963

I snapped a picture of this jade bowl while rummaging through an antique shop in Kennebunkport on break from capturing the regatta. It reminded me of you.

The dish is Japanese. Broken years ago, it was pieced back together with gold. In their culture, a flaw is viewed as a unique piece of the object's history, which adds to its beauty.

Jacob has been gone three years now. You're still broken. So am I. But I'm healing, Elizabeth. Unfortunately, it's without you. Let my love, let God's love, heal your broken pieces. You are still a beautiful, useable vessel. Let yourself be repaired.

29

Blake thought the sight of Olivia holding dessert with a frilly apron pinching her waist was mighty appealing, but watching her walk through the blueberry fields toward him in cutoffs and a long tank top with her hair knotted messily on top of her head…even better.

The last two restless nights had brought him to the conclusion he wanted something real with Olivia—a serious, let's-declare-something-make-future-plans relationship. No backstabbing brother would steal any more of Blake's thoughts when he could be focusing on winning Olivia.

He continued passing out blueberry rakes and wooden crates to the few who'd already arrived. His buddy, Abe, and Abe's son Fausto liked to start at dawn so they could find a shady spot during the heat of the day and enjoy a siesta. They each worked harder and faster than three men combined, so Blake didn't mind.

Livi sidled up beside him.

"We're starting in field three. The plots are marked, as always. A wagon is already out there. I'll be around with the tractor shortly."

The men nodded and headed toward the fields.

Blake turned toward Olivia, grateful for a moment of privacy. "I didn't expect to see you this early."

She inhaled a breath so deep it lifted her

shoulders. "Thanks to you and my new live-in help, I've gotten three glorious nights' sleep in a row. I feel like a new woman."

And that spark of contentment in her eyes was unbearably attractive. "I'm glad Jen's working out for you."

"She's fantastic."

He handed her a rake and a crate.

Olivia frowned. "I have no idea what I'm doing."

"I figured, city girl. I'll stick close until you get the hang of it." Or longer if she'd let him. Blake grabbed his Thermos from atop a barn beam. "Coffee?"

"No, thanks. I'm already fueled up and ready to go."

"I like your enthusiasm." He liked everything about her, actually.

She opened her mouth but closed it when a truckload of migrant workers parked in front of them. Probably best anyway. Today would be busy enough, and he needed to concentrate. Though, he'd love to know what she was about to say.

Blake palmed the hollow between her shoulder blades and led her to the truck overflowing with men, women, and older children. "Welcome back, guys. Today, we'll be in field three. Everything's the same as last year. Rakes and crates are in the barn. See me at the end of the day, and we'll settle up."

Several of the men's gazes, including some of the teenagers', latched onto Olivia, raising the fine hairs on the back of Blake's neck. This wasn't the first time he'd noticed her beauty being appreciated, but he didn't have to like it. He introduced her to the workers he remembered. The workers he didn't introduce did the job for him. Blake wanted to add that she was his, but he couldn't because she wasn't.

Alejandro, a decent guy who had the reputation of being the lady's man of the group, stepped too close to Olivia—as in three feet away—and dipped his chin. "Olivia, *es muy bonita.*"

Yep, but she's not interested in you pal. Blake barely kept the words from escaping. Who was he to decide for her?

Those fully awake cheeks of hers pinked right up. "Um, thank you."

Someone slapped Alejandro's back while spouting something in Spanish, and the group laughed in a good-natured razzing.

"See you guys out there." Blake smiled, despite wanting to rearrange Alejandro's face, and then put an arm around Olivia's shoulders as they walked toward field three.

When they'd walked far enough away from the others, she elbowed his ribs. "Staking your claim?"

He halted. "I've worked with Alejandro for three years. He's a good worker, great guy, but he can charm a fish out of the water. It's best to discourage him up front."

"And miss all the chest-banging? No way."

He took her rake and crate to carry them for her. "I wasn't chest-banging."

"What do you call that then?" She grinned, eyebrows lifting. The morning sun washed her face in gold.

"Protecting. But if what Alejandro is offering appeals to you, I won't stand in your way." Blake continued walking. After about ten steps, she caught up to him.

"He's very tempting, but for some reason I've

grown a soft spot for flannel." Olivia wrapped her hand around his bicep.

And he'd grown quite the sweet tooth.

~*~

Sweat dripped down the skin between Olivia's eyes, and she wiped it away with the back of her hand. She'd been picking for only a few hours, but already her legs and lower back were screaming. The August sun beat down on the workers. She'd already guzzled one bottle of water and was preparing to fill it up again from the water cooler Blake provided by the wagon.

Extending her arms, Olivia combed the rake through the bushes, collecting as much of the plump fruit as she could. Then she transferred the berries into a wooden crate. Her stomach growled. Skipping breakfast hadn't been the best idea. She popped a few berries into her mouth. The sweet juice burst on her tongue.

"I saw that."

Olivia startled at the broad shadow looming over her and knocked over her empty water bottle. She swiveled and looked up at Blake's smirking face.

"Sorry, I couldn't help myself."

"Don't let it happen again." He winked. "Feel free to take a break whenever you need to."

"Think this city girl can't hack it?"

"I guess we'll see." He pulled a baseball cap from his back pocket. "I brought you this. It's the cleanest one I could find. Your nose is getting a little pink."

He touched the tip of his nose, and she mimicked his action. The skin was tender, despite the sunscreen she'd applied.

"It's up to you if you wear it or not. Just thought I'd offer." Blake handed her the blue hat.

Moved by his attentiveness, Olivia grabbed it by the bill and tapped the embroidered red C. "At least you have good taste in ball teams." She yanked out the elastic band holding her hair, shook her fingers through the tresses, and secured it in a lower ponytail that would fit through the hole in the hat. "Thanks."

He pointed to the ground. "Looks like you could use some water."

She grabbed her bottle, took his offered hand, and stood.

They walked toward the cooler.

"What do you think of the job?" he asked.

"Honestly?" She removed her sunglasses to dab at the beads of sweat collecting on her upper cheeks. "I like baking with blueberries more than picking them."

He laughed. "And I like eating what you make."

"When are we going to start those cooking lessons? I think it's about time you cook for me." She twisted off the bottle cap, held the mouth under the cooler spout, and pressed the button. Blue liquid rushed into the plastic.

"I'd say tonight, but my mom has already taken my kitchen hostage. Why don't you stay and eat dinner with us?"

Us? As in, with his parents? Why did that thought make her stomach twist? "Oh, um, I'll need to check on Jen and Grandma first. See what they have planned." *Coward.* For the first time in a long time, she had something she wanted to pursue. But she knew how easily one's ideas could crumble. Eating dinner with Blake's parents felt constraining at the moment. She left him by the cooler and returned to the field.

A few minutes later, Blake knelt beside her holding a rake of his own. He didn't say a word, just combed the bushes alongside her.

His shoulders weren't tense. No frown lines marred his mouth or forehead. As always, he was being patient. Waiting until she was ready. Which managed to make her feel like a jerk. It was only a meal for crying out loud. "I'll call home during lunch. If Jen has dinner covered, I'll stay and eat with you."

Blake leaned closer to the bushes. "No pressure. Whatever you decide is fine."

"No, I..." *Need to stop holding myself back. Quit being afraid of everyone and everything that could happen and live again.* "I'd like to. If the offer still stands."

"Always."

The deep timbre of his voice on that one simple word made her skin pebble.

Blake sat back on his haunches. "How about a wager? Whoever picks the most berries in the next five minutes gets to decide if we eat with my parents or alone."

"Since this is my first time picking, I think we know who's going to win."

"Afraid of a challenge?"

Against him? Yes. He had a way of breaking down her defenses. "You're on."

His brows rose. "Ready?"

She stole a two second jump start. "Go!"

"Cheater!"

They raked as fast as their arms would go, combing through the bushes and filling the crates. The muscles in her arms burned, yet a smile filled her face. Every few seconds she peeked at his progress, pushing herself to move faster. She'd almost caught up to him when he pulled a second rake out of nowhere and raked with both hands.

"No fair." She transferred the rake to her other hand for relief.

A minute later, Blake dumped the contents of his rakes into his crate, now overflowing with berries. "Done."

Olivia dropped her backside onto the dirt, breathless, examining her paltry efforts. "You're the cheater."

"You never declared any rules, sweetheart." He laid a palm flat on the ground and leaned close. He lifted the bill of her hat to see her eyes. "We dine alone." Blake playfully shoved her bill back down. He stood, picked up his crate, and swaggered to the wagon.

Olivia's entire body hummed with a tangible energy. Dare she call it happiness? Yes. That was exactly what it was. And after living so long without it, it was more liberating than she'd imagined.

"I never knew blueberry picking could be such a steamy activity." Arianne nudged Olivia's shoulder and occupied the spot Blake had just vacated. "I'll keep that in mind when I need to spice things up."

Olivia couldn't deny the statement, so she greeted her friend instead. "Where have you been lately? You haven't left me for another baker, have you?"

Arianne eased her knees in the small dirt path between the rows. "I've not had much of an appetite for anything lately."

Olivia looked closer. Her friend had lost weight.

Arianne's husband called her name. Huck sidled over, gave Arianne a water, and bent to palm her cheek. "Don't push yourself. Stop if you get tired or too hot. I'll be close by."

She wrapped her hand around his wrist. "I will."

His gaze lingered on Arianne's face a few seconds longer before he joined Blake at the wagon.

To be cherished in such a way was truly a special gift. Emotion clogged Olivia's eyes, and she turned away, concentrating on the bushes. "That's sweet."

"He's normally not overprotective, but we're having a baby."

Olivia turned toward Arianne.

Her friend's eyes sparkled. "I'm due May twentieth."

"Ah!" Olivia hugged her, knowing what a rough, rocky road they'd traveled to get that precious life. "I'm happy for you."

"Thanks. Me, too." Arianne wiped at her eyes. "Sorry. No matter what I do it makes me cry."

Deep-throated laughter caught their attention. Blake slapped Huck's back while they shook hands. Olivia suspected he'd just heard the news as well.

Arianne sniffled. "He's a good guy—Blake. You should give him a chance. See where it leads."

Olivia popped another berry into her mouth. "I want to."

"But?" Arianne started raking.

Olivia moved to the next row, facing her friend. With no one else around, she was comfortable spilling the details about her parents, her treatment, and how she'd come to Stone Harbor. "In the end, Justin decided it was all too much for him to handle and left. The man was close to promising 'in sickness and in health' and in sickness he just...walked away." Olivia swallowed her emotions. "I've forgotten how to trust, I guess."

Arianne was back to crying. "I'm sorry for your loss. Justin, and especially your dad."

Olivia sighed. "I'm not sure if I'm sorry about Justin or not. I mean, of course I am. I loved him. But better to find out his failures before the wedding than after. Right?"

Arianne nodded.

"Blake has proved a million times over that he's a good man. I just…"

"Don't want to be disappointed again."

Olivia set down her rake. "Yeah."

"I understand." Arianne dumped her blueberries into Olivia's crate. "I loved my first husband, though looking back now I think the lust was stronger. We had a courthouse wedding after discovering I was pregnant with Emma. Things were great at first. Then Emma was born and things began to change. Adam began to change. He abandoned us shortly after our third anniversary.

"For a long time, I didn't want to even look at a man. They all made me want to punch something. Them. But Emma and a newfound relationship with God helped fill all those dark spaces, and, with time, it didn't hurt so much. Then Huck came strolling into my shop, waving the deed to the building under my nose as the newly inherited owner, and all those insecurities came flooding back."

Olivia plopped her backside in the dirt and wrapped her arms around her bent knees. "What did you do?"

"What any girl would do. I manipulated Huck into letting me stay in the building." Arianne chuckled. "I think he hated me for it, too. He didn't have a choice though. He'd had a motorcycle accident that took the life of his passenger and nearly killed him. With no one to care for him after they released him from the hospital, he had to accept my offer.

"As the days and months passed, I started falling in love with him, and it scared me to death. He wasn't a logical choice. But God's will isn't always logical. From a human standpoint anyway. He prods us to grow by putting things into our lives we don't expect. Sometimes that includes heartbreak. But he always works it out for good to those who love Him."

Olivia did love God. She just didn't know how to find Him anymore.

"Blake's a good man, a strong Christian. His fruit proves it." Arianne tossed a blueberry at her.

Olivia caught it before it bounced off her forehead. She gazed across the field.

Blake helped the workers dump their crates into the almost-full wagon. His back muscles rippled beneath his shirt. His smile struck her heart from way over here. He had a gift for understanding people, male and female, young and old. He was always helping others. Blake climbed onto the tractor and smoke belched from a pipe by the engine. He rolled forward, easing the machinery down the path and then fading into the distance.

Olivia craved the tenderness that was on his inside as much as the ruggedness of his outside. But he was a man, and he had the power to break her heart. Despite the raw fear that came with that territory, she didn't want to live without him.

30

Blake yawned and eased onto the porch swing, holding a Thermos of coffee.

Scooby rose from his bed in the corner and padded over to greet him.

Stars filled the pre-dawn sky, but in less than an hour, the sun would be blazing.

He poured the extra-strong brew into the lid and sipped. The liquid ran down his throat as silky-smooth as Olivia's hair had run through his fingertips when he'd hugged her goodbye the night before. It had been difficult to stop there, but he had. Even as far as she'd come, she still wore her timidity like a coat, and he refused to scare her away.

Scooby's ears perked, and he whimpered.

"What's wrong, boy?"

He whined again, gaze fixed toward the road.

Within seconds, a vehicle crunched over the gravel in Blake's driveway. The car was hard to recognize in the dim porch light. Who would be here this early?

Scooby's body language didn't indicate a threat. In fact, after the car door slammed, his backside wiggled like a worm on a hook.

As if she'd materialized from his thoughts, Olivia climbed the porch steps. Her sleepy-eyed grin sobered him faster than his coffee.

"Hey, Scoob." The dog barked and danced around Olivia's feet before calming with a rub on the head.

Blake set down his Thermos. "You're here early."

"Couldn't sleep." She joined him on the swing.

The old slats creaked beneath their weight.

Blake set them in motion with a push of his foot, leaning close enough to inhale the flowery scent of her shampoo. "Elizabeth keep you up?"

Her head moved from side to side. "Life."

Blake stretched his arm along the back of the swing. Without any coaxing, Olivia moved in and rested the back of her head on his arm. He pressed his lips to her hair. "What kept your gears turning all night?"

She shrugged. "Arianne. She gave me some things to think about yesterday."

"Is that why you were quiet during dinner last night?"

He'd told Mom at lunch there'd been a change in plans and asked if she'd pack a picnic for two. He'd thrown a couple of plastic Adirondack chairs into the back of his truck and drove them to the edge of the peninsula on the east side of his property, which offered an expansive view of the ocean.

Olivia closed her eyes. "Yes."

He ran his fingertips along her shoulder. "Care to fill me in?"

Olivia opened one eye and peeked at him. "I'm still thinking."

She nuzzled closer until she rested in the crook of his neck. "I had a great time last night. Thanks for taking me to your special place."

"It's a good spot to get away and think. We can go back tonight if you want."

She released a sleepy-sounding sigh. "Can't. Jen's going to a family reunion at four. I need to leave by three."

Too bad.

"The Machias Blueberry Festival is coming up in a couple of weeks. Why don't you come with me? I've rented a booth. Huck and Arianne will be there selling honey. People attend from all over the States and Canada. It'd be a great way to get the bakery's name out there."

She relaxed against him, eyes still closed. "I'll see if I can rearrange the schedule."

"Bring Grams along if you want. The festival only lasts two days. I can man the booth while you guys walk around."

"Why are you so different?" she whispered.

Her breathy tone made his gut ignite. "What do you mean?"

"I've never known a man who would allow a girl's grandma to tag along on their dates. You throw me off balance, Blake Hartford."

That made two of them. He kissed her head again, unable to resist. Stretching his legs, Blake rocked them in a smooth rhythm. Olivia's breaths evened. He loved this. Loved her. Not the same way he'd loved Madison, either. This wasn't a high-school-sweetheart, we-never-plan-to-leave-this-town-so-let's-get-married kind of love. This was a mature love by two people who'd witnessed the worst in others, had survived, and had become stronger and wiser for it.

Blake had no idea how deep Olivia's feelings for him ran or if she'd ever grow to love him back, but he would prove how gentle he could be with her heart.

~*~

Olivia jolted from sleep. An engine revved and rattled as it passed. She sat up and blinked against the morning sun, scrambling for equilibrium.

A whimper sounded at her feet. Scooby wagged his tail.

She was on Blake's porch. She'd fallen asleep on his swing. On him. Now Blake was gone, and the workers were filing in while she lay here under this blanket. She hadn't meant to fall asleep. In fact, when she'd arrived, her veins had been humming from three cups of coffee. Then she'd settled in next to him, and a calming force of safety and trust lulled her away.

Somewhere in the middle of the night, when sleep had fled and she'd stared at her black ceiling replaying all the events since she'd moved to Stone Harbor, she'd realized she needed Blake. Need was a strong word, but it fit. She needed his character, his strength, his affection to lift her from the quicksand pit of discouragement and remind her there was still some good in the world.

Olivia stood, folded the blanket, and stroked Scooby's head before opening the screen door and stepping inside Blake's house. Her plan to put the blanket on the couch and get out to the fields was interrupted by a blonde cooking up a storm in his kitchen.

"Did you get some rest?" Blake's mom, Rita, leaned against the kitchen door frame catching Olivia in the hall. She wiped her hands on a towel and smiled.

Was that bacon? Olivia's stomach rumbled. "I got here early and...I didn't mean to fall asleep." *On Blake's shoulder.* "I should probably get out there. I'm late."

"No worries. Blake mentioned you haven't been sleeping well. He has plenty of help." Rita used the towel to encourage Olivia to join her in the kitchen.

Blake had been discussing her sleeping habits with his mother? What other conversations had they had?

"Coffee's ready if you'd like a cup. If you wouldn't mind giving me a few minutes to finish breakfast, you can take it out to Blake and Kenneth when you go."

"Sure. Would you like any coffee?"

"Please."

Olivia opened cabinets until she found the mugs. From the corner of her eye, she noticed Rita watching her, no doubt judging Olivia's unfamiliarity with Blake's kitchen as an indication of the stage of their relationship. A typical mom move.

Olivia bit her bottom lip. She not only needed to find the cream, she needed to stop psychoanalyzing Blake's mother.

"Thank you, again, for the lovely birthday cake." Rita turned sizzling bacon slices with a fork. "I'm sorry the party got a little awkward when Lucas arrived."

Why was she apologizing to Olivia? Unless this was a foot in the door of a deeper conversation Olivia wasn't ready to have. "It's fine."

"Has Blake told you about Lucas?" Rita opened the oven and removed a tray of toasted Texas-style bread slices.

Sometimes Olivia hated being right. "Not in detail, but yes."

"Lucas..." Rita paused her task of layering breakfast food on the toast to check the ceiling for answers. "Lucas has always been strong-willed. Assertive and hard-driving. With a tendency to be critical."

Finally, the creamer. Olivia placed it and the mugs on the table. "An assertive firstborn." *Shut your therapist mouth! What are you doing?*

"Yes." Rita returned to food-stacking. "That's exactly what you'd call him. He's a special boy. Always got good grades, set lofty goals for himself, which he achieved. But he was a mess at the same time." Foil crinkled as Rita wrapped two sandwiches. She put two more on separate plates and carried them to the table. "Blake is the typical lastborn."

"The opposite," they said in unison.

Both women smiled.

Rita pushed a plate toward Olivia. "While Lucas bulldozes everything in his path to get what he wants, Blake uses a quiet strength. And his heart for people..." Rita shook her head. "I don't have favorites when it comes to my children. But Blake's always held a special spot in this mama's heart."

Olivia toyed with her napkin. "It must tear you apart to see them at odds."

Rita sipped her coffee. "It sure does. I have a good sense of what poor Eve felt with Cain and Abel."

They ate in silence for a few moments.

Rita was the first to break it. "I worry about Blake the most. When Lucas ran off with Madison, it killed Blake's spirit for a long time." She patted Olivia's hand. "Though I've seen glimpses of it lately." Rita pulled away. "Between you and me, I never thought Madison was a good match for Blake. I think he sees that now, too. However, Blake refuses to forgive his brother. That scares me. Bitterness is a cancer that devours the soul."

Olivia played with her coffee cup. "Forgiveness can be a hard thing to give. Especially if the other party isn't sorry." *When those people were perfectly satisfied with their wrong choice despite its effect on others.*

"By His stripes we are healed." Rita pointed upward. "Kenneth would advise me to stay out of it, but Blake's my baby no matter how old he is. Since he was little, I've prayed that one day a good woman who understands how special he is would steal his heart. The one God designed specifically for him." Rita touched Olivia's hand. "Will you pray for that, too?"

The question stole the air from Olivia's lungs. Pray? For Blake's future wife? Was that woman Olivia? Were their broken roads meant to lead them to each other? "Yes." The word came out as a croak.

Rita's eyes glossed over. "Thank you."

The love this woman had for her sons struck a chord inside Olivia. Did her mother still pray for her? Was her dad even concerned about the kind of man she married anymore? To keep tears from forming, Olivia concentrated on her napkin. "If you don't mind, I'll take the rest of my food with me. I have to leave at three, so I better get started."

"Of course." Rita went to the counter, ripped off a square of aluminum foil, and handed it to Olivia.

While she wrapped her sandwich, Rita retrieved two canning jars of orange juice with lids. After lowering all the goods into a small basket, she handed it to Olivia, who now stood by the kitchen door ready to flee.

"It was good to talk to you." Rita captured Olivia in a motherly hug so genuine there was no doubt who Blake got his good heart from.

"You, too." She left the house and bolted off the porch, ignoring a tail-wagging Scooby. Olivia sucked in fresh air, grateful to escape the claustrophobic conversation. As she walked past the barn and across the expanse of farmland, puffy clouds giving the day a touch of whimsy, she could feel the dynamics of her life changing once again. The change was as sure as the beat of her thumping heart, which sped at seeing Blake lift heavy crates of blueberries into the wagon. She just hoped that this time the change would be good.

31

Blake scrubbed the towel over his wet hair. He swiped a clear path on the foggy mirror and turned his face from side to side. He could forego shaving for one more day. Besides, Olivia had mentioned she liked his stubble. He yanked his shirt off the towel hook, stretched it over his head, and wrestled into it on his way down the stairs.

A hot shower had been exactly what he'd needed to loosen his tight muscles. He was dog-tired, almost tired enough to miss the fact the house felt quiet and lonely. The blanket he'd covered Olivia with that morning lay folded across the arm of the couch. He ran his hand over it. The callouses on his fingers snagged the fabric.

Blake missed her. Even though they'd spent the day picking together, even though they'd texted a few times since she'd left. It was never enough. The more he got of her, the more he wanted. And the way she'd looked at him in the field that afternoon, biting her bottom lip in concentration, cheeks and nose kissed by the sun, those vivid blues a complex mix of hope and vulnerability— that had him wanting plenty.

"Are you ever going to tell me what kept you up all night?" he'd asked.

She'd hesitated. Toyed with the rake. "Have you ever gone to pray for something specific but didn't know how?"

He chuckled. "All the time."

"No, I mean, like…" her shoulders lifted, then fell. "Like you didn't have the words. They'd gone missing, or you couldn't put the request into sentences. You just—"

"Sat there?"

"Yeah." She leaned back on her heels.

Blake combed the bottom of the bush one more time. "It's called being still."

Her brows drew together.

"God knows our hearts. He understands that humans have limitations—that they don't always know what to say or the right thing to ask for. That's why the Holy Spirit acts as intercessor for us, with groanings that cannot be uttered. During those times, we need to be still and know that He is God."

She frowned into the distance. "Be still. Jesus used those words to calm the storm on the Sea of Galilee, didn't He?"

Blake nodded. "Literal storms, storms of life. Nice analogy, huh?"

Olivia smiled, though it hadn't come close to reaching her eyes.

The conversation had then moved in another direction, but her silence indicated she'd continued to contemplate what he'd said.

Blake turned off the ceiling fan and crossed through his living room, flipping on the TV as he made his way to the recliner. The lamp illuminated the worn cushion he relaxed on every night, an eyesore compared to the other untouched pieces of furniture. He looked forward to the day when he would no longer be the only one living in this house. A desire that grew every day.

He leaned back and propped his feet, opened a bag of trail mix, and settled in for the last few innings of the ball game. A red light flashed in his peripheral vision. He tossed some peanuts into his mouth, muted the TV, then reached over and punched the button on his answering machine.

"Hey, brother."

Blake froze.

"I hoped I'd get a chance to talk to you at Mom's party, but you lit out of there. Can't say I blame you." Lucas's tone dropped. "I wanted to tell you this in person but...Maddy and I are getting married. We won't apologize for loving each other, Blake, but we'd like to apologize for how we went about it. We know we hurt you, and we're both sorry."

Blake swallowed the peanut crumbs he'd annihilated, pushing down the rising bile in his throat.

"Neither of us feels comfortable getting married without your blessing. We'd like for you to attend. Better yet, I'd like you to be my best man. I know it's asking a lot for something I don't deserve, but we were close once, and it would mean the world to me."

Was Lucas insane?

"Anyway, just think about it. Let me know." He rattled off a phone number. "Hope you're doing well. Bye."

The house fell into an eerie silence. Figures flashed across the television screen as Blake tried to decide if his brother had really just asked him to be best man or if Blake was trapped in a nightmare. Blake was already the better man. He'd never take someone's fianceé away from them.

Lucas and Madison didn't need Blake's blessing or his presence.

As for his brother's backhanded apology, Lucas was wasting his breath. Forgiveness was one thing in this life his brother could not manipulate from Blake.

~*~

Tiny, lacy slippers. Petite dresses with ruffles. Stretchy headbands with delicate flowers. Olivia let go of the shopping cart handle and grabbed three packages off the rack. "You need these in every color."

Arianne laughed and placed her palm over her growing abdomen.

Emma's mouth formed an O as she studied the items Olivia had tossed into the cart. This was the second time Olivia had visited with the girl, and she was enchanting. "Mommy, am I getting a baby sister?"

"Nope." A male voice startled Olivia, then Huck blocked her view of the girly attire with a tiny football jersey and jeans combo. "It's a boy. I can sense it."

Arianne rubbed her belly while releasing a strained breath. "You're such a baboon."

Huck grunted a monkey sound, and Emma laughed. "Daddy, you're funny."

"Don't forget handsome. And smart." He tapped the side of his head.

"And conceited," Arianne added. She leaned toward Olivia. "This is why I asked you to come along. Huck can't take anything seriously."

Olivia grinned. These two were romantic comedy at its best.

Arianne took the football outfit from him and tossed it into the cart. "What if it is a girl? Will you be disappointed?"

Huck made a face. "Of course not. She'll just have to play football on the boys team."

"I don't think so." Arianne threw in a pair of white tights.

"You're the one who's always saying girls can do anything boys can." Huck added a bib that said *Daddy's 'Lil Superstar*.

"Except play football." Arianne strolled toward the crib section, pointing out an old-fashioned style bed with a floral teal-and-purple quilt.

Olivia agreed it was sensational.

"Poor Mildred." Huck shook his head.

Arianne jerked to a stop.

Emma crashed into her back with an *umph*.

"Sorry, baby." Arianne patted the girl's head then glared at her husband. "We are *not* naming this child Mildred."

"It was your great-grandmother's name." Huck tested the sturdiness of a black crib decorated in sports gear.

"And it will forever stay in the genealogy records. If the baby is a girl, we're naming her Ainsley June."

Olivia pointed at an oak crib that claimed to double as a toddler bed. "How about this one? It grows with the child and will coordinate with either sex."

"I like it." Huck checked the price tag and whistled. "But if it's a boy, we're naming him John Wayne Anderson."

"No." Arianne, too, looked at the price tag and winced.

"Chuck Norris."

"Not happening."

"Thor."

"Lord, help me." Arianne looked heavenward.

Emma slipped her little hand into Olivia's, giggling.

Huck threw out his hands. "He'll need a good, strong name to live up to."

Arianne patted her husband's arm, smiling as if she held all the cards. "Then what about Huckleberry Anderson the second?"

Huck looked at Olivia and his face turned scarlet. He leaned closer to his wife. "Don't *ever* use my given name in public."

Arianne laughed. "It's public information."

"Diapers," Olivia blurted to break the hilarious tension. "You'll need lots of diapers."

"You're right." Arianne snapped. "That's something we can stock up on now."

Huck's cellphone pealed. He frowned, pulled it from his back pocket, and looked down at the screen. "I'll be right back." He walked toward the front of the store.

"Another reason why I asked you to come along." Arianne moved down the aisle, stealing one last look at the teal-and-purple quilt. "He wears me out," she whispered.

The two of them together wore Olivia out, but it was good to see the lighter side of marriage. It was easy to forget the second side of the coin when she only counseled the negative aspects. No one needed her services during good times. With all she'd been through, she often forgot there were good times at all.

The conversation turned to nursing pillows, which bottle design worked best to prevent gas, and if Arianne should try a home delivery in her bathtub with a midwife. None of which Olivia could give advice on.

"Maybe I should stick with a hospital." Arianne walked toward the register. "Having a baby at thirty-three is a lot different than at twenty-six."

"You're strong and healthy." Olivia followed, helping Emma push the cart. "I'm sure you'll do fine whichever you decide."

The scanner sounded a non-stop stretch of beeps as the cashier rang up the items. Huck stepped through the entrance, wallet outstretched, and joined them.

"That'll be two hundred fifty-eight dollars and sixteen cents." The redhead smiled to soften the blow.

Huck looked at Arianne, at the bags that were now settled in the cart, then back at Arianne. Arianne shrugged. With a slight shake of his head, Huck fished the bills from his wallet and gave his wife an *are you crazy?* look.

They left the store and strode through the parking lot to their cars. Olivia had met them here, only planning to stay a short time. She glanced at her watch. They'd been in there for two hours?

Arianne sniffed the air. "How about Mexican food for lunch? That place smells amazing." She gestured to the building across the street.

Emma bounced on her toes. "Can we get fried ice cream?"

Huck bent to hug the child. "Anything for you darlin'. Can't go with you though." He stood and kissed his wife's cheek.

"Why not?" Arianne pouted.

Huck opened the back door of Olivia's car, helped Emma inside, made sure she buckled in, and then met them at the trunk. "Jeff and Karen Emery's barn burned a few nights ago. The authorities say its arson. Pastor called me and a few other men to help with cleanup. They're starting in an hour. I need to go home and change."

"Arson." Arianne shivered. "I never thought we'd see something like this happen around here. And so close to home."

An echo of Olivia's thoughts. Each time she heard of an incident in the news, she wondered how safe she and grandma were living alone on their remote property.

Arianne kissed Huck's lips. "Tell them I'm praying."

"Will do." He waved at Olivia. "You don't mind running them home?"

"Nope. We have business to discuss anyway."

"Business?" His brows wrinkled. "Should I be scared?"

Arianne closed the trunk. "We're joining forces. I'm promoting her cake services to my clients, and she's promoting my shop to hers."

Huck nodded, pleased. He palmed his wife's stomach. "Later, Rambo."

"No." Arianne walked to the passenger door.

"Obi-Wan."

"Not on your life."

He sped around to his car. "James Bond?"

"Never."

He tapped the car's roof. "Indiana Jones."

"The man is insane," Arianne mumbled.

He got in his vehicle, backed out, and drove toward the stoplight.

Arianne lowered onto the seat and rested her head against the back. "He needs counseling, three times a week. Pencil him in."

Olivia chuckled and started the car. "But you love him."

Arianne sighed. "That I do."

32

The small town of Machias, Maine, would welcome fifteen-thousand people throughout festival weekend. Blake was glad Olivia had decided to work the booth with him. Spending the day with her, finding excuses to brush up against her—he couldn't think of a better way to occupy the next few days. And getting paid for it, too.

He spread the plastic tablecloth then secured his banner at the corners. The Hartford Farms logo was simple yet catchy. He was almost done transferring quarts of blueberries to the table when his phone buzzed with a text message.

We're here.

Good. That must mean she'd brought Mrs. Hudson along as well. A change of scenery might do both women some good. Blake pulled up his list of contacts, found Olivia's name, and pressed the call button.

She answered on the third ring.

"Where did you park?"

"Um...by a black pole."

"City girl. I need landmarks or a direction. Something to go off of."

"I think maybe it used to be an old gas station. There's an empty circle at the top where a porcelain globe might've been at one time."

"I know where you're at. Be right there." He took

off in that direction and met them under a line of maple trees. Jennifer, Mrs. Hudson's live-in nurse, was with them too.

Olivia gave him a lazy grin before covering it with the rim of her paper cup. Steam curled around her lips. The same reaction his gut had every time those blue eyes looked at him like that. Soft and heated.

"The booth isn't far. Can I carry anything?"

Olivia and Jen were both dragging coolers on wheels. The only other baggage was a satchel resting cross-way on Olivia's shoulder.

Olivia lowered her cup. "Nope, we're good."

On the way back to his booth, they passed a picnic area with red-and-blue picnic tables where attendees were already enjoying the blueberry pancake breakfast hosted by the Baptist church. The women passed on his offer to buy them breakfast, claiming they'd already eaten.

Underneath the shade of his tent, Blake unfolded the lawn chairs he'd brought. "What'd'ya bring?" He directed the question at Olivia.

She opened one of the coolers. "Blueberry muffins with streusel topping and honey-laced, dark chocolate fudge."

They stacked her containers at the other end of the table. The fudge looked almost as good as she did in her blue dress with those dark curls spilling across her shoulders. He was ready to kick things up a notch, and the wait was killing him.

The shadow of the tent kept the temperature at a tolerable degree. The morning passed quickly, helping customers, meeting new people, and speaking with a few potential produce buyers.

He'd never had the pleasure of observing Olivia

interact with customers. Sure, they'd worked together in a group on the town board, but during those meetings she'd been serious, almost somber. Whenever he stopped by the bakery to chat, he'd made sure to arrive during down time so his visit served its purpose. But this? The way her eyes locked onto people, studied them as if she could read their soul, paired with a smile and words that drew people in. This woman had a precious gift. Given support and the right circumstances, she would be unstoppable.

And Blake wanted to be with her every step of the way.

About the time his stomach reminded him of how late it had gotten, Arianne walked up to the booth, a roundness forming beneath her shirt that hadn't been there the last time he'd seen her. She smiled wide and glanced from him to Olivia, eyebrows arched. "Ready for a break?"

Could the woman be more obvious in her intentions? Blake wouldn't have agreed to let her run the booth for him had he known she'd announce it was pre-planned.

Olivia nibbled her bottom lip, and something silent and sneaky passed between the two females. Olivia turned to him, brows arched. "Lunch?"

Blake narrowed his eyes, attempting to decipher what had just happened. This set-up had been his idea. Or so he'd thought.

"Grandma?" Olivia knelt in front of Mrs. Hudson's chair. "Would you like to eat and walk around for a bit? See what this festival is all about?"

Mrs. Hudson stood with Olivia's assistance.

Jen offered to stay and help Arianne. Both parties probably needed the break.

Olivia pulled some bills out of her till and tucked them into her pocket. "Do you want us to bring you something back?"

Jen scrunched her nose in thought. "Maybe one of those walking tacos. Loaded."

Arianne shook her head. "I already ate, but thanks. I can't promise, however, that a piece or two of your fudge won't disappear before you get back."

"Take a container home." Olivia pointed to a cooler underneath the spare table. "There's plenty."

With Olivia sandwiched between him and Mrs. Hudson, they weaved through several aisles of primitive crafts, quilts, and antiques before reaching the food vendors on Main Street. As they were ordering, a nearby shaded picnic table vacated. Blake leaned close to Olivia's ear. "You grab that table. I'll pay."

A few minutes later, he joined them, carrying the tray of food in one hand and a stack of napkins in the other. "Chicken sandwich and water." He set the contents in front of Mrs. Hudson. "And a lobster roll with blueberry soda."

Olivia unscrewed the cap on the glass bottle. "I can't believe I let you talk me into this."

"You can't live here without at least trying it."

She took a sip and rolled it on her tongue. "Not bad. Don't you ever tire of blueberries though?"

"Do you ever tire of dessert?" Blake bit into his juicy tenderloin.

"Touché."

A group of teenage girls walked by, chatting and giggling over some guy in a dunk tank.

Blake had noticed the local library volunteers testing it on his way in this morning. Their sign stated the money would go to a new Teen Room addition. He didn't know what it was like to live anywhere else, but here, along the coast, the residents of small communities came together to fulfill a need.

He glanced at Olivia. She was too busy people-watching to finish her meal.

Every once in a while, an outsider would move in, bring fresh energy and new ideas. Fit in as if they'd always belonged. Now that Olivia had stamped her mark on Stone Harbor, on his heart, he couldn't imagine either one without her.

"How do you like your sandwich, Mrs. Hudson?"

Olivia snapped out of her daze to study her grandma.

Mrs. Hudson smacked her lips, then reached across the table and stole one of Blake's French fries. She dipped it in a blob of mayo on her foil wrapper.

Blake winked at Olivia. "I think she likes it."

Olivia picked up the remains of her lobster roll. "I saw you eyeing the blueberry pie on our way here. Is that next on your agenda?"

Blake wadded his trash into a ball and sailed it into the trashcan. "I'm too full for pie, but I'll buy you ladies a piece, if you want."

Olivia picked up her soda bottle. "I've had enough blueberries for one day. Thanks, though."

Mrs. Hudson nodded. "I'll take pie."

Olivia chuckled. The pink of embarrassment tinged her cheeks.

"Deal." Blake tapped the table twice and then stood to help Mrs. Hudson.

The woman linked her arm with his, surprising Blake.

"Pie," she said.

Olivia closed in on his other side, and they walked toward the vendor made to resemble a fifties cafe.

"If I didn't know better," she whispered, "I'd think she believed she was the one dating you." Her eyes rounded, and the sea-sick hue he hadn't seen in quite some time returned.

He knew what she meant and shouldn't tease her, but this was the open door he'd been waiting for. "Are we dating?" Blake wagged a finger between them.

Her mouth opened. Closed. Opened again. Closed. She was starting to look like a fish yanked from the sea.

He touched his fingertips to her wrist, trailed them down to her palm, then ever so lightly, tangled his fingers with hers. "If we are, I'm completely OK with that."

Goosebumps rose along the side of her neck. She started to smile but bit her bottom lip. "You're the only man I spend this much time with."

He'd take that as a yes, though it wasn't the definitive answer he was going for. Now he needed to take her on a real date without furniture shopping and festivals, and continue to practice patience until she was ready to declare exactly what she wanted.

Olivia pulled her hand from his. "Do you mind if I look around in the booths while you two are waiting? I saw one place had books. They might have some good coffee table reads for the bakery."

"Go ahead." *Backpedal from the progress we were making.* "We'll catch up with you."

Blake's gaze followed her several booths down where she stopped to rummage through crates of books. The line moved forward, and so did he. Mrs. Hudson, however, remained in place. He stepped back. The grandmother assessed him with wise eyes, the quirk of her mouth saying she knew what he was thinking, and he wasn't fooling anyone, even if she struggled to put it all together.

"Is everything all right, Mrs. Hudson?"

She stepped forward to claim their place in line, her eyes turning a soft gray as she studied him. "Love."

Blake wouldn't waste his time denying it. If it was obvious to an elderly woman with Alzheimer's, there would be no use.

After purchasing two slices of blueberry pie with fresh cream to-go, they found Olivia under the protection of the booth's shade, engrossed in a hardback book.

He bent sideways to read the title.

She pointed to a picture of a granite heart-shaped stone. "These actually exist?"

"They're all over around here. It has something to do with the tide and how they're washed to shore. My mom used to make jewelry and collectibles out of them when I was a kid. Sold them on consignment. Every Saturday morning, she'd drag us out to a different pebbled beach and make us hunt for them."

"You know where to find these?"

"It's not hard. Next free day, we'll go." That smile was exactly what he'd been after.

She closed the book and tucked it under her arm. "It's a date."

Olivia paid for her items, bought Jen a walking taco, and they walked back to their booth.

Blake, ten feet tall and bullet proof.

33

The sun hung low on the horizon, outlining the strip of highway in gold.

Olivia yawned. The combination of Blake's warm truck and the onset of dusk made her eyelids heavy.

Jen and Grandma had left the festival shortly after lunch, but Jen had encouraged Olivia to stay.

When Blake offered to drive her home, she'd accepted. They'd worked the booth until six and had grabbed a quick dinner. She agreed to work the booth again tomorrow, and then they'd watch the game on Blake's big screen. After she showed him the secret to her chicken wings.

Their first *official* date.

Olivia yawned again. Blake frowned at the road, his elbow propped against the window, hand in a loose fist. Though his features revealed nothing, her therapist instincts had latched on to the undercurrent of tension that concreted his shoulders. She'd witnessed it at times throughout the day, and, God help her, she wanted to ease his discomfort.

The day his brother had crashed the party had been the only time she'd seen anything other than compassion in Blake's eyes. Today was different. Whenever he wasn't with a customer or honing his attention on her, it played a subtle tune across his features.

Olivia shifted to a more comfortable position. One

where she could clearly read his handsome face. "I've been told I'm a good listener."

He blinked and then looked at her deadpan for a few seconds before understanding dawned. "Am I that obvious, or is reading minds your superpower?"

"It's a gift. I can also see through walls."

"Really? Good, then when you come over tomorrow, you can tell me where the studs are in the spare bedroom, and how the old electricity is laid. With your help, I could renovate a lot faster."

She crossed her arms, waiting. She was used to deflection stall tactics, and they still had at least twenty minutes on the road.

Blake blew a puff of air and reached for her hand. "Lucas called and left a message last week. They want my blessing on their marriage. Then he asked if I'd be his best man."

She reared back.

Ouch. Asking for forgiveness was one thing, but this? This was huge. "Are you considering it?"

He looked at her as if she'd grown horns. "No."

Understandable. That would be like Olivia's father asking her to officiate a marriage with his mistress. She wasn't a good enough person to do it.

The heartache, the tears Blake's mom had shed in his kitchen when Rita confessed that bitterness was eating her son's soul, made Olivia pause. Now that she was on the lookout for it, she saw exactly what Rita had been talking about. Blake walked through life ignoring the darkness growing inside him. But it was there, lying dormant, waiting for the perfect moment to unleash its ugliness. She'd seen it in his eyes the day he saw his brother.

Hatred so intense it made her skin pebble recalling

it now. Olivia rubbed her arms. "Forgiveness can be a hard thing to give."

Blake grunted and turned down the air-conditioner.

"Sometimes though"—she softened her voice—"forgiveness is necessary for us to move on with our lives."

Blake's jaw ticked along with the seconds. Finally, he glanced at her. "Have you forgiven your dad? The woman who willingly ripped your family apart?"

Time slowed.

Had she?

Olivia stared out her window. Her dad hadn't asked for forgiveness. Neither had the faceless woman who hadn't cared her actions would destroy a wife and a child.

Despite his selfish actions, he was still her daddy. She still wanted his attention, his acceptance. Still needed to hold that special place in his heart.

"Yes." Tears welled in her eyes.

Blake squeezed her hand. "Not everyone's situations are black and white."

The tone of his voice lowered on the last word, ending the conversation. He didn't like her interference into that area of his life, and he was done discussing it with her.

Rita's odd and challenging request clicked with sudden clarity. Blake would never be able to have healthy relationships as long as the wrath he had for Lucas continued to burrow into him like a termite on rotten wood. And Olivia wanted the chance to see if they could be great together.

The remaining distance home passed in a blur. Whether it was from scrambling for how to reproduce their earlier camaraderie or the pressure Blake used on the accelerator, she wasn't sure.

He parked the truck at her front door.

"Thanks for bringing me home."

"You're welcome." Blake left the truck and let down the tailgate.

She followed. Her rolling coolers were already on the ground when she reached the back of his truck. Blake grabbed the handles to carry them for her, but she stopped him with a hand to his wrist.

"It's OK. You don't need to walk me in." She tucked her new book under her arm, lifted onto her toes, and kissed his cheek. His stubble was rough against her lips, but what surprised her more was the rock-hard surface of his jaw. If the man bit down any harder, he'd crack his molars.

Maybe she shouldn't have said anything. Should've retracted her therapist antennas and minded her own business. It wasn't as if he'd asked her advice or hired her to help him take the right steps. "I'll see you in the morning."

She walked to the house, dragging her coolers behind her. She opened the door and bumped it wider with her hip. She looked back at Blake, still standing by his truck, shock evident on his face. When their gazes locked, he stepped forward as if to come after her. She smiled and gently closed the door before either of them said or did anything to ruin the progress they'd made.

Olivia slipped off her shoes, lined them against the wall, stacked her coolers out of the way, and followed the faint noises coming from the kitchen.

Grandma sat at the table, fingertips pressed against her forehead.

Jen stood on tiptoe and pulled a bottle of

ibuprofen from the cabinet. She turned and jumped when she saw Olivia.

"Sorry, didn't mean to scare you."

"Elizabeth is having one of her headaches." Jen untwisted the bottle cap.

Olivia retrieved a glass of water and set it on the table next to the pills. "Maybe taking her to the festival was a bad idea. Too stimulating. Probably wore her out."

"I think it helps to take her places. Especially on beautiful days, like today. Sunshine does the body good."

With a little coaxing, Grandma dropped the pills onto her tongue and, with a shaky hand, lifted the water and chased them down.

Olivia rubbed circles on her back. "I'm sorry you're not feeling well, Grandma. Let's get you settled in the recliner."

Both women helped Grandma stand, one supporting on each side. Olivia noticed Grandma's panties on the outside of her pajamas. She gave Jen a questioning glance.

"This is how she came out of her bedroom. I had trouble convincing her to switch them around. She got sassy with me, and that's when she started with a headache."

Ignoring the trivial plight, they led Grandma to the recliner. Sydney moseyed into the room, blinked as if the commotion had awakened her from a deep sleep, then settled at Grandma's feet. Jen placed an afghan across Grandma's lap, while Olivia went after a damp rag for her forehead.

"Have you talked to the doctor about these headaches?" Jen whispered. "I've only been here a few weeks, and she's already had four. Seems odd to me. Unless she has a history of migraines."

"She does. They did a CT scan a couple months back. There was some damage from her last stroke, which we knew about, but other than that, the doctor said everything looked good. A blood thinner, regular check-ups, and close care is about all we can do."

The dryer buzzed from the open laundry room door.

Olivia stood. "I'll fold and put away. You might as well take a breather while you have the chance." Warm air rolled across Olivia's arms as she transferred towels and washcloths from the dryer to a laundry basket. She stood at the countertop that ran adjacent to the appliances and folded. After scooping up a large stack of towels in one arm and washcloths with the other, Olivia carried them upstairs to put away.

Using her elbow, she turned on the bathroom light. The bathtub called to her, all clean and sparkly with the ledge holding a glass jar of dried lavender Arianne had grown and given her.

Grandma and Jen were resting.

She could soak for thirty minutes before finishing up a few chores. She stuffed her load into the linen closet, minus one towel and one washcloth, then retrieved her pajamas and set the water temperature for as hot as she could tolerate. She sprinkled in the lavender and breathed the calming scent deep into her lungs. She sat on the tub's ledge and pulled off her socks.

Jen's panicked voice barreled up the stairs. "Elizabeth's unresponsive. I think she's had a stroke."

34

Blake scanned the meager crowd. Checked the aisles between the booths. Ten o'clock. No Olivia.

Rain had pummeled the coast in the wee hours, encouraging festival-goers to sleep late this morning. Maybe that's why she was late. She hadn't been sleeping well for a while now. If she wasn't answering his texts because she was resting, he was grateful. However, he couldn't seem to shake the pang in his gut every time he told himself there was a reasonable explanation for her absence.

He'd been down-right gruff with her yesterday. Any mention of Lucas made his blood surge. None of it was her fault, and he should've been gentler with his words. Her intentions were good, like his mother's, but neither could fully understand.

To his surprise, Olivia had kissed him anyway, an indication—he'd thought—that she was cutting him slack. Maybe it had meant she was cutting him altogether.

The rain had cooled the temperature by at least twenty degrees. Blake was glad he'd grabbed a flannel on his way out the door, smiling at the way Olivia would razz him for it.

But she wasn't here, so Blake unfolded his lawn chair and settled in for a long day.

At three, after the already thin crowd started dispersing and with only the soggy grass beneath his boots for company, Blake packed up his space and headed home. With each passing mile, the sense that something was wrong nagged at him. Olivia wasn't the type to stand someone up without good reason. Should he stop by her house? Call the bakery? Desperation wasn't an attractive quality, so he ignored his gut and turned into his driveway.

Thunderheads made an angry backdrop against his house. He'd looked forward to filling the quiet, lonely rooms with Olivia's company tonight. Instead he'd watch the game with his best buddy and tolerate a can of mush while Scooby devoured his.

The free-picking fields were empty due to the weather. Just as well. He transferred the unsold quarts of berries from his truck to the over-size fridge he kept in his garage. There weren't many left. He'd donate them to the local food pantry first thing on Monday.

Tires on gravel caught his attention. He finished what he was doing then lowered the garage door and walked around to the front of the house.

Olivia stood on his welcome mat, knocking as though the effort took everything she had.

At the thud of his boot on the porch steps, she whirled around. Eyes, red and bloodshot. Cheeks, damp. Hair and clothes, disheveled.

"What happened?"

She didn't reply, only watched him while he climbed the rest of the way. Then she plowed into his chest. The force made him rock on his heels, but he regained balance and wrapped his arms around her.

Sobs wracked her body. "Grandma had another stroke last night."

The disjointed words were difficult to string together, but he made them out. "Did she...?"

"No."

He exhaled. Her grip around his waist grew tighter. The shiver that trembled her body ran through him too. "Here." Blake removed his flannel shirt and wrapped it around her shoulders, not wanting to break the moment by coaxing her inside. Her shoulders wilted, and she held the front closed, snuggling into its warmth. Blake rubbed his palms up and down her arms. After a few minutes, she inhaled and returned her cheek to his chest. Lightly this time.

"It's bad. The doctor said we won't know the full extent of damage for a few days. There's a good possibility she's lost partial to all control of her limbs and motor skills, but we won't know for sure until she wakes up." Hot tears soaked into his shirt. "Why isn't she waking up?"

Resting his chin on her head, he pulled her closer with one arm and used the other to stoke her hair. "I'm sure it took a lot out of her. She's just resting. Give her time, she'll come around."

"What if she's lost everything? What if I lose her? The bakery won't survive without her. She's the heart and soul of that place. I can't lose her."

He swallowed, his heart breaking for her. "You know I'll help as much as I can."

"I sound selfish right now."

"Don't. You're the most unselfish person I know."

She arched away enough to scrub the tears with the sleeve of his flannel. The fabric caught her eye, and she looked down at it and chuckled. "I'm sorry, I didn't mean to come here and blubber on you."

"I don't mind."

She closed her eyes and scrunched her face, as if trying to block it all out. "Crying is such a girl thing to do."

"From where I stand, it looks like you qualify." And the way her curves pressed against him took that statement a step further. "Stop trying to be so brave."

Olivia sighed and tucked herself beneath his chin. "My dad's coming in on the next flight."

That one sentence said everything. As hard as her dad's visit might be, Blake was grateful she wouldn't have to bear the burden of decision-making alone.

He pulled back enough to cup her cheeks, wanting so badly to make her world right. Her skin was like cream beneath his big thumbs. "Let me be here for you," he whispered.

Her hands trailed down his arms until they covered his own against her face. Her gaze dropped to his lips. That was all the answer he needed.

Their lips collided with as much gentleness as a bolt of lightning. The hint of her cinnamon chewing gum was the sweetest thing he'd tasted in years. This woman had stolen his heart, and he never wanted it back.

Her soft lips danced an urgent rhythm with his own. Her hands curled into his shirt. She mewled, and his restraint broke loose. He walked her backward until the porch post stopped them both. She mewled again. The woman was gonna have to stop before it made him crazy.

His palms had just found her waist when The Beatles "Yesterday" started playing from her back pocket. Her mouth froze against his. She tensed, pulling away slowly enough to almost kill him. Her neck bobbed with a swallow.

"Are you going to answer that?" Because if not, they should get back to kissing.

Her palm pressed against her stomach. "I have to go," she whispered.

Blake reached for her. She dodged him and jogged down the stairs.

Scooby blocked her path, tail wagging.

Stop her, boy. Don't let her leave.

But like him, the mutt stood motionless.

Unsure how to take control of the situation, what to say, Blake watched her go. Within seconds, gravel spewed beneath her tires, then the yard was empty, as if she'd never come. He wiped a hand over his face. What was wrong with him? She'd come to him for help, for comfort. Not to make out on his porch. He hadn't meant to twist her pain into his pleasure.

Those probing blue eyes, her curvy form in his shirt, the way she stared at his lips, as if she, too, were curious what they could be together, had made all rational thought flee.

She should've slapped him.

Scooby padded up the porch steps. Somber brown eyes stared him down, accusing.

Blake stretched out a hand to the porch post and leaned his weight against it. "I know, boy, I messed up."

The dog grunted.

Hang technology. If her phone hadn't gone off, she might still be in his arms right now. If anything, they'd have ended the moment mutually and then discussed it like rational adults. If that was the hospital calling to tell her Mrs. Hudson had…he'd never forgive himself.

Would Olivia have given the hospital a special ring tone? Doubtful. People only went to that kind of trouble for close friends or loved ones. Her song choice struck him as odd, and she'd stiffened like a block of ice when it pealed. Like the Olivia he'd met on the rainy street when her grandma first disappeared.

~*~

The rays of dawn split through Olivia's sheer curtains, awakening her from the bliss of sleep. She didn't want to get up. When she was sleeping she wasn't thinking or feeling. She could remain numb to the stinging reality of life and enjoy peace. She pulled the blankets to her chin and caught the faint scent of cologne. She snuggled deeper into the soft flannel of Blake's shirt.

Sitting in the hospital waiting room surrounded by unknowns, she'd craved Blake's presence, his strength. The moment she'd gotten an opportunity, she'd run to him. As she'd known he would, Blake exchanged her burdens for comfort.

And, boy, did he have a way of making it all seem bearable. She'd replayed their kiss long into the night, wanting to savor every second, wishing Justin's call hadn't sucked the bliss from the moment, hadn't awakened the sleeping dragon of fear.

Olivia rolled onto her back, wrapping the oversized shirt tighter around her middle. After she'd fled Blake's, she'd returned to the hospital to find Grandma's condition unchanged, and she'd allowed the nurse on duty to talk her into returning home to sleep. Exhaustion wouldn't help her or Grandma, so Olivia obeyed.

The lavender bathwater she'd started when Grandma's stroke hit had been waiting. After draining the cold, stagnant water, she'd scrubbed the bathtub and refilled it with steaming water. In the calming fumes and cloak of bubbles, Olivia had decided that whatever Justin's call was about—he'd only asked that she call him back—could wait. They'd walked away from each other peacefully. His *break* from their relationship had turned into ten months of silence. Whatever he needed right now wasn't on her priority list.

To her surprise, his voice playing from her inbox invoked no warm, fuzzy feelings. No longing, no regrets. They'd once had something beautiful, but that time had passed. At some point, she had to let go of what she thought should've happened and start living what was happening.

Blake was happening. A good man with a good reputation who wanted to be her rock.

She wanted to be his. For the first time in a long time, Olivia was sure of what she wanted.

She peeled off the covers, grabbed a comfortable pair of jeans and a shirt from her closet, and made her way to the bathroom to shower. She'd stop by the bakery to check on things and then return to the hospital.

The bold aroma of coffee wafted through the vents as Olivia finger-combed her damp hair. Jen was up early this morning. The poor girl was still probably blaming herself, despite Olivia's constant reassurance that it wasn't her fault. Jen would have to grow a much thicker skin if she was to make it in the medical field.

After brushing her teeth, throwing her hair into a bun, and dabbing some concealer over the dark circles under her eyes, Olivia descended the stairs and froze as she stepped into the kitchen. "Dad."

"'Morning, Livi." Steam lifted from his mug as he

poured the dark liquid.

Sydney sniffed at his feet, tail wagging.

"When did you get here?" She forced her shoulders to relax and took tentative steps to the cabinet for her own mug.

"About an hour ago. Plane landed in Bangor at four, and I drove the rest of the way."

His eyes were shadowed with dark circles too, the puffiness defining the lines. His hair was grayer than when she'd seen him a few months ago. His age had finally started to show.

And she was taken aback.

"Sorry if I woke you." He eased into a chair at the head of the table.

"You didn't."

"Whose car is that outside?"

Olivia joined him at the table, mug in hand. "I hired a live-in nurse last month. She's a local, fresh out of nursing school. I offered free room and board and meals, plus a little cash, in exchange for help with Grandma while she awaits a response to her résumé. So far, everything has worked out great."

Dad yawned. Stared into his cup as if he were completely detached from the conversation.

"Grandma has yet to wake up, in case you were wondering."

He frowned at his cup. "That's what the hospital told me when I called thirty minutes ago."

He did care. Good to know.

The kitchen grew silent. Years stretched between them like a taut and fraying rubber band. Olivia had been praying for her parents, ever since Rita had challenged her to start talking to God again. She didn't pray for her parents to get back together. After all, she was an adult and relationships were as complex as the human brain. Deeper, more specific prayer was needed, in her life and in theirs. In Blake's life, too. So she prayed for the tough things like forgiveness, healing, and God's will despite their own wishes. And, yes, she even prayed for Blake's future wife.

With an open heart, the Bible had started speaking to her again. Not that it had ever stopped. The passages never forced themselves upon people. The reader simply had to open the book and read. Sometimes the verses whispered, and sometimes they roared. With a loud, audible voice to her heart, they'd been teaching her that even the best of men can fall.

King David, a man after God's own heart, was not immune to the temptation of a beautiful woman. When he'd messed up, he'd messed up big. His choices had forced deadly consequences. He fell into depression and asked God to take his life, but he was still King David, a man after God's own heart. A title he'd earned after receiving forgiveness for committing adultery and murder.

And the man sitting next to her was still her daddy.

Olivia had no power to fix what was broken, but God did. All she could do was find her bearings, move on with her life, and trust God to orchestrate the rest. She took a deep breath, sent her daily prayer to God asking Him to take away her hurt, then placed her hand over her father's. "I'm glad you came, Daddy."

35

Brown sugar. Vanilla. Yeast. Olivia breathed in the scent of her old friends and rubbed the knot from her shoulder. The heat and bustle of the bakery were a welcome change to the long days sitting in the hospital.

Dad had taken residency in the spare bedroom and had kept her company during most visits.

Grandma had woken Monday night but failed to comprehend commands. Her condition was still serious, and the extent of neurological damage unknown.

Blake hadn't attempted to call or text since their kiss four days ago. She'd started to contact him several times but decided it was best to leave the proverbial ball in his court. He'd initiated the kiss. Blake knew where to find her, and if he had no regrets, could lead the relationship from here.

"I'm praying for you all." Brittany added a blueberry cream pie to the chilled display case. "We hated to hear about Elizabeth. It's good to see you though."

Olivia counted the till to make sure they were opening with enough change. "It's good to be back. I feel like I haven't worked in months." She closed the drawer with her hip. "Thank you for taking charge. How are things going?"

"Fine." Brittany propped her elbow on the case. "Darlene's been surlier than usual. We have a few new recipes we'd like your approval on whenever you have extra time. No rush." She turned for the kitchen. "Oh, and I put an ad in the paper for a prep-assistant like you asked. Hopefully, we'll get some applicants soon."

"What would I do without you?"

"I have no idea." Brittany winked and disappeared through the swinging doors.

A prep-assistant would really free their time. The position was offered to any reliable high-school student who could work after school, measuring ingredients that would be used in recipes the next day, restocking the supply shelves, and helping with cleanup. That would allow the bakers to concentrate on fulfilling demand, and give Olivia freedom to concentrate on finances, a new website, and better advertising. Now that the *Mayberry of Maine* campaign was complete, and successful, she could send those letters she'd written to several travel magazines in hopes of some exposure.

The rest of the day passed quickly with a steady rush of customers and three consultations for cake orders.

Dad had called an hour ago to inform her Grandma was now responding to voices by turning her head, but was still unable to move any limbs or follow commands.

Olivia locked the front door and turned over the closed sign, prepared to swap shifts with Dad at the hospital.

Teresa and Casey were clocking out when Olivia reached the kitchen. Brittany filled the mop bucket with hot soapy water, a few bubbles escaping with the force of the spray. Darlene washed the flour coating from her hands.

Olivia turned down the radio. "Go home and enjoy your evening, ladies. I'll clean up."

Everyone expressed thanks and moved for the time clock except Darlene, who fidgeted in front of Olivia like a kid in a long line for a roller coaster. "Sorry to hear about Elizabeth. If I can help in any way, please, let me know."

Olivia blinked, shocked. Had Darlene actually exhibited something other than resistance? "Thank you. I will."

The woman left without another word.

Brittany turned off the water and rolled the mop bucket her way. "I can stay and help."

Olivia took the mop handle and smiled. "Get outta here. I've got this."

A knock rapped on the open back door. Blake filled the doorframe, hands in the pockets of his worn jeans, his white T-shirt peeking out from beneath a light weight athletic jacket. A spark zipped between them as his gaze locked on hers.

Brittany smirked. "Yes, you do." She clocked out, and Blake stepped into the room. "Nice to see you again, Blake. Come to satisfy your sweet tooth?"

Blake blushed. Actually blushed! And it was one of the cutest things Olivia had ever seen.

Brittany chuckled and left out the back door.

Olivia trapped the mop into the upper portion of the wheeled bucket and squeezed out the water. Blake's tentative stance told her he had something to say and wasn't sure how she would take it. She'd fret if he didn't look miserably love sick and uncomfortable, leaning against the wall, waiting to be invited in. He'd taken long enough to make his move, and it wouldn't hurt for her to have a little fun.

"Um…" Blake rubbed the back of his neck and shifted in the doorway. "Can I do something to help?"

Olivia yanked a damp rag hanging on the faucet to dry and tossed it to him.

He eased inside and wiped the remnants of flour and sugar from the stainless steel table into his hand. "How's Grams?"

"She woke up, but it could still be days before we know how much damage the stroke caused." Olivia scrubbed the floor by the still-cooling ovens, double-checking to make sure they'd been turned off.

"How are you holding up?" Blake asked.

"Fine."

Blake exhaled. "You're not making this easy on me, are you?" Now that the table was clean, he draped the rag over the faucet again and rinsed his hands. "I came to apologize."

She leaned against the mop handle. "For what?"

"For…kissing you."

Oh, no he didn't. He did not just admit he regretted kissing her.

Her thoughts must've played across her face because he backed up and shook his head. "I mean, I'm not sorry for kissing you—I thoroughly enjoyed kissing you—but you needed me to be here for you."

"You can't be supportive and kiss me at the same time?"

"What? No, I…" He rubbed his chest. Had she twisted him up to the point of acid reflux?

"Let me start over." He inched closer, took the mop from her hands, propped it against the sink, and palmed her shoulders. "What I'm trying to say is that I know you need a friend right now. I want to be that friend and not do anything selfishly because I want more. Please, let me be here for you. I won't cross any lines again. You have my word."

Heat filled her face. "What if I want those lines crossed? What if I want to date you, and only you?"

Well, that was bold. And completely out of character, even if it was the truth.

Blake studied her. The second hand on the time clock ticked by for what seemed like an hour. Finally, one corner of his mouth lifted, followed by the other. "I can agree to those terms." He stroked her cheek. "As long as there will be chicken wings involved."

She laughed.

Blake placed a chaste kiss to her cheek. "I'm glad that's over. How about I buy you dinner?"

"My dad's in town. I promised him we'd eat before switching places at the hospital."

"I understand." Though his disappointment was evident. "Here. Let me." Blake reclaimed the mop and within a few minutes had the floor sparkling. He dumped the dirty water.

She wheeled the contraption into the utility closet. "Thank you."

He held her hand as they walked outside. She locked up, tested the door, and then slipped her arms into her sweater. "It's chilly."

"Summer doesn't last here." Blake walked her to her car. He leaned against the door and wrapped her in his arms, as if he couldn't get enough. "Drive safe. Tell Grams I said hi."

Olivia loved how perfectly he fit into her life, even though they'd been strangers less than a year ago. "I will."

He started to pull away, but she latched onto his waist. "Hold me."

"Gladly." He hugged her closer.

It felt good to be held. To have a physical connection to another human being. Such a simple thing made the world more tolerable.

He kissed the top of her head. "How's your dad doing?"

She shrugged. "I don't know. He acts indifferent, but I don't think he really is. They've always had a strange relationship, though. I gave up trying to figure them out a long time ago. He'll probably leave in a couple days, and I won't hear from him again for a while."

"I'd like to meet him before he leaves. If he has time."

Olivia looked up at him. "You want to meet my dad?"

"Why not?"

His words were casual, but she knew Blake well enough now to know he did everything for a purpose. If he wanted to meet her dad, he was serious about her. The idea both thrilled her and scared her to death. "OK."

"Good." He kissed the tip of her nose, and then opened her door. "You really think he'll leave so soon after his mother's stroke?"

"Probably. He hasn't been very involved in her care thus far. As he's said, 'it's his turn to be happy.'" They released each other, and Olivia opened her door and tossed her purse into the passenger seat. "Either way, Grandma needs me. I came here to make sure she has the best care, and I'll continue doing just that."

"She's blessed to have you." Blake pressed his lips against hers. "We all are."

36

Pink floral wallpaper wrapped the foyer walls. A large oak desk was the focal point of the room beneath a chandelier that washed the room in a soft glow.

Bile rose in Olivia's throat. "This doesn't feel right."

Dad kneaded his forehead, impatience sagging his body. "This is the nicest place so far. It's clean, the odors are minimal, and the staff appear hardworking."

"I don't want to put Grandma in a nursing home." She crossed her arms around her middle, a cold chill rising from her feet. In some strange way, Grandma helped her hold everything together.

Dad held his arms out, the thick folder given to them by the director clasped in one palm. "What are your other options, Liv? Mom will never walk again. She has the arm strength of a newborn, she doesn't remember who we are, and she can hardly speak." The folder slapped against his thigh. "Your nurse friend told you yesterday she'd accepted the pediatric ward position. What other options do you have?"

His tone reminded her of adolescence. Her teenage rebellion had worn him thin. They'd been at a T in the road then too. Either direction would change their lives, one for the better, one for the worst. Though her mind was telling her this choice was for the better, her heart disagreed. Her chin quivered.

Dad sighed and clamped a hand on her shoulder.

"You've done an amazing job taking care of her, you really have. I'm proud of you for resurrecting the bakery. But, Livi, your over-achieving nature will put you in your grave one of these days. You can only do so much. Things happen that are out of your control and you just have to deal." He inhaled, aging ten years in one soliloquy. He dropped his chin to his chest and continued kneading his forehead. "You just have to deal."

Something in his mannerisms and the hollowness of his eyes made her think he was talking as much to himself as he was to her. She lowered her voice. "Is everything all right? In your...new life I mean?"

His head jerked up. "Everything's great. Great." He patted her back and pasted on a smile as artificial as wax fruit. "Come on; let's meet this Blake of yours."

He was out the door before she could catch up.

September had sneaked up on them, ushering mild days and cool nights.

She'd washed Blake's flannel but had yet to give it back. He hadn't asked for it, and she enjoyed snuggling into its soft warmth after dark.

The car was already running when Olivia sank into the passenger seat. She put a hand over her dad's fist, white knuckling the gear shift. "I want you to be safe." She swallowed. "And...happy. Are you sure things are OK?"

"I said I'm fine." His gruffness nipped at her emotions.

Dad backed out slowly, giving the nursing home another long glance. "I think this is the place. They'll take good care of her."

Olivia envisioned moving day, and her stomach churned again. "I don't know."

Dad braked, jolting them forward. "You're Power of Attorney, do whatever you want. I'm leaving in three days whether you have this all figured out or not."

Tears blurred the view in her side-view mirror of the plantation-style building adorned with giant ferns and white wave petunias. Grandma was the one constant in her life right now. Olivia wasn't ready to let go.

~*~

Blake shifted on the pew beside Olivia. He couldn't wait until church was over to tell her the news. No disrespect toward God. He was simply eager to see her face after many months of hard work. His thigh brushed hers. A rumble besides the one in his empty gut set him off. She wanted him, exclusively. He still couldn't believe she'd said it. Blake stretched his arm behind her and forced his brain to concentrate on the message.

When the service ended, several church members filed over for introductions. Blake received more handshakes and back slaps than the senator had when he'd visited. Apparently, Blake Hartford bringing a woman around after his last embarrassing relationship deserved honorary attention.

The crowd thinned, and Olivia handed Blake her Bible then slipped her arms into her black sweater. The white, flowy dress she wore whispered over her curves and ended just above her calves. Black heels gave her a couple extra inches, bringing her to eye level with his nose. "You look gorgeous."

She tugged on his tie. "You look pretty good yourself, Flannel Man."

"I'm not wearing flannel. A pretty girl stole my best shirt."

Her eyes lowered to her shoes. "I need to give that back, don't I?"

"Nah. Keep it. I've got twenty more where that came from." He linked her fingers with his and led them out of the auditorium.

When they reached his truck, Blake opened her door and helped her climb in. They were meeting her dad for lunch in Winter Harbor. Blake had met the man yesterday and though Jonathan was nice enough, something didn't sit well with Blake. Something more than animosity over hurting Olivia.

Blake got in the vehicle and defrosted the windshield. Fog clung to the treetops despite the noon hour. It wasn't cold to him, but Olivia was shivering, so he turned up the heat. Switching gears to drive, Blake patted the space between them. She grinned, slid next to him, and buckled in. Now would be the perfect time to tell her, but he wanted to do it in front of her dad. Remind the guy how special his daughter was. He put his arm around her and backed out of the tight space. She shivered. "Are you still cold?"

"It's my nerves. I always get cold when I'm nervous." She held out her palms to warm them by the panel vents.

"Is this about me meeting your dad?"

"It's Grandma. Dad's set on the nursing home we toured yesterday. It's all he talked about last night. I don't want to make any hasty decisions, but with Jen taking that new job, I'm under a lot of pressure. The hospital plans to release Grandma on Wednesday."

"Are you worried it's not the right facility, or is it having to live apart?"

Olivia laid her head on his shoulder. "The facility is great. The nicest we've found. I'm just not ready to make this decision."

"I don't think anyone is ever *ready*. You'll just have to decide where she'll receive the best care and be brave."

Olivia nodded and looked away.

He decided to let it go for now.

Betty's Country Diner wasn't as crowded as usual for a Sunday afternoon. They must've beaten the church rush. The smell of mashed potatoes and chicken fried steak greeted them from the sidewalk.

He held the door for her, and the hostess led them to a table in the back.

Olivia sat across from him and leaned conspiratorially over the table. "I overheard someone at church say that the family sitting in front of us has had the stomach flu. I'm going to wash my hands."

"Good idea." The last thing he wanted was to be sick.

She tucked her small red purse beneath her arm and disappeared into the ladies' room.

After ordering their drinks, Blake went to the bathroom to wash his hands too and stopped short when he saw Olivia's dad.

Jonathan faced the opposite wall, his left hand rubbing his temple. "I know Jade. I miss you, too." The words sounded forced. "As soon as I get Mom moved Wednesday, I'll be home."

Should Blake leave the man to his conversation? He certainly wanted to stay out of the details. However, this was a public restroom, and anything he could do to shield Olivia from any more pain was worth a little eavesdropping.

Jonathan sighed. "Yes, then we'll get you settled in."

Blake moved toward the sink.

"I know. This has been hard on me too." A pause. "And I wasn't expecting you to get—" His words died at the sight of Blake.

Get what? Blake turned on the water and pumped soap into his palm.

"I'll call you later." Jonathan ended the call, then pressed and held the top button to shut it off completely.

Blake rinsed and then yanked a few paper towels from the holding rack. "We've got a table in the back whenever you're ready." Blake left Jonathan standing there, hands on his hips. He wasn't about to make excuses for overhearing. He lowered into the booth and picked up a menu. "Your dad's here." Blake pointed to the restroom. "He'll be out in a minute."

She stiffened but smiled anyway. "The buttermilk shrimp looks good."

He agreed, though the bulk of his appetite had vanished.

"Thanks for waiting." Jonathan scooted in next to Olivia.

The waitress took their order.

Olivia returned their menus to the rack at the opposite end of the table.

Perfect time.

Blake pulled a folded newspaper page from his back pocket and slid it across the table. "I found this in the *Portland Press*. Sunday Edition, Food and Dining section. Thought you might be interested."

She scanned the page, then reached for his hand, cheeks glowing. "Bakery Puts Stone Harbor Back on the Map."

Blake bumped her foot with his. "Read it."

She nibbled her bottom lip before returning to the article. "Harbor Town Bakery, once the buzz in several food magazines, and winner of three prestigious awards, lost its credentials during the recession, and the desserts lost their spark with the onset of owner and head baker's Alzheimer's disease three years later. Granddaughter, Olivia Hudson, has sprinkled a new generation of magic on the bakery, putting the place back into the limelight of dessert lovers everywhere.

"Food critic, Angela Bloomsbury, announced in the *Chicago Times* she was delighted to see the bakery had survived. 'I visited Maine fifteen years ago and stumbled upon Harbor Town Bakery on my way through blueberry country. From my first bite of pie, I was transported back to my grandmother's kitchen where a simple dessert could wash all my cares away. I was disheartened to see the bakery's fall and, truthfully, hadn't thought of the place for years. During my visit to the Annual Blueberry Festival in Machias, Maine, last month, I came across a flyer lying on the ground advertising the bakery's new menu. I drove to Stone Harbor, which is now known as 'The *Mayberry of Maine*,' and was delighted at what I'd found.

"The place still held its old charms, along with a few updates like free Wi-Fi and comfortable furniture if you plan to stay a while. As for the desserts, there's a plethora of new items, from a simple chocolate chip cookie to an elegant cheesecake or fruit tart, which all get an A+ in my book. The sky is the limit, and I can't wait to see how high Miss Hudson flies." Olivia put a hand to her heart, staring at the print in disbelief.

Blake stroked her wrist with his thumb. "It isn't just my attention you've captured."

She looked up at him, eyes teary.

"Congratulations."

Enough time passed without a reaction from Jonathan, Blake wondered if the man would acknowledge it at all.

Then his mouth grew pensive, his eyes clear but somber, and he reached for his daughter's other hand. "Congratulations, sweetheart. I'm proud of you."

Jonathan met Blake's gaze and nodded.

37

Sydney jumped awake from her morning nap when Olivia's cell phone blared. The dog hadn't acted right since Grandma's stroke. She'd paced the house on anxious paws the day Olivia and her father had packed some of Grandma's things for the nursing home. Like the canine knew these new arrangements weren't right, and there was a good possibility she'd never see her owner again.

No pets allowed.

Olivia set her full coffee mug on the table and answered the call.

"Hey, Mom."

"Did I wake you?"

"No. Just relaxing a bit before I get ready for work."

"Congratulations on your success. Your dad emailed me a copy of the article."

Olivia slipped the satiny ribbon between the pages of her Bible and set it aside. "That was nice of him."

"It was." Mom's voice trailed off as usual when Dad came up in conversation. "Did you get your grandma settled in?"

"We did." Though she still hated the situation, Olivia was starting to understand it was probably best. "How have you been?"

"Oh…I'm fine. Volunteer work at the library is

keeping me busy. Busy is good."

Olivia understood. "Rest is good, too. Why don't you fly up here and stay for a while? Relax. See the sights."

"I don't think that's a good idea." Something rustled in the background. "The area holds a lot of memories. Besides, I don't want to interfere with your new roommate."

"Jen won't mind."

The idea of Olivia living in this big house alone had her begging Jen to stay on. She worked days and Jen worked nights, so the arrangement was perfect. It wasn't too far from the hospital, and rent was cheap. "At least think about it."

"I will. How does it feel to be another year older?"

"Ugh, you would bring that up, wouldn't you?" Olivia stretched her legs along the couch.

"Am I not supposed to wish my only child a happy birthday?"

Not when that child was twenty-nine and didn't have her life together. "With everything going on, I hadn't even noticed."

Mom laughed. "I hardly believe that coming from the girl who thinks her birthday should be a week-long celebration."

That was a child's mentality. Back when problems were black and white and life hadn't left its dirty footprints on her soul. "It's just not that important this year." Especially when she was spending it alone. Blake had to leave town, so she'd scheduled herself to work.

"I know I haven't said as much, but I admire what you're doing. You're successful at everything you touch. I wish I could be more like you."

Olivia swallowed, unsure what to say. "Please, come visit, Mama."

"We'll see. In the meantime, you bake yourself a big ole cake and eat every bite."

"No deal. Calories aren't as kind to me as they used to be."

"Wait until you're fifty. Eat them now while you still can."

The doorbell rang.

Sydney jumped to the ground and barked all the way down the hall to the front door.

Olivia threw her feet to the ground, hoping the noise hadn't woken Jen. Phone in hand, she jogged on tip-toe to the front door and swung it wide. "Uh, can I call you back later?"

"All right, sweetheart. Enjoy your day."

"Thanks. Love you." Olivia ended the call, trying to comprehend why Blake would be on her front stoop, grinning as though he'd gotten away with something naughty. Horrified by the sudden realization of her unkempt appearance, she ran her fingers through her hair and crossed her arms over her yellow tee. "What are you doing here?"

"Well, that's rude, little miss sunshine." Blake patted the dog's head.

Sydney circled his feet, and then left to inspect the row of landscaping bushes.

"Sorry, I'm just surprised to see you this early in the morning."

"Nice pajamas."

She peered down at her bubble gum pink toes peeking out from beneath pajama bottoms covered in cupcakes. Olivia glowered and gave him a playful kick. Blake snatched her waist and pulled her close.

"Someone told me today is your birthday. I came by to see if you have plans."

"I'm scheduled to work."

"No, you're not. You've got fifteen minutes to get ready and climb in my truck. I'll be waiting." He slapped her hip and walked away.

"I can't, I—"

"I talked to Brittany. She's got it covered," he called over his shoulder. "Hurry up. Clock's ticking."

Her feet danced on the cold slab of concrete. "Where are we going?"

Blake turned to her and grinned. "I've got our whole day planned, and I can guarantee you don't want to miss it. Dress warm. Bring a sweatshirt."

Well, it would be nice not to spend her birthday alone. She scooped up the dog, now waiting at her feet.

"And do something with that hair."

Her mouth fell open. His laughter chased her all the way inside and up to the second floor. Fourteen and a half minutes later, she climbed into Blake's truck, showered, dressed, and in full makeup. She doubted Superwoman could beat that record.

"You're late." Blake fired the engine.

"I am not."

They rumbled down the driveway.

He pulled his gaze from the windshield and gave her an ornery grin. "I'm just trying to get a rise out of you, so your gift seems more appropriate." He bent to retrieve something from underneath his seat.

She stared at the red-wrapped package he offered. "You didn't have to get me a gift."

"Open it."

Olivia took it and peeled back the tape.

"It's not much, but I couldn't pass it up. It was so

you."

An apron fell onto her lap. An embroidered moose with a sassy scowl and crossed arms said *Don't Moose with Me*. She laughed, holding it up for further inspection.

"I found it appropriate."

"Thanks. I love it." She set the gift aside, claimed the middle seat beside him, and kissed the corner of his mouth. He slowed to a stop at the end of her drive and turned his head for a real kiss.

Thirty minutes later, after discussing their favorite childhood birthdays, Blake turned onto a side road that led to a dead end. He parked, reached into the truck bed, and held out a metal pail.

"What's this for?" She finished zipping her sweatshirt then gripped the handle.

"Collecting your heart-shaped stones."

Her own heart melted into a puddle right there on the grassy hill. The breeze drifting off the water lifted her hair.

Blake tucked a strand behind her ear. His hand lingered near her cheek, the callouses on his fingertips causing her heart to beat a wild rhythm. "Come on." Blake took her hand and led her down to the water.

Their feet crunched the pebbles beneath their shoes. She'd never been to a beach without sand before, but it was more beautiful than anything she'd witnessed in the south. Waves crashed against jagged boulders jutting from the water. Luscious, green pines lined the high cliffs, contrasting their beauty against dark, wet rocks and deep blue water.

She closed her eyes and listened to the waves' melody. Blake wrapped his arms around her from behind. She leaned into him. "I don't ever want to leave."

"This spot gets wicked in the winter."

"It's chilly now. I'm glad you told me to bring a sweatshirt."

"I'll gladly keep you warm." He kissed her cheek.

Olivia held up the pail. "About these stones…"

Blake released her. "You have to hunt for them, search the rocks until you find one."

Olivia went to work, kneeling to scour through rocks of all different sizes and colors. They were cold and slick in her hand, wet from the tide.

Blake moved farther down the beach.

After several minutes of sorting, she jumped to her feet. "I found one!"

Blake pivoted in her direction. "Keep looking," he yelled. "There's more."

She rubbed her thumb over the smooth, gray surface of the stone. The center was indented, making a perfect heart. Not symmetrical, but perfect all the same.

For what seemed like hours, they scanned the shoreline, flirting, picking up anything that resembled a heart. Keeping the good ones.

After a while, Blake rested on a boulder a safe distance from the water and waited.

Her bucket nearly full, Olivia searched one last place that earlier had been surrounded by bubbly surf. A deep groove at the base of the boulder held a pile of stones inside, and she picked through them, squealing with delight. "Look at this one, it's huge." She placed a rock the size of her hand in the top of the pail.

Blake jumped. "Livi, watch out!"

A wave of icy water crashed into her backside. She sucked in a breath. White foam swirled around her tennis shoes. She stood still, frozen.

Blake's deep laugh echoed along the beach. He approached her, arm outstretched.

"You think that's funny?" Her body trembled.

"I do." He continued laughing.

From the sound of it, another wave was rolling in. She yanked his hand as hard as she could. He tumbled forward into the surf. The shoulder and chest of his shirt soaked in water.

"You're right." She beamed. "It is funny."

Water clung to his lashes. "You're in trouble now."

Olivia scrambled to her feet, clutching her pail, and ran as fast as she could up the hill to the truck, squealing as Blake's footsteps neared. They reached the vehicle, both out of breath and shivering.

He took the pail from her hand, balanced it on the truck bed, and trapped her against the vehicle. "That wasn't very nice."

"But it was sure satisfying."

"So is this." His lips pressed against hers, warming her instantly. When desire threatened to dominate their good sense, Blake pulled away. "Happy Birthday."

She shivered, more from the aftershock of that amazing kiss than from her wet clothes.

Blake opened her door. "Let's drive around and warm up. Then I have another place I'd like to show you before your birthday dinner."

"You're spoiling me."

"You're worth it."

She peeled off her wet sweatshirt, draped it over the dash, and strapped into the middle seat. Blessed heat flowed from the vents. They huddled together, and Blake rubbed her arms.

"I hope we don't ruin your seats."

"They'll dry." He nuzzled her neck.

"Your nose is like an ice cube."

"I know. It's your fault."

They drove along the coast for close to an hour, covering everything from their favorite movies to their worst college experience. Olivia laughed harder than she had in months. She could truly define this day as happy. Blake parked at an overlook where Coleman's Lighthouse towered in the distance.

She dug around in her bucket. "This one's my favorite."

A light gray, speckled heart.

Blake inspected it between his fingers. "Granite."

"The book I bought at the festival said they're formed when a weak layer of rock breaks off something larger, like a cliff or a boulder, in a V-shape, and falls into the ocean. Their edges are rounded by tumbling along streambeds or rolling surf."

Blake nodded. "Something beautiful created from something broken." He lifted her chin and gazed deep into her eyes. "It went through a lot of adversity to get there but now it's polished to perfection."

A flood of warmth as intense as sunshine blasted any remaining doubt she had about giving her whole heart to his man. Blake saw *her*, even when she couldn't see herself. The best part, he was offering himself to her, something he didn't do to just any woman, according to the town. He was a rare and beautiful gift. Like this stone. Emotion clouded her eyes. "Thank you, Blake."

He rubbed his thumb beneath her eye. "For what?"

"For being you." She kissed him. The stubble on

his upper lip was rough on her lips. Then she pulled away and curled her arms around his neck, squeezing. He returned the embrace, pulling her closer. After months of wandering lost and alone, Blake felt like home.

"There's another place I'd like to show you." His deep tenor rumbled in her ear. "We could hike. Work up an appetite."

Anywhere with him was fine with her. "Sounds good."

Blake drove a few miles farther to Lubec, where they toured the famous red and white striped West Quoddy Lighthouse. Mostly dry, they hiked a few of the smaller trails.

Blake asked if he could go with her the next time she went to visit Grandma at the nursing home. She offered to help him paint the spare bedroom he'd been working on, and they rescheduled the chicken wings and baseball date they'd missed.

"All this food talk is making me hungry," Blake said. "You up for an early dinner? It's close to four."

"Let's do it."

He chose a cozy restaurant on Water Street, claiming the view was like no other.

The waitress gave them a window table that overlooked the rippling cove, protected by a short lighthouse the locals called Spark Plug.

The savory seafood hit the spot. Olivia was too stuffed for dessert, but Blake insisted she have birthday cake. She forked a bite of dark chocolate cake in her mouth and moaned. "I can't remember when I've had such a fun day."

The small lines around his eyes crinkled as he pulled a corner of his mouth into a sideways grin.

"Anything for you."

"Anything?" She set down her fork and wiped her mouth with a napkin.

"Anything."

"Can we go see what all those people are staring at?"

Blake followed her finger out the window to the large group that was gathered at the cove. People pointed and took pictures with their phones. Blake paid and then led her by the hand to an empty space along the fence an elderly couple had just vacated.

"Blake, look!" She pointed.

On a heap of rocks harbor seals were sunbathing. Their slippery skins glistened in the sunlight. At least ten seals chased each other in the water. An occasional bark ensued, joined by the click of cameras and clapping children. A seal on shore stole a fish from the one resting beside it.

Blake's laugh stamped perfection on the day.

They watched the marine show until the sun began its descent, and the group of seals thinned.

Blake drove her home and walked her to the doorstep. She stared up at his rich, dark eyes. "Thank you for an incredible day."

That heart-stopping smile was every bit as intoxicating as wine. "You're welcome."

Her muscles were relaxed, her mind clear. She fought a yawn as she slid the key into the lock. Sydney's bark sounded through the door. "Do you want to come in? Hang out for a while? Grandma has a large collection of old movies. I can make popcorn." Yes, she was practically begging, but she didn't want him to go.

Blake joined her on the stoop, his close proximity

sending awareness through every nerve. He pecked her lips. "As long as there's popcorn."

Olivia prepared the snack while Blake picked out the movie.

Sydney staked her territory beside Blake on the couch. Apparently no female was immune to his charms.

Olivia set the popcorn bowl on the coffee table. "'Old Yeller'? This movie makes me cry."

"It's one of my favorites."

Of course it was.

"All right, you win." She settled in on his other side and turned off the lamp. While the bond between a boy and his dog played across the TV screen, Olivia curled into his side, relishing the connection to this man. She'd fallen in love with Blake, whether she'd intended to or not.

38

Fall entered like a lioness stalking its prey. Each day the air grew colder, the mornings darker, the days shorter. Red, gold, and orange leaves turned the countryside into an autumn paradise.

Olivia slowed the car. Clouds of black smoke belched in the distance. Odd. To her knowledge there was nothing up ahead other than blueberry fields and Blake's house.

Her stomach did a summersault. The arsonist!

Blake's house had been built in 1898 by a wealthy lumber baron. Though it wasn't a registered historic site, it fit the arsonist's profile, as described on the evening news.

Olivia mashed the gas pedal, willing her sluggish engine to speed faster. She turned into Blake's driveway a little too fast. The car rocked to the left and spit gravel beneath the tires. A haze of dust collected behind her as she gained momentum to the house.

A house that appeared to be fine.

She threw the gears into park, turned the key, and got out, scanning every detail of the large home. Quiet. Peaceful as usual.

Scooby lumbered to the top of the stairs, backside wiggling, waiting for her approach. The mesquite smell of smoke still hung in the air, though the dark clouds were barely distinguishable from her current vantage point.

"Blake?"

Olivia took the stairs two at a time, grazed a palm over Scooby's head, and gave the door two quick knocks before bursting inside. "Blake, it's me...I—*oomph*." She smacked into Blake's solid frame as she went around the corner toward the kitchen.

"Steady, girl. You that excited to see me?"

That sexy side grin she loved made the last ten minutes' events more confusing.

He lifted his hand and bit into a grilled cheese sandwich.

"I saw smoke, a fire. I thought..." The heat of embarrassment filled her body. "I was afraid something bad happened."

Blake swallowed his bite. "We're burning the fields today."

The blueberry fields?

Over the last month, the bushes had turned a beautiful reddish-brown in preparation of winter's slumber. "Why on earth would you burn them?"

"It keeps them healthy." Blake nodded toward the kitchen, indicating for her to follow. He opened the fridge for a soda. "We rotate the fields, burning the bushes every other year. It kills any pests and unwanted growth, and allows the plants to grow fuller and thicker the next year. Putting them through the fire make them stronger."

"We?"

"Some friends of mine from the fire department help every fall. We're almost done. I just came in for a quick bite to hold me over until dinner."

Olivia relaxed against the countertop. "I was scared to death."

"Concerned for me?" The can hissed as he popped

the tab.

"Yes."

"How concerned?"

The toes of his boots met hers. He bent until their noses touched.

"Very."

Blake's lips grazed hers.

"You taste like cheddar cheese."

"Aren't you sweet?" He backed away and drank his soda.

"Cheddar cheese happens to be my favorite."

"Really?"

"No." She giggled.

Blake chewed his last bite. "As soon as they leave, I'll pull your car into the barn and get to work."

"And I'll get started in here."

Blake wiped his hand on the thigh of his jeans. "Big plans?"

"Very big."

"Mmm, can't wait."

After a little more kissing, Blake put on his coat and left her alone in his quiet house.

She retrieved the grocery bags from her trunk and left her keys laying in the driver's seat. She prepped the ingredients for dinner then started on dessert, her brain in a fog of giddy daydreams. Mentally, she'd come so far in the last six months. Many things factored in—the calming coastline, the supportive town, the distance between her and the ugliness back home. But most of the credit went to Blake.

He'd shown her there was still good in the world with his big heart and never-ending patience. How to reconnect with God. How one's identity didn't come from their circumstances, their career, or even their family, but in the choices they made and their relationship with Christ.

She wanted to spend forever with this man.

Her cell buzzed with an incoming text. She pulled her hands from the soapy dish water, dried them, and went for the phone. An icy dose of reality slapped her in the face.

I've called several times. Need to talk, Livi. I miss you.

The delicious scent of the kitchen was suddenly unappealing. She hadn't returned Justin's calls on purpose. She missed what they'd once had, but she didn't miss him. Not after the way he'd discarded her during her most critical time. Not after meeting Blake and discovering true love. Olivia deleted the thread. Justin was career-driven and would eventually let her go. That part of her life was in the past, and that's where it would remain.

An hour later, she trekked to the barn where Blake was enduring the chill to change her oil. Olivia gripped the Thermos of coffee and burrowed deeper into her scarf, blocking the wind's whispering guilt over Justin's text.

She should tell Blake she'd been engaged. That her faith in men had not only been destroyed by her father's actions, but also by her fiancé's. The subject had never seemed important enough to discuss before, since their goal had been to keep her moving forward and away from the past. Sure, the subject would come up eventually, but in her mind it hadn't seemed important.

Until now.

Blake had a right to know all her secrets. She wanted him to know. She loved him and wanted to do things right. She opened the barn door to the scent of hay and oil.

Blake looked up from his crouched position beneath her car's hood. "Almost done."

Olivia peered at the mass of components stuffed into the small front section of her vehicle. "I brought something to warm you up."

He swiped a shop rag from the top of his toolbox and began wiping the grease from his fingers. "I changed your oil and topped off your fluids. Tire pressure is good, however, the tread on the rear driver's side is wearing faster than the others. Next good day we get, I'll investigate."

Guilt punched her chest. "You're too good to me."

"You're too good *for* me." He threw down the rag and came at her.

"Don't touch me with those dirty hands."

"These dirty hands?" He stalked closer, palms out.

"I'm serious. Don't do it, Blake. You'll ruin my new shirt."

"Mmm, and flannel looks good on you." He captured her lips. "Told you I'd win you over."

She scowled. "Don't let it go to your head."

He shrugged.

"Dinner in twenty."

"I'll clean up and be right in."

Olivia went back to the house, calling herself all kinds of coward. The evening was too sweet to taint it with confessions. They had plenty of time to cover those things. Why bring it up tonight? She went inside and added a few more logs to the living room fire. She washed her hands, slipped on her oven mitts, and pulled a steaming deep-dish pizza from the oven. The barn door closed and Blake was visible from the window. Olivia debated whether her decision to keep silent about Justin was wise or not.

Instead of coming inside, Blake stayed on the porch, his phone pressed to his ear, one hand braced against a porch post. Though she couldn't hear what he was saying, his posture and the somber expression on his face said something was wrong.

Olivia put the pizza back into the oven to warm and wondered if the call had anything to do with his brother's wedding invitation she'd seen in the trashcan earlier.

The front door opened then closed. The thud of boots being removed echoed from the hall. Footsteps neared. Blake appeared. A large crease marred his forehead.

Olivia waited as he washed up and busied herself removing the salad from the fridge, pouring drinks, and retrieving utensils. A tug on her apron strings stopped her from passing him. She turned to find he'd unraveled the bow, one string still gripped in his fingers.

"This is one of the things about you that first got to me."

"My apron?"

He nodded. "The way the bow sits perfectly in the small of your back. The way the strings sway against you when you walk."

She raised a brow. "Blake Hartford has a dark side."

He shrugged. "I'm a guy." He tugged her closer, untying the rest of the bow and lifting the apron from around her neck. "I could get used to you cooking in my kitchen all the time."

"*All the time*? You're one of those guys, huh?" She was teasing, of course, but the crimp between his brows deepened.

"You know what I mean."

She nodded, liking the idea as well. "I could get used to cooking for you all the time."

Their vague confessions said so much. Like how fast and how serious this relationship was progressing. Olivia was no longer scared. She could trust Blake with her heart. Blake was her home. She stared into his dark eyes, full of love. And sadness. She put her hands on his cheeks. "What's wrong?"

Blake swallowed. "I just got off the phone with Brent Nichols, a buddy from high school. He owns the lumber yard where I get stuff for the house. His wife was five months pregnant with their third. She lost the baby."

Her hands fell to her sides. "Oh, how awful."

Blake's grip at her waist tightened. "I guess it happened a few weeks ago. Her appendix burst. The doctor said under normal circumstances, the rupture would've killed her. Apparently, her uterus helped cushion the blow, but it broke her water. There was nothing they could do." He sighed. "They've been through a lot over the years. Right after they got married, she was in a car wreck that almost took her life."

Why did things like this happen to good people?

Blake cradled Olivia's head against his chest. God caused the sun to shine, the rain to fall on the just and the unjust. Blessings fell upon God's children and to those who refused His love. Same for trials and tribulations.

Sometimes bad things just happened.

Her grip on him tightened. "It's amazing how severe a beating the human heart can withstand and still survive."

Blake kissed the top of her head. "God promises to restore the years the locusts have eaten."

"I've never heard that before."

"Old Testament. Joel."

Is that what God was doing, using Blake to restore the last year and a half of her hellish existence? Her conversation with Arianne in the blueberry field sprang to her mind. Was Blake the oasis at the end of her proverbial wilderness?

He gazed deep into her eyes, communicating things she longed to hear.

"I..." The breathiness of her own voice stopped her from confessing her feelings too soon. "I'll pray for them."

"Me, too." His gaze flicked to the counter where the salad and breadsticks waited.

She pulled away and retrieved the pizza from the oven, then set to work cutting the slices, her mind reeling. She'd almost told Blake she loved him. But this wasn't a marathon. There'd be plenty of time for confessions and endearments and details of failed relationships.

No need to rush.

39

Olivia tipped the dustpan, dumping dirt and crumbs in the trash. In a few minutes, she'd clock-out and say goodbye to the longest week ever. They'd been working non-stop since the end of October creating a holiday menu, baking festive treats, taking pie orders for Thanksgiving, which was now only two weeks away. They'd been so busy it was hard to find time for lunch breaks most days.

Feet and back aching, she turned to her employees standing single-file at the time clock. "Thank you all again for your help and hard work. Enjoy the rest of your weekend."

"Thanks for the bonus checks." Teresa held up her envelope and smiled.

The rest of the group thanked Olivia again, as if they hadn't already told her a hundred times. Including Darlene. Maybe the woman was softening with holiday spirit.

Olivia put a hand in the small of her back and stretched. Yawned. She returned the broom and dustpan to the utility closet and looked down at her rumpled work clothes. She was supposed to meet Blake for dinner tonight at a new seafood restaurant in Machias. Staying awake during the meal would be a challenge, however. Another yawn spilled from her mouth.

Brittany slung her purse over shoulder and rubbed

the back of her neck. "I have a feeling we'll be baking nonstop until the ball drops in Time Square."

"I think you're right."

"That review in the newspaper was exactly what we needed. I think."

Olivia chuckled. Since the original article in the *Bangor Times* in August, five other newspapers had printed the review. Their reputation had spread throughout the coast, skyrocketing business for the holidays.

Olivia turned off the main lights, dimming the room to the visibility of the security lights. "I bought the cutest nautical Christmas ornaments last week. I'm going to go ahead and start decorating the dining room Monday."

Brittany silenced the radio. "Christmas is my favorite holiday. Roaring fireplaces, sweaters, snuggling by the tree."

Warmth crept into Olivia's neck. She and Blake had been doing plenty of snuggling lately. Nothing too far, of course. Just enjoying the flow of the relationship. She appreciated the way he showed both his affection and respect for her.

"Well, I'm outta here." Brittany waved and exited to the parking lot.

A rush of cold air barreled into the room.

Olivia stepped into the dining area to make sure the elderly couple who had come in seconds before closing had gone so she could lock up. Just past the swinging doors, her blood froze at the figure sitting in the nook, scrolling on his phone. Her lungs refused to take in air.

The room swayed.

Justin.

He saw her and stood, confident and cavalier as always in gray dress pants, a white shirt rolled up at the sleeves, and a perfectly coordinated tie. Cropped, honey-colored hair tousled at the ends as if he'd recently run his fingers through it.

She was going to be sick.

"Hi, Livi."

The familiarity with which he spoke made her stomach twist harder. Blake had whispered that same pet name in her ear hours earlier, and she much preferred it coming from his lips. The swinging door smacked her backside on its return trip, prompting her to action. She jumped and stumbled forward. "What are you doing here?"

Justin cowered slightly and rubbed the back of his neck. "You wouldn't return my calls or texts. I thought, maybe, I should come to you."

She'd needed him to come to her a year ago when she'd been sitting in a recovery room, her insides dark and cold, while patients with far worse conditions than hers rambled and begged for help as they paced the halls all night long.

He took a tentative step closer.

Olivia closed her eyes. *God, please, let this be a nightmare.* She'd finally found her footing on the slippery slope of her life. Created a new beginning. She didn't want to revisit the past.

"I've missed you."

She opened her eyes. This man standing before her, hands buried in his pockets, feet apart, had once been her whole world. Best friend first, then future husband. Those gray-green eyes and his self-assured smile used to turn her knees to jelly. She'd put him on a pedestal. Given him her all.

That was her mistake. She'd put her entire trust and confidence—her happiness—in the people she loved, like Justin and her parents, only for them to let her down. From day one in their relationship, perhaps even before, Blake insisted she love the Lord more than him. God was a safe place to put her trust, her confidence, her happiness.

Justin rocked back on his heels. "Say something," he whispered.

Olivia took a deep breath, the previous unknowns in her life shifting and locking into place. "I don't know what to say."

He studied the floor. Nodded. Looked back at her with love. Fear. "You look good. Content. Happy."

"I am."

"Good. I want you to be happy."

"Is that why you're here?"

A loud *whoosh* of air left his lips. "I asked for some time to clear my head, assess life, make sure we were doing the right thing." He closed the distance and covered her elbows with his palms. "I've no doubt now how much I love you, how much I want to spend the rest of my life with you."

Now that the hard part was over. "I haven't heard from you in almost a year."

"I know." His thumbs rubbed her arms, forehead knotted in a frown. "I know. I just…wanted to be a hundred percent sure. You deserve that. And…you needed time to heal." His forehead pressed against hers. "I'm sorry, Livi."

Sorry? An apology didn't erase the scary uncertainty of her future, the months of loneliness he'd forced her to endure. Yet, it was strangely OK. God had given her something better. "I forgive you, Justin."

His palms went to her face and his smile of relief turned serious as he bent to kiss her.

Olivia pushed at his chest. "I forgive you, but we can't go back."

He leaned away, still holding her.

"It took me a long time to find my identity again. It's not in you, or my parents, or my job. It's in God. I've started over. And started seeing myself through God's eyes. I don't want my past anymore."

Justin's hands fell away. "How can you say that? We've always been together. A team since we were kids."

"Where was my teammate when my life was spiraling out of control? Where was he at during those black days and even darker nights after I left the hospital? I could've used some help. You left."

His fingers curled into his hair. "I didn't know what to do. How to help you. I'd never seen you like that—talking but not making any sense, that strange, hollow look in your eyes. And visiting a mental facility…" He threw his hands out. "Yes, I'm a coward."

The word hung in the air like thick morning fog over the harbor. After several seconds, Justin ran his hand over his tie. "It was a lot for a guy to take in."

"Try being the one living it." She curled her arms around herself. "You can't come back now that the worst is over and expect to continue our plans. You'll always hold a special place inside me, Justin, but you'll never be my *person*."

"Please don't say that." He grabbed her arms again. "You're my person. I don't know how to live without you."

"You'll find your way, just as I did. I'll pray for a

wonderful woman to come into your life who can give you all the things I can't."

Justin's lips tightened in hard line, his jaw like granite. "I don't want anyone else. I want you."

Too late.

Olivia gazed around the bakery, the stillness eerie compared to the day's crazy rush. "I'm with someone."

"I know."

Olivia studied his features for motive.

Justin swallowed. "Your dad told me. Three months ago."

She pulled her hoodie tighter around her middle. That's when he'd started texting her. "Yet you waited to come."

He looked at her, his eyes so fierce with determination it made her spine turn cold. "I told you. I wanted to be absolutely sure I knew what I'd be fighting for."

Her heart broke for him.

Before her fuzzy brain could comprehend what was happening, Justin had a hold on her waist, pulling her hard against him. She could hardly move.

"You've known him for a year. We've known each other our whole lives." His mouth crashed down on hers, the desperation of his kiss stealing her breath. She tried to get away, but it all happened too fast to keep up with.

"I love you, Livi," he said, breathing hard. "Let me try again. Let me prove myself. Please."

She couldn't think within the confines of his arms, her lips still recouping from the pressure of his. Olivia turned her face away for clarity.

Blake was standing outside the windows, his gaze boring into hers.

40

Blake went hot. Whatever dandy was driving the red Jaguar was kissing his girl. And Olivia was allowing it. The sky broke loose, and cold rain pelted Blake's hat, his shoulders, and pooled at his feet. Yet all he could do was stand outside the bakery and watch this nightmare play out. A plot he'd lived once before.

Olivia's gaze met his through the glass. Her face paled to a ghostly white. Yep, caught. He hadn't for one second suspected her to be the playing type. She was too honest. Too fragile. Too broken.

Or he was an idiot.

Olivia yanked free from the man's embrace and flung open the door. She met Blake in the rain. "I'm glad you're here."

Interesting. Not the first sentence he would've expected to come from her lying mouth. Then again, she sounded genuinely relieved to see him.

"Did he hurt you?" Blake pointed to the jerk dressed like he'd just come from a board meeting.

She turned to look back inside the open front door. "No."

Then Blake's eyes weren't tricking him after all. Only his heart. "Who is he?"

The man leaned against the door frame, staying under the protection of the awning. He tucked his hands in his pockets, crossed his ankles, and looked at Blake as if he were a roach. "Her fiancé."

Blake's gut churned. "Your what?"

The last word came out in a growl.

"It's not like that." Olivia started toward him but stopped when he backed away.

"What's it like, then?"

Rain plastered her hair to her cheeks. Soaked into her thin shirt. She shivered. "We *were* engaged. We broke up before I moved here."

Now the nameless man—a stylish, manicured city guy perfect for a city girl—walked up behind her and placed his hand on her shoulder. Marking his territory. "We put the wedding on hold. Took some time to regroup. We never broke up."

Olivia jerked away from the man's hold. A cloud of breath formed in front of her lips. "You asked for time, and then I didn't hear one word from you for a year. That's a breakup in my book."

Engaged? The truth curled around Blake's heart and squeezed. Of course there'd been other men. He'd known that. But he'd been living in the moment, figured there was plenty of time to explore her past. Her current healing was more important than rehashing old events. However, he'd never expected she belonged to another man. Not one so recently anyway.

"Yeah, well, it wasn't." The guys white dress shirt was now clinging to his torso. "You agreed to give me that time. What am I supposed to think?"

"I heard nothing from you, Justin. *Nothing*. You never once in all that time asked how I was doing, or inquired if I'd settled in nicely here. No communication whatsoever."

"I've been texting and calling for the last three months!" The man threw his palms out.

Another blow to Blake's world. "Is that true?"

Her wilting body told him the answer.

Three months ago would mark the blueberry festival, Mrs. Hudson's stroke, their first kiss. The moment she and Blake started a relationship. How coincidental.

"You never thought to mention him to me?" Blake pointed to the guy then let his hand fall against his cold, wet leg.

"It was over for me." Her voice broke. "I didn't think rehashing it was as important as building on us."

As if just noticing the rain, Justin looked at the sky, then smoothed his tie and went back into the bakery, shaking his head.

Blake almost felt sorry for him. He knew exactly what it was like to have the woman he'd planned to marry stolen by another man without warning.

Anger seared Blake's vision. "With my past, it was important."

Olivia moved toward him, placing her hand over his heart. "I'm not like Madison."

Blake wrapped his fingers around her cold wrist and removed her hand. "Yes, you are." Blake turned for his truck. Dampness from his boots seeped into his socks with every step. So much for a romantic dinner in Machias, where he'd planned to audibly confess how deeply he'd fallen in love with her. So much for planning a future with a woman he wanted to spend the rest of his life with. Again.

~*~

The light bulb buzzed overhead. Grandma's closet

had always made a great hiding spot when Olivia was a child. Tonight was no different. Blouses, slacks, and sweaters surrounded her from all sides. Shoe boxes and file storage containers filled the long shelf above the clothes. She inhaled the scent of Grandma, an old-fashioned floral scent that reminded her of a bygone Hollywood era.

She could stay in here for weeks. Hide from the world as she used to when she was in elementary school, and they'd visit during the summer. Not wanting to go home, she'd hide amongst the clothes, hoping they'd miss their plane, which infuriated her father. She'd loved her Indiana home, but something about this place had called to her even then.

Tonight, she wanted to enclose herself in the tiny space, escape from the pain of her parents' choices, her grandma's illness, and the loss of another good man.

Blake refused to take her calls, return her texts, or answer his door. Apparently, he'd said everything he needed to say when he'd accused her of being just like Madison. The vicious spark in his eyes, the poison in his voice, had been directed at her heart.

It hit the target.

Rita Hartford was right. Until Blake could forgive his brother, give the bitterness to God, Blake couldn't have a healthy relationship with anyone.

So Olivia prayed. Prayed that Blake would give it over, prayed that Blake would understand her reason for not mentioning Justin, and prayed that whether it was God's will for them to be together or not, their relationship with the Lord wouldn't falter. And, yes, she continued to pray for Blake's future wife just as she'd promised. Even though that woman apparently wasn't her.

Today marked another untraditional Thanksgiving spent alone in a room full of strangers. She'd spent the day with Grandma, who no longer remembered Olivia, and after a mini-stroke shortly after moving to the nursing home, could no longer communicate.

Continually wiping the white, pasty gravy from Grandma's chin at dinner, Olivia had discussed the bakery, all the happenings around town, and how much Sydney missed her. It wasn't how Olivia would've preferred to spend the holiday, but she was thankful to still have her Grandma.

Which was why she was cocooning herself away now, to gather more items to keep Grandma comfortable and retrieve some paperwork the nursing home director had asked for. Anything to keep her mind off Blake and the emotional sendoff she'd given Justin after three days of him attempting to change her mind. They'd separated peacefully, and she wished him all the best.

Olivia started on the left side of the closet and rummaged her way right, pulling down and opening boxes, intrigued by the things Grandma had chosen to keep over the years—birthday cards, Polaroid photos of her and Grandpa in the seventies, shells, half-sewn cross-stitch designs, magazine recipes, and newspaper clippings. She lifted the items off the closet floor and piled them on the bed while she scanned the clothes rack and shelves.

After collecting a few pairs of fleece-lined pants, a couple of long-sleeved shirts, and an extra quilt, Olivia worked her way through the shoeboxes in hopes of finding house slippers or a comfortable pair of loafers.

She opened an old hat box to find it bursting with

photos and newspaper clippings. Most were articles written about the bakery and obituaries of people Grandma had known.

Beneath the mementos rested a leather-bound journal. Olivia flipped through the pages, stopping when a glossy black-and-white photo slipped from the pages. Her grandpa, mid-thirties she'd guess, was holding a fishing pole in front of a glass lake with looming mountains in the distance. The photo had faded with age, but the handsome planes of Grandpa's face were evident. Dressed in tailored pants and a white shirt, he grinned at the camera.

The profiles of two small boys were in the bottom left-hand corner. Olivia turned the photograph over, but it gave no indication as to the year or who the boys were. The clothing appeared to be late 1950s.

Similar pictures were tucked inside. A few included Grandma and two boys around the ages of two and four. The same ones in the photograph, judging by their striped shirts. Olivia recognized the older boy as her father, the stubborn set of his chin unchanging.

A brittle newspaper clipping wedged a few pages over had Olivia's pulse racing.

Tragedy on Moosehead Lake, dated July 1957.

Olivia absorbed every word of the article, filling in blanks where the ink had smudged. The local sheriff was quoted giving his condolences to the Hudson family for their loss. It went on to give details regarding the date and time of death of the toddler belonging to Clifford and Elizabeth Hudson of Kennebeck—Jacob Hudson.

Olivia went cold with shock. Her grandparents had lost a child? She'd had an uncle? How unimaginable to hold a child in your arms, nurture him, and raise him, only for that child to be taken from you.

After all these years, that same loss still stood sentinel inside Grandma despite her declining brain activity. Olivia couldn't recall how many times her grandma had mentioned Jacob. That grief had become part of Grandma's DNA. Out of all the things her sweet grandma had forgotten, why did this tragedy have to haunt her?

Olivia settled cross-legged on the floor, setting the photos aside. Her family history had remained silent long enough. If this journal was anything like the one Grandpa had made, Olivia would get answers.

She opened the front cover to her grandma's perfect scroll.

1962

Cliff suggested I pour my heart into these pages. He thinks it will cure my grief. I promised to try.

Grandma recalled a few vague memories and mentioned her irrational anger at Olivia's dad over the situation, but nothing that really connected any dots for Olivia. The pages were mostly filled with doodles and drawings.

Halfway through the journal, two silver photo triangles meant to hold in a picture, rested empty in the middle of the page above a caption.

Some mountains cannot be moved.

Olivia fingered through the pictures and stopped at the one of her grandpa with the fishing pole. She slipped it into the photo triangles. Perfect fit.

Bile burned in Olivia's throat. How had she gone twenty-nine years unaware of such a tragedy?

How had her grandparents handled the aftermath? What steps had they taken to move forward with their lives? How had Olivia's father been affected?

Counseling held such a stigma back then. Things that happened in a person's childhood could alter how they looked at the world later in life.

Was this the case with her father? Were there other secrets Olivia didn't know?

Olivia closed the book and curled her arms around her legs. She leaned against the closet wall, shrouded by her grandma's clothes, took a step back in her mind and took a therapist approach to her life.

People made choices. Those choices affected others. Some for good, some for bad. Olivia saw it every day in her practice, and patients spent large amounts of money for help overcoming the effect of choices.

Now, Olivia had a choice. She could take her father's adultery, Justin's betrayal, and Blake's abandonment and slip back into a depression that sucked joy from her life, or she could give it all to God. Let *Him* fight for her.

She chose to live.

41

"It isn't until we learn to forgive that we can be truly free." The words scrawled on a sticky note in Olivia's handwriting he'd found attached to his door refused to stop their taunting.

The last stroke of blue faded into the black night as Blake put away his maul in the tool shed. Hardly night. It was only five-thirty. Time to begin the long, grueling motions of pretending he wasn't lonely, that his heart wasn't devastatingly broken.

Nights were the hardest. Especially tonight, knowing she'd been here. She should be sitting with him now by the fire, curled up in his arms. They should be laughing together, cooking food and eating 'til they popped. Kissing.

Instead, after he carried in this load of firewood, he'd mark off his thirty-fourth day without her and wonder, once again, how he'd made it through another day.

He loaded wood chunks in his left arm and maneuvered through the door. He added two logs to the already blazing fire. The wood, covered with a dusting of snow, hissed when it met the flames. Blake added the remaining logs to the rack in the corner and then stirred the fire with a poker, sending orange sparks up the chimney.

He plopped down in front of the radiating heat,

coat, boots, and all. Blake hadn't needed to split any more firewood. He already had enough to last him two winters. But it gave him something to do while he waited for the new upstairs flooring to arrive. If it didn't come soon, he'd have every tree on his property scalped, cut, and stacked.

Scooby moaned from his bed by the couch. The dog lay on his side, twitching and jerking in a deep state of REM.

Blake wished he could sleep that well. Most nights, he stared at his dark ceiling, a breath away from giving in and calling Olivia.

What good would that do? She'd been engaged to another man the entire time they'd been dating. There were no words of reconciliation, no words to stitch up the wound.

Sure, the guy was a loser for putting things on hold and not contacting her for months. Still, she could've told Blake. At least mentioned she'd been engaged. Especially, knowing how delicate the situation was with his brother. But she'd chosen to keep that secret to herself.

Blake stood and hung his coat on the rack, pulled off his boots, and went to the kitchen. He eyed the contents of his fridge. Sliced turkey, sliced ham, and an almost empty carton of yogurt. He grabbed a soda and closed the door, deciding to go hungry. He really should get some groceries in the house. Empty cabinets during a Maine winter was just plain stupid.

Blake opened the soda's tab and took a sip on his way back to the living room. His nightly routine—pace the floor between TV and fridge, pretending he wasn't a fool who'd been fooled twice.

This house was just a house again. Not the home it

had morphed into when Livi had been part of his life.

He stared at the couch, untouched for thirty-four days. Blake missed her. So much it hurt to breathe sometimes. And the proposal he'd been considering for Christmas was now nothing more than a pipe dream.

~*~

"Merry Christmas, everyone. See you next year!" Olivia pumped more enthusiasm into her words than she felt. She handed each of her employees a red envelope with their names written in cursive on the front. Bakery profits had doubled since her arrival, and she couldn't have done it without these ladies. Even grumpy Darlene.

As soon as the last chore was done, Olivia shooed them out the door to enjoy time off with their families. Tomorrow was Christmas Eve, and the bakery would remain closed until after the New Year. Eight days off. How would she ever survive without distraction?

She'd considered flying home and spending the holiday with her mother, but the nursing home had called, concerned with how much Grandma had been sleeping and the CBC count of her latest blood test. Olivia had decided it was best to stay.

Once she was entirely alone in the bakery, she glanced around the sparkling kitchen, and sighed. The kitchen was still warm, and when she donned her apron in this room, her life made sense.

Stepping out the back door would throw it off kilter again.

Olivia collected her purse and keys and took her time bundling herself against the elements. When one last walk-through proved the doors were all locked, the ovens off, and that nothing had been overlooked, she decided she'd stalled long enough and braved the cold.

Her cheeks burned. She shrank further into her alpaca wool scarf like a turtle retreating to the protection of its shell. The winters here were brutal. This was a land where having a man to keep you warm at night would be helpful.

How she missed Blake. His smile. His selfless, easy-going nature. His conversation. The very thought of his name rocked her insides with an ache she'd hoped would dull after six weeks without him. Yet, he was still her first thought upon waking each day. Her last thought before sleep gave her a short reprieve.

Would he ever learn to forgive?

As Olivia started her car and cleaned the dusting of snow from her windshield, a taxi pulled up behind her. The tinted windows made it impossible to see the passenger's face, but a shadow in the back seat paid the driver and then opened the door. A man emerged, suitcase in hand, his scarf wrapped around his face and head like a mummy. Only the weathered skin around his eyes gave her any indication as to his identity.

She smiled the best she could with frozen cheeks. "Hey, Daddy."

He tugged the scarf off his mouth. "Hey, sunshine."

Sunshine. Another one of her nicknames he hadn't used in years.

The cab pulled away, leaving them alone in the wind and snow.

Dad shrugged. "I thought we should spend Christmas together. Unless you have other plans."

Olivia's heart swelled. He had no idea how much she didn't want to spend the holiday alone. "No plans. That's a great idea." She opened her trunk.

Dad dropped the suitcase inside.

Maybe they'd actually enjoy the holiday together. Like old times.

42

The bold colors of Grandma's old Christmas bulbs reflected off the living room window. Night had swallowed the daylight. Flames flickered from the fireplace where two empty stockings hung. This morning, after the glorious experience of sleeping until eight o'clock, Olivia had woken to a fresh brewed pot of coffee and steaming biscuits and sausage gravy. The meal was about the only thing her father knew how to make, but he made it well.

Jen had joined them, and they'd spent an hour discussing the best and worst Christmas presents they'd received.

Olivia laughed until she nearly cried, not only from the humorous responses but because, for a quick moment in time, Dad had seemed like Dad again, despite the heavy cloud that hovered over him. Wanting the temporary normalcy to become permanent was too much to hope for, so she didn't let the desire grow roots.

Since the winter storm hadn't been as harsh as predicted, Jen left at noon to spend the weekend with her family.

Olivia and her father had searched the attic for Grandma's artificial Christmas tree and then left to do some light, last minute shopping. They'd each enjoyed a mocha and a warm yeast donut from Katie's Kitchen before heading back home. Somehow they'd made a silent truce to designate conversation to subjects that wouldn't stir controversy or raw emotion.

It was the most enjoyable time she'd spent with her dad in a few years. A Christmas present all in itself.

Of course, he'd asked about Blake, figuring she'd be spending part of the holiday with him. She'd given her dad the gist of their breakup then quickly changed the subject. While the dinner brisket cooked, filling the house with the delicious smell of seasoned beef, they'd put up the tree and lights, deciding to forgo the ornaments. Now, they both relaxed in front of the TV, bellies full, four presents wrapped and tucked beneath the tree.

It was easy to dwell on things she didn't have, like a Maine blueberry farmer, instead of the blessings she did possess: her health, her family—dysfunctional as it was—the bakery, and her friends.

"What's wrong?" Dad asked.

That's when she noticed the downward pull of her brows. A lone tear snaked down her cheek. Olivia swiped it away, trying to act nonchalant.

Dad blew out a loud breath. "I'm sorry about Blake. He seemed like a really decent guy."

"He is." She offered a wobbly smile.

"It's my fault. I never should have encouraged Justin. I didn't think you were all that serious with Blake, and I have to admit, I hated to see you grow roots here. I thought you and Justin would work things out, and you'd come home." He shook his head. "But what do I know?"

The comment wasn't sarcastic or condescending. It was genuine.

Olivia sat up and curled her legs beneath her.

"This is my home now. I know it holds no ties for you anymore, but this town, the people, the bakery—I need them."

Dad nodded. "I really am sorry. For everything." He scrubbed a hand down his weary face.

This might not be the right time to ask, but Olivia had been dying to since her dad's arrival. "I'm sorry about your brother. Jacob." The name was foreign on her tongue.

Dad's gaze sharpened on her. "That's a name I try to forget."

"Why?" She put her hand over his, encouraging him to open up to her.

He sighed. "Because his death is my fault."

"How? You were only five."

"I'm going to tell you this once, and then I don't ever want to hear about him again."

Olivia agreed.

Dad shifted forward, resting his elbows on his knees. "We were camping at Moosehead Lake. Dad had gone fishing, and Mom was hanging clothes out on the line. I started whining that I was hungry, so Mom put me in charge of Jacob while she went in and made me a sandwich.

"I got distracted by a butterfly. Chased it, completely forgetting about Jacob. I followed it pretty far, I'm not sure how far really. When I heard Mom yelling my name, I remembered I was supposed to be watching over Jacob." Dad closed his eyes and swallowed.

Olivia squeezed his hand.

"He'd tried to follow me, but he was only two so he didn't get far. He must've seen something he wanted in the lake."

Her stomach turned. "And that's when he drowned?"

Dad nodded.

"How did you all cope?"

He shrugged. "I don't know. I was young. I knew my brother was gone, but I didn't understand death. I learned quickly not to ask too many questions.

"Dad eventually became Dad again. Mom—she was angry with me for not obeying her instructions. She never looked at me the same way again."

A part of Olivia wished she hadn't asked. What a tragic, private, personal thing. But knowing made certain aspects of her father click into place.

Dad rubbed at the lines in his forehead. "I didn't want to tell you this tonight, since it's Christmas and all, but we're on the subject of siblings so…"

His odd choice of words caused her stomach to twist. What other earth-shattering news could he possibly add to this situation?

His aging face contorted as if he'd tasted something sour. "Jade's pregnant. She's nine weeks along."

Earth shattered.

Jade, who'd had a part in almost completely destroying Olivia's existence, was having a baby. Her father's baby. Olivia's half-sibling. *God, help me.* Olivia didn't speak. Simply concentrated on breathing in and out. Sometimes there just weren't words.

The musical on TV continued to play while she watched the dynamics of her life shift once again. Why did her feet keep gaining traction only for the ground beneath her to change course? Would the nightmarish ripples of this infidelity ever stop?

By the time the couple on TV announced their

engagement, shock had given way to fury inside Olivia's chest. She opened her mouth to voice her feelings when the black-and-white image of a little boy flashed into her memory.

She closed her mouth. Her new sibling didn't deserve her wrath any more than Olivia's father deserved blame for his brother's death. His childhood scars were probably the reason he had trouble functioning in female relationships now.

Choices had consequences. So did the way people chose to react to situations. She could feed the bitter emotions roiling inside and let another person's actions control her, or she could strive to handle it the way Jesus would have, with forgiveness and love.

Saying congratulations didn't seem like the appropriate phrase for this situation, so she choked out the only response she could speak with honesty. "That gives me the next six months to get used to the idea of being a big sister."

He snapped out of the daze he'd settled into. Surprise lit his face. "You want to be part of this child's life?" The bit of hope shining in his eyes spoke the depth of his regrets.

She wrapped her arms around herself. "It's a baby, Dad. Not cancer."

Only three times in Olivia's life had she seen her dad cry. This was the third.

Not a dramatic show, but his eyes welled up with tears. "Thank you, sweetheart."

Her own emotions started. She curled up next to him. "Are you happy with Jade? Have you finally gotten what you wanted?"

He chuckled, humorless. "I got what I wanted. But I lost everything I had."

~*~

Groceries were a must. Blake had already blown through the leftovers from his parents' Christmas dinner. The dinner he'd arrived at after Lucas and Madison had left. His brother had tried contacting him again, twice over the phone and once through Blake's website.

Persistence had always been one of Lucas's strongest qualities.

A cold, rainy mist clung to Blake's face and coat as he crossed the parking lot to the store. Head down, Blake stepped inside the automatic doors. Christmas music sung by a cheesy pop artist played over the speakers. Fifty-percent-off holiday displays were everywhere.

Blake wanted to forget this Christmas and get started with a new year. He wiped the bottom of his slick boots on the mat, grabbed an available shopping cart, and moved toward aisle one for milk and sour cream. A flash of red caught his eye as he passed aisle four.

Olivia?

He halted and backed up. She stood on tip-toe to reach something on the top shelf. Then she tossed it in her cart and turned to go down the back end of the store.

Blake's palms began to sweat. His heart raced. Over the last two months, he'd had moments when the loss of her was so great his body physically ached. Moments when he'd been angry and dead sure breaking things off had been the right move. Other times, he was pretty sure God was telling him to make things right with her. Was this his chance? Blake walked in her direction. He had no idea what he was going to say, but he had to see her. Like it or not, he still loved her. Before he could get three feet, Olivia disappeared down another aisle. Blake sped to catch her.

His cellphone rang.

He looked down at the screen, intending to punch the ignore button, but the number originated from Portland, and he'd been playing phone tag with a business contact there. Blake groaned inwardly. He'd take the call and trail far enough behind her that he wouldn't be seen, but he wouldn't lose her, either. "Hartford Farms."

"Blake?"

The female voice stopped his progress. Something dark and familiar curled in his chest.

"It's Madison. Please, don't hang up."

He scowled. "What do you want?"

"I want…" She sighed. "I want your forgiveness. Lucas wants your forgiveness. We both want you at our wedding, but if you can't give us that, at least forgive us for hurting you. We want to be a family, Blake."

"I can't do this right now." He had to get to Olivia. Tell her they'd both been wrong. Make up for the miserable weeks they'd spent apart. "I'm hanging up now." Blake tucked the phone back into his pocket, abandoned his cart, and followed after Olivia. Where was she? He'd been on the phone less than a minute. How could she have gotten away so fast? He sped along the back of the store, searching every aisle as he passed. There. At the checkout. Slowing his steps so as not to appear aggressive, disappointment rose inside him as he neared.

The woman wasn't Olivia.

Same red coat. Same dark hair. Same height. But this woman had dark eyes and a pointed chin.

His shoulders dropped. It was probably for the best. What would he say anyway? He didn't have an 'I'm-an-idiot' speech prepared. No valiant way to sweep her off her feet, convince her they belonged together.

At least now he knew how he truly felt. Despite her deception, despite his shortcomings, he wanted to be with her. Wanted her. Forever.

Blake returned to his cart, collected enough food to last the week and then drove home. As he put away his groceries, Blake's mind reeled over Madison's call, the pleading desperation in her familiar voice. The two of them were relentless. Did reconciliation really matter that much to them?

He loved Olivia. Wanted to spend the rest of his days, and nights, with her. He wanted children. Someday. He wanted his own family to be a part of a larger one.

Knowing that, what did it matter if he let go of the past? With Olivia in his life, his relationship with Madison no longer mattered. And the bitterness he held onto was pointless. *"It isn't until we learn to forgive that we can be truly free."*

Blake slid a cereal box into the cabinet, closed the door, and leaned against the countertop. *Where do I start, Lord?* He just couldn't get past the betrayal coming from his own brother. Someone he'd grown up with, laughed with, cried with. Shared meals with.

Jesus.

The name tumbled through Blake's mind. Yes, if anyone knew how Blake felt, it was Jesus. Betrayed by a man he'd taught, grown with, broke bread with. Someone he'd called brother. Death in exchange for a few measly bucks.

What did Jesus do? Forgave. Everyone and everything. He took on the entire sin of the world.

Yet Blake was so superficial, he couldn't forgive losing a girlfriend when God had a better woman out there for him anyway.

Pride.

Blake released a long, slow breath. *I'm sorry, God, for harboring bitterness and hatred in my heart. A heart that should be filled with nothing but You. I give this all to You, Lord. I forgive them.*

And, boy, did forgiveness feel good. His whole body felt lighter. His soul, cleaner than it had been in years. He had a fresh start.

And three days to secure a tux, a hotel, and make it to Boston in time for a wedding. What better way to prove to Olivia he'd let go of the past and opened his heart to the future—their future—than going to his brother's wedding?

43

Death packed a mighty punch. Even when one saw it coming. There was no ducking, no running. No escape.

Grandma's blankets rose and fell with every raspy, shallow breath. Despite the aggressive antibiotics, her lungs were continuing to fill with bacterial fluid. Grandma had refused to cooperate with breathing exercises, and had given up.

The hospital room offered no comfort with its muted walls, flashing medical equipment, and stiff furniture.

Dad sat in the corner chair and stared at his mother asleep in the bed. The knowledge that he was a new dad at fifty-three had crash-landed him into reality after his stint in mid-life crisis land. Over the last few days, they'd discussed it all at length, vented, cried, forgave, repented, and hugged.

Neither liked the curves their lives had travelled, many of which were caused by poor decision making. But here they stood, and all they could do was move forward. Dad with his new family, Olivia without Blake. And in less than twenty-four hours, as the doctor predicted, without Grandma, too.

Loss was a natural part of life. It was hard, and it hurt. Death packed a mighty punch, even when one saw it coming.

~*~

Blake sat at the reception table covered in fancy white linen, sipping punch that surprisingly held the perfect amount of sweetness.

Lucas and Madison swayed on the dance floor, their first dance as husband and wife coming to a close. The white dress, the love radiating from both their faces made Blake's chest squeeze.

He wanted this with Olivia. The right to hold her, kiss her whenever he wanted to. He loved her and wanted to spend the rest of his life proving it. He tugged at his tight collar. The catered meal of lemon chicken breast, asparagus, roasted red potatoes, and yeast rolls was delicious, but it was mediocre compared to his favorite cook's dishes. Especially when Olivia's apron strings bounced along her hips as she strode around the kitchen. The memory had him guzzling more of the cool punch.

He checked his phone. Still no response.

Blake had texted her that morning, in the quiet of the church after some soul-searching and a long, arduous prayer.

Can we meet? Talk?

She was probably busy with the bakery. Or wanted nothing more to do with him after he'd reacted so terribly. Or maybe all that forgiveness talk was one-sided.

Lucas had joined him in the silent sanctuary and encouraged Blake not to give up. Then they'd prayed together. Man, it felt good to have his brother back.

"You look a little lonely over here all by yourself. Would you care to dance?" The soft-spoken redhead shifted her punch glass to her other hand. She was attractive in her slinky black dress, but he wasn't interested.

"I'm not much of a dancer, but you're welcome to join me." Blake pulled out the chair next to him, not wanting to be rude.

She hesitated, then set down her punch and smoothed her dress as she accepted his offer. "I'm Stacey."

"Blake."

Awkward silence.

Her gaze drifted around the room. "You seem as distant to the festivities as I am. I thought I'd come over."

He twirled his empty punch glass in his hand. "Great celebration. My mind's just elsewhere."

Her attention once again focused on the other side of the room.

Ah. Blake smiled. "Which one is he?"

Stacey turned back to him, mouth slightly open. "Am I that obvious?"

"Just a little."

She blushed. "Jefferson. He's in the blue shirt and tie. He works with the groom. I work with the bride. Anyway, they set us up once. Things were great for a while. Then I did something stupid and lost the best thing I'd ever had."

Blake would toast her if he had anything left in his cup. "Join the club. I'm king of stupid right now."

Stacey tucked her hair behind her ear. "You lost someone, too?"

He nodded.

She leaned back in her seat. "Good to know I'm not the only idiot on the planet." Her eyes widened. "I mean…"

"It's OK." Blake chuckled. "No offense taken."

They talked through the next three songs while Blake sneaked glances at the dark screen on his phone. "I changed my mind. I think I'd like to dance after all."

She took his offered hand, and he led her out on the dance floor. "Can we manage to dance in Jefferson's general direction?"

He swept her into his arms. "Absolutely."

~*~

Olivia's eyes refused to stay open. The strain of tears, of saying goodbye to her last living grandparent, of signing paperwork, and carrying out Grandma's last wishes had beaten her like an amateur in a professional boxing ring.

Dad drove, his stony features highlighted by the glowing dash lights. He hadn't said much after asking for time alone with Grandma that afternoon.

Olivia didn't feel up to talking anyway. All she could do was hurt right now. Her eyes slid closed again, and her head bobbed to the side. She jerked upright, blinked her eyes against the pull of sleep, and sucked in a breath. Deep, restful sleep wouldn't elude her tonight.

Dad reached over and patted her knee.

She should let Mom know Grandma had passed away. After all, they'd been in-laws for thirty-one years. Besides, Mom had asked for updates on Grandma's prognosis. She bent and grabbed her purse off the floorboard. She retrieved her cell tucked in the front pocket. She'd missed a text from Blake. Her heart rate kicked. Her attention sharpened. It was probably nothing more than his condolences. Except no one knew.

Can we meet? Talk?

After ten long weeks of silence, he finally wanted to talk? It was like deja vu all over again. Why did it take men so long to get their thoughts together?

Yes, she wanted to meet. To talk. But first, she had to get through the memorial service on Tuesday. What they had to say could wait a few more days.

44

Tears nearly froze to Olivia's cheeks. She burrowed further into her blanket scarf and held it closed over her mouth. The graveside tent was packed with people but it wasn't enough to ward off the icy blast of January.

She stared at the spray of red roses splayed across the oak casket, the preacher's words mere noise in her ears. The woman who'd offered her a refuge, who'd taught her much in such a short time, was gone. The house, the bakery, all seemed hollow without her.

Even Sydney mourned, pacing the rooms as if in search for her old friend.

An arm came around her shoulders and squeezed. Arianne, all red nose and cheeks, pressed the side of her head to Olivia's. "If you need anything at all, call me."

The movement of bodies and whispers registered in Olivia's ears, and she realized the service was over. "Thank you."

Huck thrust out his gloved hand. "I'm sorry for your loss."

Olivia returned the gesture. She appreciated the phrase but had heard it a thousand times. Minus one. Not a word from Blake. Another ache swelled in her chest. She slipped her hands in the pockets of her wool dress coat and swallowed the lump in her throat. "How is he?"

Arianne's brow crinkled for a moment before it smoothed again. "Oh! Good. Really good." She leaned closer to Olivia's ear. "He's at his brother's wedding."

Stunned was not strong enough a word to describe Olivia's reaction.

"He called to let me know before he left." Huck rubbed the back of his neck. His ears were scarlet from the cold. "I texted him as soon as we found out," he glanced at the casket, "but he's not responded. Heard there's a nor'easter hitting Boston right now."

At least Blake's absence didn't mean he didn't care. Of course he cared. After all, he'd nicknamed her grandma. He'd have come, even if he didn't want to reconcile their relationship. Blake was that kind of man. One of the many reasons she loved him.

Arthur and Eugenia Greene stepped up to give their condolences.

"Thank you for coming." Olivia wrapped her arms around the woman. Her powder-scented perfume tickled Olivia's throat.

Eugenia sniffed and dabbed at her nose with a lace hankie. "She's with her Jacob now."

From the corner of her eye, Olivia saw her dad stiffen and walk away. Olivia winced but covered it with a false smile.

Others made their way over. Arianne rubbed a circle on Olivia's back, the lump beneath her coat swaying. "I'll check in on you soon."

The crowd began to thin. Shivering, Olivia walked to her car, already spewing heat from the exhaust. Her heel snagged on a frozen patch of grass. She caught herself, thinking of the blessed warmth awaiting her.

Dad sat in the driver's seat, rubbing his forehead. He looked up when she opened the passenger door.

She settled onto the seat, adjusting the panel vents to blow directly on her. Dad reached over and held her hand, keeping his focus on the windshield. All she wanted to do was go home, put on her pajamas, crawl under her blankets, and sleep for days.

After thawing from the shock of Blake reconciling with his brother. The only joy to be had on such a dark day.

~*~

Delayed.

Blake hung his head and blew out a frustrated breath.

They'd been at the airport for six hours, praying the status of their flight would change. Boston was getting hit with a wicked amount of snow, the final total predicted to be around two feet.

After almost a week in Boston, Blake wanted to go home. Grab a shower, maybe a little caffeine, then head straight to Olivia's. She'd yet to answer his text. He'd given her time to think about it, consider her reply. But after three days without word, Blake was about to go crazy.

Was she busy? Had she blocked his number? Had she responded but forgot to hit send? Had she decided to get back together with her ex?

Blake hadn't really considered that possibility until now, and it made the hotel's continental breakfast churn in his stomach. Blake glanced at his watch then paced some more. Airport waiting areas were restricting enough without hundreds of people trying to get home after the holidays. And half of those people were using all the outlets to recharge their phones and tablets, while Blake's battery was dead.

"Honey." Mom wrapped her hand around his arm. "Are you all right? You're prowling like a lion waiting to be loosed from its cage."

Blake glanced around the airport. He had been prowling. "Yeah, I'm fine. I'm just...ready to get home."

Mom smiled, her mother's intuition knowing exactly why he wanted to get home. "I know I've said it a thousand times, but I'm glad you and Lucas have set things right. It does my heart good." She placed her palm over her chest.

Blake gave her a side-arm hug. It felt good to finally let it all go. He'd held on to his anger way too long. "Where's Dad?"

"Getting a snack from the food court. He's addicted to those cinnamon rolls."

"Who isn't?" Though it wasn't post-heart attack food.

"I'm heading that direction myself. There's a bookstore I'd like to check out, since it's looking like we're going to be here several more hours. I'm hoping they comp us a hotel for the night instead of making us sleep in these uncomfortable chairs." She rubbed at the small of her back.

Another night in Boston? Blake sighed. "I need to get home."

She reached up and smoothed the hair at his temple the way she used to when he was a boy. "She's a good girl, and you obviously love her very much. If it's God's will for you to be together, there will be plenty of time for making up."

Easier said, than done.

"Now, seeing as our flight is canceled," Mom

pointed to the schedule board, "let's get us a treat."

Blake howled inwardly. He retrieved their carry-ons from the seat they'd been occupying after another long glance at his phone. Any attempt to vacate an outlet would probably prove futile anyway.

"Don't worry, hon. That girl's put down roots. Olivia isn't going anywhere."

~*~

When it rains, it pours.

The age-old cliché held truth, except in Olivia's case it flooded to biblical proportions. And figuratively, all she had was a dinghy and one oar. And shore was five miles upstream. Olivia stood in the mind-numbing cold, staring as tiny flecks of white coated the charred remains of the bakery. Would the adversity in her life ever end?

She'd placed her faith, her trust, her identity in Christ. She no longer questioned if God cared, if He were present in her life, who she was or where she came from. Now, it seemed as if God was testing her to make sure she was legit.

But did it have to hurt so much?

She'd spent months caring for Grandma, pouring her life into a woman she wished she'd gotten the opportunity to know long before the Alzheimer's stole Grandma away. Only for Olivia to lose her.

She'd spent months pulling the bakery out of debt, saving jobs, and restoring it to a place the community could fellowship. To lose it.

She'd lost her parents, she'd lost her fiancé, she'd lost Blake. Olivia felt just plain lost.

"Ms. Hudson?" She turned.

An older gentleman with a rounded stomach, a thick, white beard, and gold-rimmed glasses returned her stare. "I'm Luther Crane, Chief Fire Inspector for Washington County. May I ask a few questions?"

"Of course."

"Would you prefer to talk privately inside the library? They've reserved a meeting room for us. I'd rather not be the cause of your hypothermia."

Olivia swallowed against the pain in her throat. A reaction from days of endless sobbing. She nodded, noting the crust of ice on the harbor through the smoke of the still-smoldering timbers.

Once they were settled inside the small room of the library, Olivia barely had enough time to remove her coat before the inspector attacked her with questions.

"You'd taken charge over the bakery after your grandmother, Elizabeth Hudson, appointed you durable power of attorney, correct?"

"Yes, sir."

"Do you keep insurance coverage on the bakery?"

"Yes."

"Your policy covers a total loss of five-hundred-thousand dollars, am I correct?"

Olivia recoiled at the suspicion in his tone. "That's correct. It also covers employee wages for six months or until the bakery reopens, whichever comes first."

"Do you plan to reopen?"

She hesitated. She wanted to but there hadn't been enough time to consult God on His will in this yet. Did He want her to rebuild, or was He telling her to go home to Indiana? "I don't know."

The chief's head lifted slightly, and he leaned back

in his chair, writing notes on his notepad. "Where were you at approximately eight-forty-five last night?"

Unbelievable. They suspected she'd started the fire? The fireman on scene had told her it was likely a faulty oven. Which was odd, since they'd been closed for the past week. Did they suspect her of arson?

She chose her words carefully and kept her voice soft. "I was at my grandmother's memorial service. It started at seven at Starks Funeral home. It lasted until eight-thirty. My father and I stayed a little longer to say one last goodbye. As we were leaving, Jaunita Brown ran out of her home across the street to inform us the bakery was on fire. Her husband is a volunteer fireman."

The chief wasn't good at hiding his surprise at her confession. He scratched his chin.

Another fireman walked in.

The chief frowned. His busy eyebrows nearly covered his eyes. "What's this about, Mr. Crane?"

"Arson." He made a few more notes. "Accelerant was found along the east perimeter of the foundation."

Olivia gasped. Someone *purposely* set fire to her business? On the night of her grandma's memorial service?

The chief grunted. "Do you have any enemies, Ms. Hudson?"

Her mind immediately went to Darlene, but Olivia didn't think the woman had it in her to be an arsonist. Justin had left for Indianapolis weeks ago, and she'd overheard that Blake was with his family in Boston attending his brother's wedding. She was reeling over that news almost as much as that of the fire. "No."

The second fireman leaned his hands on the back of a chair. "We've been dealing with a serial arsonist in the area for a while. This particular fire doesn't follow the individual's signature pattern, but that doesn't mean he or she isn't involved."

Olivia wished the room—her life—would stop spinning. "Now what?"

The chief stood. "We'll have to confirm your alibi while you file some reports. We'll continue our investigation. In the meantime, I suggest you inform your employees, discuss things with your insurance company, and meet with a contractor if you decide to rebuild."

Her brain could barely compute all the things being thrown at her.

They ended the meeting, shook hands, and exchanged contact information.

The chief offered to walk her back to her car, but she refused. She needed space to think. The arctic air would keep her from curling into a ball and sleeping the remainder of her life away. She walked around the bakery, keeping clear of the restricted area blocked by yellow caution tape. *Where do I go from here, Lord? What am I supposed to do now?*

The only sound that hit Olivia's ears was the icy sludge smacking into boat hulls as the wind teased the water. Suddenly, an overwhelming ache to see her mother possessed Olivia. She hadn't seen her mother in a year. She'd go home. Visit her mom. Spend some time away from Maine to clear her head. To clear her heart.

Olivia retreated to her car and the warmth of the heater. She pulled out her phone and responded to the text Blake had sent days ago.

Grandma passed away. Bakery burned down. Going home.

45

Olivia was gone.

Blake trudged back to his truck. Jen still hovered in the open doorway of the Hudson house, arms crossed over her middle to ward off the cold, her face full of pity. She'd just informed him that Olivia had left for Indiana this morning.

While Blake had been descending into Bangor, Olivia had been ascending from Portland. Jen had just gotten back from driving Olivia to the airport a couple hours ago, while Blake had been showering and settling up with the neighbor boy for taking care of Scooby in his absence.

Irony was a cruel, cruel thing.

His cell battery had remained dead at the airport while he'd slept upright in a hard, plastic chair. Mom and Dad had accepted the comp hotel, but Blake chose to stay for a guaranteed spot on the first available flight. He'd gotten Olivia's text too late.

He drove past where the bakery used to stand, unable to believe it, too, was gone. The morning paper declared it was arson. Whoever was responsible better hope the authorities found them first because if Blake did, it wouldn't end well.

Jen had no idea if Olivia planned to rebuild, when she'd be back, or if she planned to come back. She did, however, have the address to her mother's house where she'd be staying, though Blake had to practically beg Jen to share it with him.

He needed to do something to convince Olivia to give him another chance. To prove how committed he was to making their relationship work. He needed to make it and fast, before she spent too much time in Indiana.

Where Justin lived.

Problem was Blake wasn't a romantic. He didn't know what made a woman swoon or how to write a love poem. He was capable of buying flowers, of protecting her, holding her, kissing her, but none of those things were enough. He went home and made a fire, all the while praying over what to do.

Scooby sat on his pallet in the corner, spying on him with his head on his paws.

Blake put his hands on his waist. "What would you do if it was your girl?"

Scooby lifted his head and barked. Twice.

"Thanks for the advice, buddy, but I don't speak canine." A picture on the mantel caught Blake's eye. The selfie he and Olivia had taken on her birthday, a mass of harbor seals sunbathing in the background.

And then it clicked. Blake knew exactly how to bring Olivia home.

~*~

All play and no work made Olivia a very lazy woman. Not that she'd been playing. Sending referral letters to her former clients and signing her third of the practice over to her to fellow therapists had kept her busy during the past week. Not including keeping up on the dozens of emails sent back and forth between her and the contractor for the bakery.

Olivia had decided to rebuild. She'd known it all along, actually; she just hadn't realized it. But after forty-eight hours in the heartland, and she knew this was no longer home. Home was in a small harbor town on the coast of Maine, with its colorful buildings and quirky residents. Home was on a blueberry farm, in an old Victorian house, in the arms of a flannel-wearing farmer.

The town and bakery didn't have a choice in her homecoming. Blake, however, wasn't a given. No doubt, he was back from Boston by now. He hadn't attempted to contact her after she'd told him she was coming home. He was either giving her space or moving on. Her plan was to tie up all her loose ends here and then return to Maine and figure out the rest later.

She stretched out in bed, arching her back for full effect. The two-hour nap had been exactly what she'd needed. Dusk approached, which meant it was nearing five o'clock. The long, long nights of an Indiana winter. Olivia walked in to the living room.

Mom sat up from her lounged position on the couch. "This is interesting. Apparently, our sense of smell is linked to our psyche. Where some scents can indicate euphoria, others can trigger anxiety, depending on the past memory those scents are linked to in our brains." Mom was watching Dr. Feel, the famous syndicated television network psychologist and best-selling author. He told Olivia's mother things every day that Olivia had been telling her for years. But they were only true if they came from the celebrity's lips.

Thank God he'd filmed an episode about the

behavioral dangers of a divorcee over fifty in which he refuted the health of getting tattoos, bar-hopping, and dressing like a teenager.

Mom was back to jeans and slacks and her closet of three-quarter length sleeve sweater sets in every color of the rainbow. And scarves. Feminine, age-appropriate scarves.

"Amazing. I had no idea." Olivia joined her on the couch.

Mom rested her feet on the coffee table and covered up with a blanket. "Baked spaghetti is in the oven. How can you run around in just a T-shirt? It's freezing."

Olivia mimicked her mother's stance. "Spend a winter in Maine and this will feel like a tropical climate."

"No thanks." Mom muted the TV. "Are you sure you want to rebuild? I just can't see you being happy there now that..."

"A person can be happy living anywhere if they choose. I'm choosing happiness."

Mom sighed. "It's your life." She picked up a stack of letters from the end table beside her. "Mail. All forwarded from Stone Harbor."

Olivia took the stack and flipped through the letters first, saving the 5x8 cushioned package for last. Hartford Farms was stamped as the return address. Olivia bolted forward. Her pulse kicked into high gear. Heartbeat pounded in her ears. This package wasn't forwarded. Her mother's address was printed neatly on the label in Blake's handwriting. Olivia ripped it open. She pulled out a small hardback book with a picture of her and Blake inserted into the clear pouch on the front cover. A journal.

Mom looked at her, eyebrows knotted.

Paper stuck out from the top of the book.

Olivia pulled it out and read in silence.

Olivia,

My condolences for Grams. She was a wonderful lady and will be greatly missed by all.

I'm sorry about the bakery. It's a terrible loss, and I pray they find the scumbag and bring him to justice.

Lastly, I'm sorry for how I reacted that night. Or should I say overreacted. I let my anger, my bitterness toward my brother cloud my judgment. A choice I'll forever regret.

Lucas and I have resolved the situation, and I made it to his wedding on time. Two feet of snow kept me from getting home and apologizing to you in person.

Let me assure you my heart is now clean and full of room to fill. I want to fill it with you. I want to fill my home with you. My life with you. So much so that I've been working to rearrange the house for two. I've even fired up the antique Mayflower range in my kitchen, hoping that, if nothing else, it will convince you to come back to me.

I love you, Olivia. Marry me. And, like your grandfather, fill this journal with pictures and words of our own love story.

— Love, Blake

Olivia couldn't breathe. Her mind was full of Blake's words, so impacted by the rawness of them, it forgot to remind her lungs to contract. When her vision went fuzzy around the edges, Olivia shook herself awake from the shock fog. Blake loved her. Wanted to marry her. She tightened her grip on the package and discovered there was more inside. Holding it upside down, a weighty object fell into her lap.

A heart stone. She clasped it in her fingertips and rubbed her thumb over the smooth surface, her tears darkening its color. She rolled it in her palm.

Come home was written on one side in black permanent marker.

Olivia leaned her head back and giggled. Everything was going to be all right. She wiped her tears with the back of her hand.

Mom was now skimming the letter, tears filling her eyes, too. "That's romantic."

"Isn't it?" Olivia rubbed her chest, unable to contain the elation expanding inside.

"What are you going to say? Never mind. I'll get you a pen and paper."

Olivia placed a staying arm on her mother's shoulder. "I'm saying yes. But I'm not doing it in a letter." She hugged her mom, gently patting her back. "I'll tell him in person."

EPILOGUE

August 8

Here it is! Journal entry number one—our first day as husband and wife. See that picture? Those smiles! That's Mr. and Mrs. Blake Hartford, standing in front of their completely renovated Victorian treasure, AKA honeymoon destination. What better way to spend our first night together than in our own house?

In case you're wondering, yes, those are blueberries in my bouquet. Isn't it fantastic? My dear friend Arianne blended the perfect mix of white Indiana-grown peonies, white roses, and fresh blueberry sprigs. She also designed and sewed my dress, planned a menu and booked a caterer, and coordinated the entire wedding (with my input, of course) in six months, all while carrying the very active Baby Anderson, a boy she safely delivered in May, who never lets her sleep.

My favorite baker, Brittany, made an absolutely scrumptious almond-flavored Italian wedding cake in the kitchen of the new and improved Harbor Town Bakery. A perpetrator has yet to be found, but justice doesn't always come swiftly. Despite it, our grand opening in June was more successful than we ever imagined. Life is good.

God is good.

When hard times come, it often feels as if the heavens have opened up and dumped a tsunami amount of rain on your life. The same can be said about blessed times too, though. Rain puts out fire, and my family sure has risen from the ashes.

I met my new baby sister for the first time today. She's beautiful and perfect. Our dad looked exhausted, but that's to be expected from a new husband and father. Mom looked fantastic. Her boyfriend, a widower from the church I grew up in, tagged along, and it was nice to see her happy again.

Oh, and did I mention Blake's brother, Lucas, was our best man? We truly have a new start.

Philippians 4:8 "Finally, brethren, whatsoever things are true, whatsoever things are honest, whatsoever things are just, whatsoever things are pure, whatsoever things are lovely, whatsoever things are of good report; if there by any virtue, and if there be any praise, think on these things."

Author's Note:

I hope you enjoyed Blake and Olivia's story. More than anything, I pray the message of hope spoke to you that there's light even in our darkest moments.

This story was written during a long stretch of what I consider the darkest part of my life, a time where circumstances out of my control beat me up and continued kicking me while I was down. Through it all, I felt God's presence, His gentle voice telling me I hadn't been forsaken. That I needed to "be still" and know that He is God. That in His timing, He would make all things new again. And He did. I'm on the other side now. I still don't understand, but I survived to tell the tale.

If you ever find yourself in the pit of depression, whether as the patient or the caregiver, I encourage you to dig into the Bible and read the hundreds of uplifting scriptures, the promises God makes to His children, and the hope that lies within. It may take reading them over and over but eventually they will print themselves on your heart.

I also recommend reading Hope Prevails by Dr. Michelle Bengtson. She not only shares her own personal journey through depression, but she guides readers on how to successfully overcome it the Bible way.

Hope truly does prevail, dear reader. "These things I have spoken unto you, that **in me** you might have **peace**. In the world ye shall have tribulation: but be of good cheer; I have overcome the world." John 16:33 (emphasis mine)

A Devotional Moment

But if a widow has children or grandchildren, these should learn first of all to put their religion into practice by caring for their own family and so repaying their parents and grandparents, for this is pleasing to God. ~ 1 Timothy 5:4

In times past, three generations of families often lived under one roof. Over time, in our western world, the practice died away, but recently, we've seen an upsurge in this practice again. Because of financial life events and other constraints, families are learning to rely on and take care of each another. In some cases, the issue is age. We care for our elderly parents and grandparents in recognition of the way they cared for us. When we meet this obligation and challenge with the same love that God has for us, it pleases Him.

In **How to Stir a Baker's Heart** the protagonist must meet the needs of her grandmother when her own heart is already broken. She pours herself into running her grandmother's business, but must deal with obstacles while trying to lift her own depression. Matters come to a head when obligation crashes into local community, and a resolution must encompass the needs of many.

Have you ever been burdened with the responsibility of caring for others even while you feel unequipped to handle your own situation? Obligation piled on top of depression or other responsibilities can feel overwhelming, but the opposite can be true. If we help others with a joyful intention—even when we don't feel joyful—and give our own sorrows to God, we often find that what we thought was overwhelming dissolves into something easily handled. When we cast our cares on God and when we repay our parents and grandparents, we please Him and open ourselves to receive abundant blessings.

LORD, HELP ME TO SHARE MY HEART WITH LOVE AND HONOR FOR THOSE WHO ONCE NURTURED ME. TEACH ME TO RETURN THE LOVE YOU HAVE FOR US. IN JESUS' NAME I PRAY, AMEN.

Thank you

We appreciate you reading this White Rose Publishing title. For other inspirational stories, please visit our on-line bookstore at www.pelicanbookgroup.com.

For questions or more information, contact us at customer@pelicanbookgroup.com.

White Rose Publishing
Where Faith is the Cornerstone of Love™
an imprint of Pelican Book Group
www.PelicanBookGroup.com

Connect with Us
www.facebook.com/Pelicanbookgroup
www.twitter.com/pelicanbookgrp

To receive news and specials, subscribe to our bulletin
http://pelink.us/bulletin

May God's glory shine through
this inspirational work of fiction.

AMDG

You Can Help!

At Pelican Book Group it is our mission to entertain readers with fiction that uplifts the Gospel. It is our privilege to spend time with you awhile as you read our stories.

We believe you can help us to bring Christ into the lives of people across the globe. And you don't have to open your wallet or even leave your house!

Here are 3 simple things you can do to help us bring illuminating fiction™ to people everywhere.

1. If you enjoyed this book, write a positive review. Post it at online retailers and websites where readers gather. And share your review with us at <u>reviews@pelicanbookgroup.com</u> (this does give us permission to reprint your review in whole or in part.)

2. If you enjoyed this book, recommend it to a friend in person, at a book club or on social media.

3. If you have suggestions on how we can improve or expand our selection, let us know. We value your opinion. Use the contact form on our web site or e-mail us at

<u>customer@pelicanbookgroup.com</u>

God Can Help!

Are you in need? The Almighty can do great things for you. Holy is His Name! He has mercy in every generation. He can lift up the lowly and accomplish all things. Reach out today.

Do not fear: I am with you; do not be anxious: I am your God. I will strengthen you, I will help you, I will uphold you with my victorious right hand.

~Isaiah 41:10 (NAB)

We pray daily, and we especially pray for everyone connected to Pelican Book Group—that includes you! If you have a specific need, we welcome the opportunity to pray for you. Share your needs or praise reports at http://pelink.us/pray4us

Free Book Offer

We're looking for booklovers like you to partner with us! Join our team of influencers today and periodically receive free eBooks!

For more information
Visit http://pelicanbookgroup.com/booklovers